# PURSUED BY PERIL

## TRACKING TROUBLE
### BOOK 4

## LINDSAY BUROKER

# ACKNOWLEDGMENTS

Thank you, good reader, for continuing along on Arwen's journey. She needs all the support she can get!

Thank you, also, to my editor, Shelley Holloway, my beta readers, Cindy Wilkinson and Sarah Engelke, and my cover designer, Gene Mollica Studio. Lastly, thank you to my audiobook narrator, Vivienne Leheny, for bringing the characters to life. She does the best goblin voice around.

# 1

THE SPIDER-SHAPED ARTIFACT GLOWED A MALEVOLENT PURPLE AS half-dwarf enchanter Matti Puletasi sipped coffee and studied it from a safe distance. At least Arwen *hoped* it was a safe distance. So far, it hadn't hurled chaotic energy around the private room in the back of the Coffee Dragon, nor had it struck anyone with lightning, but dark-elven artifacts weren't known for doing nothing.

"Maybe it's a calling card." Matti pushed a hand through her tousled black hair, yawned, and took a long drink, the goblin-fuel blend wafting steam and its intense coffee aroma into the air.

Given that it had only been a few days since Matti delivered her twins, Arwen was impressed she had the energy to help out. But the recently kidnapped Zoltan, the vampire alchemist who lived across the street from Matti, had assisted her from time to time. Like Arwen, she probably felt she owed him.

Arwen had *thought* it would be a simple matter to track down the dark elf who'd left the artifact, but nothing was simple when dealing with her mother's people. Now, she paced around the room, hoping Matti would see something that Arwen hadn't.

She'd already asked Amber to research the internet for

matches, and she'd shown the device to Val, Colonel Willard, and Gondo, but they hadn't been willing to touch it, much less study it assiduously. Since dark elves had a propensity for creating deadly artifacts, Arwen couldn't blame them, but she found the situation frustrating. Yet again, someone had been harmed because of her.

"Or it could be a warning." Matti tapped the edge of the table where the spider rested. "Maybe your people *want* you to know they were responsible."

"My *mother's* people." Arwen grimaced, hating any suggestion that she was linked to their kind, even if she had equal parts dark-elven and human blood. "And I would have known it was them whether they'd left that or not. They've been trying to keep me from getting this removed all along." Arwen pushed up her sleeve to show her loathed spider tattoo, its red eyes almost glowing, its black legs curling around her forearm. "I wouldn't have asked Zoltan to help if I'd thought he would be in danger. I assumed all the wards around Val's house—and the dragon living in the turret —would deter even powerful dark elves."

"Well, Zavryd is pretty busy serving his mother, the queen, so he's part-time in the turret. The wards, though, yeah. It's disturbing that someone got through. We've got similar wards and defenses around our house, and I don't like knowing that a dark elf could waltz in, especially now." Matti waved in the direction of her home in Green Lake. She'd said her elven mate, the former assassin Sarrlevi, was watching their newborns.

Arwen had offered to bring the artifact to Matti, so she wouldn't have to leave home, but Matti had been quick to say she didn't want anything dark-elven near her kids. Since she'd been cursed by one of their artifacts the year before, Arwen couldn't blame her for an abundance of caution.

"Understandable," Arwen said. "I knew powerful mages could break wards, but I *didn't* know it would be possible to bypass them and slip through without disturbing them."

"Yeah. Val said you weren't able to track the person who left this?"

"I tracked a female dark elf to the backyard, but I believe she left via a portal, because I lost the trail at the patio."

"Was it... your mother?" Matti raised her eyebrows.

"No. Even though it's been twenty-three years since my father and I escaped from her tunnels, I would have recognized her aura."

When Arwen had first called upon her soul-tracking magic, she'd thought she might find trace of Harlik-van, the brother she'd only recently learned she had. But the aura had been female, and Arwen hadn't recognized the owner of the ghostly footprints that had appeared. It was possible her brother was dead and her mother had sent another minion. Whoever it had been, the dark elf had been powerful enough to force Zoltan up the stairs ahead of her—the tracks had shown that he'd walked out of the basement.

"Put up a barrier." Matti set her coffee on the table and used her magic to form a translucent bubble around herself.

Arwen, who'd only recently learned how to do so, raised a barrier of her own.

While keeping her distance, Matti probed the spider with her magic. Its purple glow brightened, and an angry lash of power whipped from it. It struck Matti's barrier, and the air buzzed as dwarven and dark-elven magic clashed.

Arwen's bow and quiver leaned by the door, but she reached for the magical multitool that Azerdash Starblade had made for her. He'd finally gone over most of its magical capabilities with her, but all she wanted now was the knife. She flicked open one of the blades. If that artifact hurt Matti, Arwen would slam the knife into it, feeling no remorse about destroying it.

But the attack faded without penetrating Matti's barrier. She calmly picked up her coffee and took another sip. "It doesn't like being probed."

"I'm tempted to see how it likes being thrown off the Space Needle."

"I don't think the windows up there open."

"I could get a half-dragon to fly me to the top so I could chuck it off."

"You might be fined for littering. Besides, isn't your half-dragon MIA?" Matti looked at the multitool.

"Azerdash is on another world, avoiding dragons who want to kill him and..." Arwen didn't know what exactly. When Azerdash had been reunited with his long-lost galaxy blade, a weapon of tremendous power, he'd spoken of accepting his destiny, but he hadn't given her a lot of details. Understandable, since she'd become a magnet for enemy dragons who liked to read her mind to find out where he was. "I'm not sure, but there was talk of uniting the various intelligent species, raising a huge army, and convincing the Dragon Council and all the dragons who've been ruling the Cosmic Realms for ages to butt out and let people govern their own worlds."

"An ambitious task."

"Yeah." From the beginning, Arwen had worried it would be a *suicidal* task for Azerdash. Even though searching for Zoltan had kept her mind busy these past few days, at night, she'd lain awake and worried about Azerdash. It wasn't fair that the universe had finally given her a man who didn't think she was a freak, who liked her cooking, and who had quirky passions, just like she did, and then driven him away.

"Is he coming back?" Matti asked.

"He said he would visit."

But would he? He'd said he would, but... might he stay away to keep Arwen safe? Or because he was busy? Or... in danger?

Arwen grimaced again, adding, "I promised to make him tacos."

"Is that a favorite food for half-dragons?"

"We don't know yet. He's open to experimentation."

"That must come from his elven half," Matti said. "Zavryd inciner-ates Val's dipping sauces and breading when they get chicken strips."

"He would be difficult to bake for."

"As long as you make all-meat dishes, I hear he's happy." Matti trickled a little more power toward the spider, something that felt different from before.

Arwen wasn't familiar with enchanting magic, but she assumed Matti was using various methods to try to learn from the artifact. It had to do something besides exist. But since it hadn't cursed or attacked anyone yet, reacting only in self-defense, Arwen didn't know what.

"You don't know where your— your mother's people live now, right?"

Arwen shook her head. Matti had asked that the year before when she'd needed someone capable of lifting her curse. At the time, Arwen had only known of a dark-elf priest who'd had a labo-ratory near the goblin sanctuary where Azerdash and his friend Yendral had lived until recently.

"When my father and I escaped, he caved in their tunnels and started a wildfire. The flames spread, and people and helicopters dropping water and retardants descended upon the area. That put an end to their habitation." Arwen didn't clearly remember the events of that night and the day after, but her father had given her his accounting when she'd asked. She'd had trouble sleeping those first few years, always afraid the dark elves would come for them, and he'd been trying to assure her that they'd left the area and didn't know where his farm was. "As a teenager, I visited the spot out of curiosity, and to make sure they hadn't come back, and nobody was around. But they have to be somewhere. We didn't encounter that many in the basement of the building in Bellevue."

"I don't know much about dark-elven enchanting magic." Matti gazed contemplatively at the artifact. "But I can sense that there's more there than... Well, I think you're right that it's more than a calling card. I thought it might be a beacon to let them find you easily."

"Unfortunately, they don't have trouble finding me whenever they wish."

"Isn't it nice to have them care?" Matti lifted a hand, altering the magic trickling toward the device.

"It's not, no. And they don't care. They want to use me for some reason. Apparently, they always have and were waiting for me to be old enough to do..." Arwen shrugged, not wanting to share what they'd admitted in her presence, that they essentially wanted a spy, if not more, someone who looked human and could walk on the surface, blending in while doing the work of the dark elves.

Whatever Matti was doing prompted the artifact to lash out again, this time with a thrust of power that struck their barriers and knocked books off the case built into the wall behind them.

Arwen was about to suggest that they stop tinkering with the artifact—or take it to an empty beach where it could do little damage—when Nin, one of the owners of the Coffee Dragon, opened the door to peek in.

"It is difficult to make excellent espresso and satisfy one's demanding guests when ominous dark-elven magic is pulsing and throbbing in the back room." Nin, her hair swept back in a blue ponytail, gave Matti a stern look instead of Arwen.

"I'm sorry." Since she was responsible, Arwen stepped forward to nod apologetically. "We'll stop."

"Good." Nin walked in, revealing that she carried a flat rectangle wrapped in tissue paper and tied with a ribbon. "Already, we have had explosions here that forced us to remodel.

The improvements were desirable but not inexpensive, and it is impossible to get insurance for a building that serves the magical community."

"Because insurance agents hate magical beings?" Matti asked. "Or because the illusion that keeps mundane humans from finding the shop means nobody can appraise it?"

"I believe both of those instances are true. We do, however, receive payment instructions for the property taxes, so the government has *some* idea as to the value of the building. And its existence."

"It's hard to elude the IRS." Matti pointed at the package. "If that's another baby gift from the goblins, I'd like you to have it. Or possibly for the dumpster in the alley to have it."

"What have they given you?" Arwen, who'd been the recipient of a magical arrow made from a recycled stop sign, had found goblin gifts could be useful. Clunky but useful.

"The ones that live down the street made us a crib that can collapse for easy storage."

"That sounds practical."

"It would be if it didn't *spontaneously* collapse, sometimes when in use."

Arwen blinked. "I hope you didn't find that out the hard way."

Matti's babies were only a few days old, far too young to expose to iffy goblin engineering.

"Natia and Laki weren't in it. We'd set it up and put a mattress and blanket inside when—" Matti clapped her hands together dramatically.

"Did the mattress survive?"

"It would have, but a rather incensed Varlesh incinerated the entire thing and removed goblin access to our property."

"I didn't know elves were as prone to incineration as dragons."

"When it comes to protecting their offspring, yes." Matti smiled fondly. "I think we chose the right names for them. I vetoed

Elven names with six syllables that teachers wouldn't be able to pronounce—I dealt with that myself growing up—and talked Varlesh into pulling from my father's Samoan culture. Natia means hidden, and Laki means lucky. I have a feeling our kids will need to be lucky."

"And to hide? From goblins?"

"From all magical beings with inimical intent. Or at least inimical gifts."

"Not an adjective usually applied to a crib."

Matti turned a palm toward the ceiling. "Goblins."

Nin turned not toward Matti but toward Arwen and held out the package. "This is from the half-troll tattoo artist temporarily leasing space in the loft. He asked if I would give it to you the next time you came to sell your delicious desserts here." Nin looked wistfully at Arwen but didn't ask when she would do that again.

For now, finding Zoltan was Arwen's priority, so she had put baking on hold. Her father wasn't pleased that she also wasn't helping out much at the farm, which made her feel guilty. Arwen wanted to find Zoltan and put an end to the dark-elf threat as soon as possible. She hoped he was still alive—inasmuch as a vampire *lived*—and that her mother's people hadn't driven a wooden stake through his heart for presuming to craft a formula capable of removing a magical tattoo.

"Thank you." Arwen eyed the package, hesitating to open it, since Mark had been trying to get her to go out with him. He was nice enough, but she'd given her heart to another.

"It looks like a framed picture," Matti said. "Hopefully not of himself shirtless. Unless you're into that."

Arwen remembered *Azerdash* standing shirtless on her property as he'd sweated while constructing the rejuvenation pool that now wafted its appealing eucalyptus scent into the air near the pumpkin patch.

"I'm not." Arwen risked unwrapping the gift and found framed and signed tattoo art of two crossed arrows. Two of *her* crossed arrows, she realized. Glacier and Ghoster. In addition to having unique fletchings, they had blue shafts. She read an included card.

*Most beautiful Arwen, I maintain hope that you shall join me for a cup of coffee and that we can get to know each other better. Whether you agree to that or not, I'd like to offer you a version of this for your arm once we've removed the other. It would make a much more appealing tattoo, in my humble opinion. I am confident that you will complete your quest, and we'll be able to break your tie to the dark elves.*
*~ Mark*

"I appreciate his confidence," she murmured.

When Nin raised her eyebrows, Arwen showed her the card. Matti started to lean in to read it but paused, her head swiveling toward the front of the coffee shop, though they couldn't see anything from the private room.

"Perhaps he would be a safer mate to pursue than a half-dragon whom many wish to kill," Nin said.

Arwen shook her head bleakly, not wanting to think about what she would do if Azerdash died. She'd barely gotten to know him. She'd barely admitted that she was falling in love with him and—

"Uh-oh, who is that?" Matti frowned.

Arwen started to ask but sensed what Matti had sensed. The aura of an unfamiliar dragon.

# 2

"Any chance Val and Zavryd are in the area?" Arwen whispered.

Why she whispered, she didn't know. Her senses told her the dragon was flying high in the sky over Lake Union—well out of earshot. But he was arrowing in their direction and coming fast.

Dread hollowed Arwen's belly with the certainty that yet another dragon had come to question her about Azerdash's whereabouts, another dragon too powerful for her to fight.

"Val is up in Edmonds giving a sword-fighting lesson to Amber." Matti, who never went anywhere without her dwarven war hammer, plucked it up from the wall it leaned against. "Zavryd hasn't been around for a couple of days. I hear some upstart half-dragon is plotting a rebellion, and all the full-blooded ones are having long and frequent powwows about it in their Council valley." Matti eyed Arwen.

Arwen shook her head, well aware that Azerdash's hand had been forced, that the *rumor* of that plotting had long preceded his acceptance of the quest. She wasn't even positive he *had* accepted the quest. All she knew was he was being hunted and, thanks to a magical dragon tattoo that his creators had inked on his chest, he struggled to fully camouflage himself, even with his impressive power.

"I assume this guy is a Silverclaw and coming to talk to me about him." Arwen took a deep breath and grabbed her bow and quiver.

Matti gripped her arm. "Camo yourself, girl. It's never a good idea to *talk* to dragons."

"Oh, I am." Arwen rubbed her thumb over an oval embedded in the handle of the multitool. "And you should too."

It was bad enough that Arwen had risked exposing Matti to dark-elven magic. Exposing her to an enemy dragon was even worse. Oh, Matti was strong enough to do a lot of damage with that hammer, but dragons were almost impossible for lesser species to kill, and Arwen hated the thought of something happening to a new mother.

They looked at Nin.

"Do you want me to extend my protection?" Arwen offered, sensing the dragon gliding closer to the coffee shop, coming in for a landing. Unfortunately, the illusion that hid the building from human appraisers did nothing to mask it from magical beings. "To hide you too?"

Nin hesitated. "I am the only owner of the Coffee Dragon present."

"So... you can't hide?"

"One must be available to one's customers."

"I doubt that dragon is here for a mochaccino."

"An all-protein shake, maybe," Matti murmured, then led the way into the hall.

Arwen started to pick up the dark-elven artifact before following her but worried its magic would break her camouflage and the dragon would sense her. She left it on the table. Of course the dragon, with his superior senses, probably already knew she was in the shop. Why else would he be coming?

As Arwen stepped into the crowded main room, with the tables full of ogres, shifters, goblins, and other refugees and visitors to Earth, she sensed the dragon landing in the street. His powerful aura was as great as Zavryd's, and she dreaded facing him. She crossed her fingers that she wouldn't have to, but what if he grabbed Nin or some of the patrons and threatened to hurt them if Arwen didn't reveal herself?

Tires screeched in the street outside, followed by a wrenching of metal.

"I'm guessing someone at the wheel has enough magical blood to see dragons." Matti peered out one of the large windows, but the crash wasn't visible from their position. "Or this guy is choosing to make himself visible to mundane humans."

The dragon's aura changed slightly. Had he shifted forms?

"Shit." Matti frowned toward one of the side walls of the shop. "What is he doing?"

Though the dragon had Arwen's attention—he was heading for the front door—she swept out with her senses in the direction Matti was looking and picked up the powerful aura of her elven mate, Sarrlevi.

Arwen's first thought was to be relieved. If needed, they would have the assistance of a strong warrior and mage. Then she detected the smaller and less formed auras of their newborns and remembered he was the babysitter today.

Matti made a shooing motion at the wall, though Sarrlevi was still a few blocks away. Arwen trusted she was telepathically warning him not to come in and to keep their twins safe.

The numerous conversations stopped, every gaze swinging toward the front door as it opened. Even the raucous goblin gaming noise that usually came from the loft, no matter what the hour, fell silent. Everyone inside the shop could sense the dragon.

The fit human male who stepped inside wore magical chain-mail armor and black trousers, with a dirk and rapier hanging at his hips. His raven hair was swept back into a knot, save for a braided streak of gray that dangled down in front of one ear. He had bronze skin and topaz eyes that gazed around the shop as his hands rested on the hilts of his weapons.

Even though Arwen was confident she was camouflaged and too far away for him to see through it, she tensed. Beside her, Matti only glanced at the dragon as she continued to frown at the wall. Sarrlevi was continuing closer, walking faster than he had been before.

After perusing the patrons, the shape-shifted dragon strode toward the coffee counter.

Three goblins had been standing in line, but two scurried away at top speed. The third grabbed a muffin from a display basket and dropped to his knees, bowed his head, and lifted it toward the dragon.

"An offering for a mighty visitor," the goblin squeaked.

The barista lifted a finger, as if she might object to him giving away muffins that he hadn't paid for, but Nin, who stood by her side, pressed her employee's hand down and shook her head.

"I have called Val," Nin murmured to the barista.

"Even she cannot handle a dragon," came the return murmur. The barista had a quarter gnomish blood and could doubtless sense the power of their visitor.

"Val is not only a business partner but she is the *muscle*, as she calls it."

"Which she will use to bring her mate?"

"That is the hope."

They must not have heard that Zavryd wasn't in town—wasn't on the *planet*.

Arwen wiped a sweaty palm on her trousers and wished she were wearing her armored jumpsuit. If the dragon attacked Nin or anyone here, Arwen would feel obligated to leap into battle to protect them. But after the jumpsuit had been damaged by fae arrows, she'd left it with the gnome Imoshuan to repair.

The dragon wore a bemused expression as he accepted the muffin.

*This offering is not made from meat.* He spoke telepathically, the words for everyone in the shop, fewer people now since more than one customer had sneaked past Arwen and Matti and down the hall to the back door.

The goblin who'd proffered the muffin smacked his palm to his forehead, then sprang to the display of food for sale, perusing the items with a shaking finger. The barista's lips thinned, but she didn't object when he snatched a beef stick wrapped in cellophane and offered it to the dragon.

Nin looked toward Matti, though she shouldn't have been able to see her or Arwen. Maybe they were having a telepathic conversation. Arwen had a feeling strange dragons didn't saunter into the coffee shop that often.

The newcomer lifted the beef stick, turned it in numerous directions, and sniffed it through the wrapper. With the faintest poof of magic, he incinerated the cellophane, then sniffed the stick again. He took a small bite from the end, chewed once, then spat it onto the floor and incinerated the rest of the beef stick.

The goblin squeaked and ran behind the counter.

*This world is as primitive and inferior as I always heard.* The dragon looked around, coolly eyeing every patron who hadn't sneaked away, before turning back to Nin and the barista. *Create a beverage for me.*

*Maybe he did come for a mochaccino.* Arwen thought to Matti.

Matti was busy gaping at the front of the shop, where Sarrlevi was now visible through the window. Sarrlevi and their newborns, the babies swaddled against his chest in a sling made from woven leaves. Arwen wagered they hadn't found that at Babies R Us.

"What kind of drink would you like?" Nin asked. "We don't have meat-based beverages."

*What about the protein shakes?* Arwen asked Nin silently, though maybe she shouldn't have spoken, even telepathically. The powerful dragon might have the ability to intercept words meant for another.

*They are made from whey and soy isolate,* Nin replied.

*Tasty.*

*Lord Zavryd has assured me they are not acceptable to the dragon palate.*

*You will also tell me,* the dragon continued, holding Nin's gaze, *where I may find the dark-elven mongrel who holds Azerdash Starblade's tail.*

Arwen tightened her grip on her bow. She'd been right.

Nin's lips parted slightly as she stared at the dragon, as if mesmerized by him. Or under his magical power. When she winced, her brow furrowing, Arwen knew without a doubt that the bastard was reading her mind.

She drew an arrow, though she didn't know whether to attack or flee. Or attack and *then* flee. She couldn't leave the dragon here to mind-scour everyone—or worse. If they didn't cooperate, he might hurt them and tear down the coffee shop.

Before she'd decided on an action, the door opened. Sarrlevi walked in with his twin long swords in his hands, held out to his sides so he didn't bump his snoozing cargo. He wore black trousers and a forest-green shirt, the swords glowing menacingly, and would have looked like the badass assassin he'd once been if not for the babies nestled against his chest.

He wouldn't jump into a *battle* with them, would he? Or challenge this new dragon to a duel, the way he so often did Zavryd?

Matti must have been worried about the same thing, because she left Arwen's side. She skirted tables to give the dragon a wide berth, heading toward Sarrlevi before she disappeared, moving too far away for Arwen to see her through her camouflaging magic.

"Lord Saruknorath," Sarrlevi stated, stopping a few feet inside the shop.

His words didn't elicit surprise from the dragon. As a full-blooded elf, Sarrlevi had a powerful aura, so their visitor had to have noticed his arrival. Only when he—Saruknorath—turned and saw the babies did surprise lift his brows. For a moment, he only stared. Then his head tilted back, and he laughed.

Arwen blinked. Few dragons had ever laughed in her presence, even Zavryd, who was the least uptight of their kind she'd met.

*I'd heard you retired,* Saruknorath told Sarrlevi. *Now I see the reason why. What mongrels. Have they any potential at all?*

Jaw tightening, Sarrlevi glared at the dragon. If not for the babies, he might already have challenged Saruknorath to a duel. Arwen hoped Matti could grab them before anything happened.

*Between my power and that of their grandmother, the dwarven Princess Rodarska, they are certain to become great mages and warriors.*

"My power is okay too," came Matti's affronted voice from Sarrlevi's side, though she remained invisible to Arwen.

"It is." Sarrlevi levitated his swords in the air as he carefully removed the babies in their sling to transfer to Matti. He didn't take his gaze from the dragon as he did so. Speaking telepathically again, he said, *This establishment is claimed by Lord Zavryd'nokquetal.*

*Yes.* Saruknorath lowered his head and curled a lip. *I sense his sanctimonious aura lingering here. For his sake, I shall hope he does not consume the dreadful food. It would cause his body and power to deteriorate. Should I fail in my mission, he may need all the power he can muster. But I, as you're aware, never fail to complete a mission.* The dragon held Sarrlevi's gaze.

Nin, touching her temple, as if released from a spell, pointed the barista toward the back hall. The woman hurried away as the dragon faced Sarrlevi. Most of the rest of the patrons had also done so, some leaving their mugs behind, others taking them. Upstairs, goblins hunkered by a window. Or maybe they were climbing *out* the window.

Soon, only Nin remained behind the counter, the espresso machine hissing as she made a drink. What would she give to the haughty dragon?

*I have heard that,* Sarrlevi replied, taking a step forward now that Matti held the babies. Or Arwen assumed she did. Her camouflaging magic extended to hide them, and she'd probably stepped back out of the way. *You have been hired to hunt the half-dragons?*

*I have. Will you simplify my assignment by telling me their location?*

*I will not. You reputedly enjoy a challenge.*

*This is true.*

*I also do not know where they are,* Sarrlevi said. *Once, they took refuge here, but I do not believe they are on this world presently.*

*No doubt someone offered them odious meat products pulverized and re-formed into chemical-laden sticks.*

*Yes,* Sarrlevi said, *that is most certainly what prompted them to leave, not the Silverclaw dragons constantly attacking them.*

Saruknorath laughed again. Arwen had no idea what to make of the dragon, but his personality didn't matter as much as the fact that he was looking for her.

With his laughter complete, Saruknorath turned his back on Sarrlevi and faced Nin again. Would he resume trying to mind-scour her? Why hadn't she fled? Out of a stubborn refusal to leave her business?

"Many enjoy our goblin-fuel dark, *dark* roast espresso." Nin offered the dragon a tiny cup on a saucer.

*You have poisoned it?* Saruknorath asked telepathically. He might not understand English, but he must have gotten the gist from her thoughts.

"Of course not."

He took the saucer from her and sniffed it. Behind him, Sarrlevi crouched, his swords back in his hands.

Saruknorath sipped from the small cup, then drained it and rested the saucer on the counter. *A bracing beverage.*

"Many find it stimulating." Nin eyed the tablet and card reader on the counter, as if she might ring him up, but thought better of it.

*Leave, Forester,* Sarrlevi spoke into Arwen's mind. *He will soon learn that you are here.*

Nin gasped, clutching her forehead.

Frustration made Arwen lift her bow, longing to fire into the dragon's back. If he caught and questioned her, so be it—she didn't know where Azerdash had gone and couldn't betray him—but this was unacceptable. She had to do something to stop him from hurting Nin.

Magic wrapped around Nin, not the dragon's but Sarrlevi's. Protection magic?

Saruknorath whirled back toward him. *You seek to aid the half-dragon criminal? And risk my ire? When you have offspring nearby?*

*I seek to protect the friend of my mate.* Sarrlevi pointed his chin toward Nin. *And I do not believe from your reputation that you would assault my offspring. They would not be worthy opponents for a dragon. Even I, you do not likely consider worthy.* More magic wrapped around Sarrlevi as he established a defensive barrier.

Arwen used the distraction to creep toward the espresso stand. After that second invasion of her mind, Nin must have decided she had better get out of the dragon's clutches, because she was easing from behind the counter.

*Few are worthy,* Saruknorath said, *but elves are not as limited as some.*

*We are not.* Sarrlevi didn't look like he truly wanted to fight the dragon, but his aura flared with power, perhaps to keep Saruknorath's attention.

Arwen intercepted Nin and gripped her arm, sharing her camouflaging magic.

*You should check dark-elven tunnels if you seek a dark-elf mongrel,* Sarrlevi added. *You are more likely to find such a person there rather than in this well-lit coffee house.*

*There are such tunnels on this world?*

*Certainly. There are dark elves, so there must be tunnels.*

*I believe you seek to distract me from my quest, retired assassin.* Saruknorath stepped toward Sarrlevi, his aura noticeably more powerful. *It is acceptable to quash one who interferes with one's quest.* Smiling, Saruknorath drew his dirk and rapier.

Sarrlevi was ready for a fight, but Arwen feared this would be a far more deadly battle than the duels he engaged in with Zavryd. This dragon didn't consider Sarrlevi a neighbor and a friend of his mate.

More, Arwen couldn't let Sarrlevi be hurt. Matti and their children needed him.

*Hide,* Arwen told Nin, releasing her to raise her bow.

Though she was tempted to try for a killing shot, she doubted she could land one. In all her battles with dragons, she hadn't yet. They were too powerful, and this guy was ready to start a fight with Sarrlevi, so he had a barrier up. More likely, her projectile would bounce off.

Aware of Nin giving her a worried look, Arwen fired.

The arrow skimmed above the dragon's barrier and sank into the wall over the doorway.

When Saruknorath glanced in surprise at it, Arwen sprinted down the hall and out the back door.

## 3

———

ARWEN SENSED THE DRAGON ON THE MOVE, CHASING HER OUT OF THE coffee shop. Debating whether she was brave or an idiot, she sprinted down the alley with her bow in one hand and Azerdash's multitool in the other, her thumb pressed to the oval that would activate the camouflaging magic. Running had broken her cover, and she would have to slow down for a reactivation attempt to work, but she wanted to lure Saruknorath away from the coffee shop—from her *friends*—first.

The back door banged open behind her.

She raced around a corner and down a sidewalk crowded with human passersby interspersed with goblins and other patrons who'd fled the shop. Those with magical blood gaped at her, then ran in the other direction. They could sense the dragon after her.

His aura grew more significant, and her own senses told her that he'd shifted into his natural form instead of chasing her on foot. As he rose into the air to hunt her from above, Arwen made herself slow to a stop before activating her camouflage.

Only a second passed before he appeared, a black-scaled dragon with a gray scar that ran from his brow and halfway down the side of his long neck. His topaz eyes glowed as his wings flapped slowly, taking him low over the street in the same direction that Arwen had been running.

Heart hammering, she made herself stand still and trust the magic to hide her.

Nearby, a manhole cover flew into the air, startling her. Several humans who couldn't see the dragon witnessed the cover sailing upward, and they rushed away.

Saruknorath tucked his wings in tight to land in the street. Even with the effort to make his body compact, he knocked over a traffic sign, and his tail took out a pair of hanging baskets on stands.

Terrified he would smell her, even if he couldn't sense her aura through the camouflage, Arwen was tempted to sprint in the opposite direction. Instead, she made herself step slowly away so her cover would hold.

Saruknorath pressed one glowing topaz eye to the manhole he'd revealed. Did he think she'd gone into the stormwater or sewer tunnels that were down there? Maybe she could thank Sarrlevi for putting the notion in the dragon's head. Dark-elf tunnels, indeed.

Sniffs sounded as Saruknorath waved his snout over the hole. Maybe he caught some faint scent of her, because his eyes narrowed, as if he'd found something.

Heavy clouds promised rain, which would help wash away scents, but it hadn't started yet.

Abruptly, the dragon whirled, his tail smashing into a car and breaking the side windows. He didn't glance at it, instead looking down the street in Arwen's direction.

On the sidewalk, she froze. She was fifteen or twenty feet away, far enough that camouflaging magic *should* hide her, but she feared he did indeed smell her.

His gaze locked on another manhole cover that was closer to

her. It flew into the air. Saruknorath sprang past Arwen to land in front of it. Once again, he tilted his head sideways to peer into the hole.

While the dragon searched, Arwen turned toward a brick building and carefully slung her bow across her back. As more sniffs sounded, Saruknorath searching around the hole for her scent, she climbed up the wall. If he believed she'd taken to tunnels, maybe hiding on a rooftop would make sense.

*Arwen?* Matti asked telepathically into her mind. *Are you all right? Do you need help?*

After pulling herself onto the roof, Arwen peered down at the dragon investigating the hole. *I don't know.*

She padded across the flat roof, putting more space between her and Saruknorath.

*I had my hammer cocked, ready to throw at the dragon if he attacked Varlesh,* Matti said.

*I didn't want you or him to have to fight on my behalf, especially not with your babies right there.*

*We were more worried about Nin being mind-scoured. You were hiding. Or so we thought.*

*I didn't want* anyone *having to fight a dragon who came for me.* Arwen reached the far side of the building and crouched, debating on her next action. *And I don't want anyone mind-scoured. That hurts.*

*Tell me about it.*

Movement in her peripheral vision made Arwen jump. Saruknorath remained in the street, talons on the ground, but he'd lifted his long neck so that he could see above the roof.

Arwen started to reach for her bow, but his head turned slowly back and forth. His gaze skimmed over her as he searched, but he didn't see her. His nostrils flared. Sniffing.

*Mongrel dark elf,* Saruknorath projected all around, and Arwen imagined mundane humans looking about in confusion. *I know*

*Starblade has selected you as a mate and that you have information on his whereabouts. I may be a visitor to this world, but I have the where-withal to find you. I assure you. Come to me, and let us end our encounter swiftly. I will not harm you if you allow me to read your mind.*

Compulsion magic laced those last two sentences, and Arwen's muscles twitched, her body wanting to obey the perfectly reasonable request.

No. She rooted her feet to the rooftop. It was *not* reasonable, and she wouldn't do anything to help a dragon find Azerdash.

Saruknorath's mental tone grew colder when he added, *Should I have to spend many days on this odious world, I will feel less amenable toward you when I inevitably find you. You fired an arrow at me. Even if you missed—and* meant *to miss—that is a great crime, one that necessitates you be brought to the Dragon Council for punishment and rehabilitation.* He shared a vision of her lying prone in a verdant valley with dragons perched on rock pillars, looking down at her. They tortured her, then erased all of her memories and instilled new ones, making her a compliant servant to their kind. *All you need to do is come to me and tell me what you know of Starblade and his plans for his new sword, and I shall overlook your crime.*

The magical compulsion continued, and Arwen stood and took a step toward him before catching herself. Scowling, she hunkered down again, willing her power to be enough to resist his.

The tattoo on her forearm itched, and her desire to obey the dragon lessened. As always, she hated when her dark-elven magic helped her, but, in this instance, she would accept its assistance without complaint.

Saruknorath's head swiveled toward her, his gaze almost upon her, his nostrils twitching. He opened his maw, revealing long white fangs, then flicked his tongue. Something flew from his mouth and hit the roof twenty feet away. It bounced a few times before settling. The spider-shaped, dark-elven artifact.

Hell, what message was he sending with *that*? That he knew it was hers? That he knew she was close? It couldn't be coincidence that he'd chosen this rooftop to spit it upon.

His head lifted further, his gaze shifting toward the south.

Whether he sensed another dragon or some different threat, Arwen didn't know, but with a smashing of glass—his tail hitting another innocent window—he leaped into the air. The wind from his wingbeats stirred Arwen's hair as he flew away.

Unfortunately, he didn't open a portal and leave Earth. Instead, he soared off to the north.

Aware that Val and Matti lived in that direction, Arwen hoped he didn't pester them further. She also hoped he didn't know where she lived.

Arwen's phone buzzed. It heated abruptly in her pocket, and when she pulled it out, the display flashed several times, as if it were on the fritz.

She rested it on the rooftop, and it settled down, showing only that Amber was texting.

*Delivery for you at the coffee shop.*

Arwen looked in the direction the dragon had flown before picking up the phone and—more reluctantly—the artifact. She climbed down from the roof and headed for the coffee shop.

Who Saruknorath was, she didn't know, but she was positive she hadn't seen the last of him.

# 4

SINCE HER FRIENDS RELIED ON THE INCOME FROM THE COFFEE Dragon, Arwen shouldn't have been relieved when she walked in and found that the customers hadn't returned, but the part of her that felt panic in crowds was glad only Nin, Matti, Sarrlevi, their babies, and Amber and Imoshaun were in the main room. Once, she would have considered even that many people a crowd, but her anxiety was less likely to rise among those she knew. Usually. She stutter-stepped when all of their gazes swung toward her. Well, not *all* of them. The babies were looking up at their mother, or maybe the hammer slung over her shoulder, and ignored her.

"I apologize for the interruption to your business." Arwen nodded to Nin, who'd removed the arrow from above the door frame and held it out to her.

Arwen winced at the hole it had left. Though numerous enchantments made the Coffee Dragon sturdier than *most* buildings, her arrows were magical and tended to pierce such defenses.

"It is not your fault," Nin said. "The *dragon* is to blame."

"Technically, all he did was come in and have a drink." True, but Arwen thought he'd been about to pick a fight with Sarrlevi.

"Which he did not pay for. That makes him a criminal. Also, he mind-scoured me and insulted the beef sticks."

"That second thing is clearly the most egregious affront."

"They are made from grass-fed, free-range cows and do *not* contain chemicals." Nin sniffed.

Arwen looked at Amber, who had her hands on her hips as she watched Imoshaun, the gnome inventor, wander around the front of the shop, peering through her glasses at the enchanted yard art and other knickknacks inside magically protected display cases. Price tags promised they could be purchased alongside coffee and chemical-free beef sticks, but Arwen had never seen anyone buy the art.

"I thought you were going to pick up the armor, not the armorer," she told Amber.

"I *was*. But she wanted to come along and see the business of the great Ruin Bringer." Amber rolled her eyes. "Don't forget my payment, FYI. It's only because you're a good client that I was willing to run an errand to Bellevue for you during rush hour. *And* take on a chatty passenger who crawled into the back and disassembled my recently installed speakers. She's worse than your half-dragon."

"Really?" Arwen raised her eyebrows.

"Well, I guess not. She stayed out of my glove compartment and didn't call me an irreverent mongrel. Still, I'd charge an extra fee if you hadn't just paid me a bunch of gold coins. Even if it was a pain in the ass to get them exchanged for *real* money, they turned out to be worth a lot, so I'm being extra tolerant."

Arwen smiled sadly, thinking of how Azerdash had supplied those gold coins. An ache tightened her throat. She already missed him.

"Here." Amber handed the jumpsuit to Arwen. "I had to watch her add even *more* sequins and weird shimmery bits to it as part of the repairs."

"Thank you," was all Arwen said, not sure if the comment meant Amber disapproved vehemently of the fashion statement the jumpsuit made or was still upset that the garment, which had previously been hers, had been altered so greatly that she no longer wanted it.

Since its value was immense to Arwen, she was glad to have it. She did, however, continue to feel guilty that acquiring it had involved maiming something of value to Amber.

Though she wanted to ask Sarrlevi who that dragon was, Arwen held up a finger to Amber and jogged to the back room to retrieve her pack. Fortunately, the dragon hadn't bothered *it* while he'd been absconding with the artifact. She still didn't know why he'd picked that up, but it made her nervous. What if he had the ability to track people—or find their homes—by examining items they'd touched?

Arwen nodded to Amber when she returned with the pack. "Here's your payment. I brought more than we agreed to." Arwen withdrew two jars and a container holding multiple batches of cookies. "Our cherries aren't ready to harvest yet, so I pickled some red huckleberries for you. It's a similar recipe, and they sell quickly at the market. People say they're delicious. And these cookies appeased even the fae queen. They're blueberry and chocolate chip."

"I thought your half-dragon's sexually vigorous friend appeased the fae queen," Matti said when Amber stepped away to look at a text message.

Arwen hadn't spent much time with Matti these past few days and hadn't mentioned that part of the story to her, but she wasn't surprised the tale had gotten around. She *had* told Val. "I'd like to think the cookies helped."

"Probably." Matti peered over her babies' heads and into the open pack. "Do you have anything for anybody else? My appetite isn't quite as voracious as it was when I was eating for three, but I *am* nursing now. That's hard work."

Amber glanced up from her phone. "Don't you just sit there while they do the, uh, milking?"

She waved her fingers, a faint lip curl suggesting she thought the whole thing too unpleasantly biological to discuss.

Arwen recalled Val saying her daughter didn't have maternal instincts, at least not yet.

"My body has to *make* the milk," Matti said. "It's very challenging."

"More so than hurling a hammer around all day?" Amber asked.

"For sure. My half-dwarven body is built for hammer hurling." Matti patted her stout thigh.

Amber snatched the cookies from Arwen's grip before Matti could suggest sharing. She also grabbed the jars, though she eyed the huckleberries a little skeptically. "I'll let you know if these are a fair exchange for the cherries. They're kind of small."

"The weight of the food in the jars is the same. I have a scale. I make sure to give customers a fair deal. Matti, I can make you some when I get a chance."

Arwen pulled another tin of cookies from the bottom of her pack. She'd intended to leave them at the Coffee Dragon for the staff and patrons to enjoy until she had time to bake and sell here again, but Matti had helped Azerdash unlock the chest holding the galaxy blade. She deserved a reward.

When Sarrlevi approached, walking up to Matti's side and gazing fondly at her and their babies, Arwen said, "You seemed to know that dragon. Will you tell me who he is? Another Silverclaw?"

Val walked through the front door with her magical silver tiger, Sindari, at her side and her hand resting on the butt of the semi-automatic pistol in her thigh holster.

"He is, in fact, a Starsinger dragon." When a grasping baby hand appeared in the air, Sarrlevi extended a finger to touch it.

"A Starsinger?" Val asked, joining the group. "Like Xilneth? Did he croon love songs to anyone?" Val looked at Arwen.

Arwen, who'd heard of but didn't have experience with Xilnethgarish, shook her head. "Definitely not. He was mind-scouring Nin and wanted to do the same to me. He's looking for Azerdash."

"He is also a member of the Assassins' Guild," Sarrlevi said, "though it was always my understanding that Nesheeva, the guild leader, doesn't charge him dues, so he's more of an honorary member. A couple of times, he's tried to claim the guild should be his and that its members should serve him and bring him regular offerings."

"How did Nesheeva keep him from enforcing that?" Matti asked. "He was pretty powerful."

"I believe she went into great detail about all the paperwork that a guild leader must do, and Saruknorath decided that was not of interest to him."

"Now he sounds like a Starsinger dragon," Val said.

*I do not see a threat present,* a telepathic male voice said. Sindari, the tiger.

"You said you'd gnaw off my foot if you had to fight another dragon," Val told him.

*I did, and the words were true. I was, however, prepared to battle lesser foes, if necessary, while you drew the dragon's ire.*

"Well, wait ten minutes, and the goblins will be back. You know how you enjoy dodging the dice that ricochet down the stairs."

The tiger's green eyes gazed coolly at Val. *You know I do not enjoy the crowded mayhem of this place. You should have become a business owner of a serene grotto or sunny beach, a more appealing place for great Del'nothian tigers.*

"Didn't you get sand up your butt the last time we were on a beach?" Val asked.

*Because we were battling a hydra from the shallows, not relaxing in the sun.*

Arwen cleared her throat. She liked Sindari, but she was more concerned about the dragon assassin than sand in tiger orifices. "Does Saruknorath's presence here mean the entire Assassins' Guild is after the half-dragons or that someone hired him alone to... take care of Azerdash?"

She winced at the thought. Even though dragons had been trying to kill Azerdash for weeks, learning of a new one in the hunt disturbed her.

"It may mean either of those things," Sarrlevi said. "I am no longer in the Assassins' Guild and have not visited their head-quarters in some time."

"Nesheeva doesn't send you the guild newsletter anymore?" Matti asked. "That's a shame."

Sarrlevi gazed at her through his lashes. "Assassins do not have *news*letters."

"Is there any chance you would be able to find out more about why Saruknorath is after Azerdash?" Arwen asked Sarrlevi. "And if others are? I don't know where he is now, but I'd like to warn him if I can figure out how."

Sarrlevi didn't owe her any favors, but, in the past, he'd assisted her in small ways, and he'd also seemed inclined to help Azerdash and Yendral avoid notice while they were on Earth.

"I will speak with Nesheeva on this matter. Perhaps I will show her the portrait we had done of our new family."

"She might tease you about settling down to have kids," Matti told him. "She's on the snarky side."

Sarrlevi lifted his chin. "You are magnificent in the portrait, and the half-elven artist captured the impressive healthy glow of our babies."

"She might tease you *a lot*." Matti looked to Val, as if seeking her opinion.

"Is he wearing the baby sling in the portrait?" Val asked.

"Oh, yes," Matti said. "Outside of feeding time, I barely get to hold the kids."

Sarrlevi only raised his chin higher. "As a father, it is my duty to protect our offspring."

One started crying.

"Maybe we should take them home for nap time." Matti peered down at the kids. "Or possibly a diaper change."

"They do require that often." To his credit, Sarrlevi didn't step back and lift his hands to imply he wanted to avoid handling the task.

"It's all that good food you keep bringing us," Matti said, though Arwen doubted the babies would be able to consume anything but milk for some time.

"Another duty of the father." Sarrlevi offered his arm, and they walked out together.

"I suppose I can put my tiger away if the dragon isn't coming back," Val said.

"He may be back," Arwen said. "Nin gave him some of that goblin-fuel coffee. It's meant to cause an addiction, isn't it?"

"I'm not sure *encourages chemical-substance dependency* is on the bags that come from the roaster, but it has been known to have that effect. Willard hasn't visited Starbucks in ages. She doesn't even like this place, but she shows up every morning with a huge mug to fill for the day."

Four-foot-tall Imoshaun approached the group, tools clanking in the pockets of her overalls, but she eyed Sindari warily and didn't get too close. She lifted a pamphlet and raised her brows toward Arwen.

Arwen started to walk over to join her, in case she wanted to charge for the armor repair or had come along to discuss another matter, but she realized she hadn't fulfilled a social obligation to introduce Imoshaun to the group. The gnome knew Val, who'd been to her workshop before, but Arwen didn't think Imoshaun had met the others.

She shared everyone's name and finished with, "And this is Imoshaun, a renowned inventor on the gnomish home world."

"And also here." Imoshaun smiled, waved the pamphlet, and opened it to a dog-eared page. "Look at this." She held it up to display rows of text above drawings of machines or maybe magical artifacts. Or a combination of both? The writing wasn't in English —or *any* Earth language.

"I've seen those brochures before at Willard's office but have no idea what they say," Val said.

"Is that Elven?" Arwen asked.

"I think so," Val said. "My sister, Freysha, is visiting and could translate it."

"No need," Imoshaun said. "It's the prestigious *New Realm, New Moon Journal* published by two elven scribes who are refugees living in the arboretum, where they set up their printshop among the gardens. Camouflaged, of course. It is a central location where they can report on all the important work magical beings are doing in this area. This is an article about the project Gruflen and I are engaged in. It combines dragon magic with gnomish inventions. We have built a memory-enhancement device for those with brain damage who are losing their recollections of the past. Incorporating dragon magic with gnomish technology has never been done before! Of course, it is quite challenging to obtain the assistance of a dragon for such endeavors, but when one can find rare dragon artifacts to study and use..." Imoshaun beamed a smile at Val.

"Are you talking about the dog whistle—*dragon* whistle—that was driving Zav nuts in the dark-elf parking garage?" Val asked.

"Yes. After I rescued my husband, we took samples of it."

"Mangled samples?" Arwen asked. "I shot it."

"Before Zav smashed it into hundreds of pieces," Val added.

"Yes." Imoshaun clasped her hands to her chest. "It was not completely pulverized or incinerated. It was wonderful and has been so useful in our work. Ruin Bringer, is there any chance your mate would consider bringing us more artifacts from the dragon home world? We do not mind if they don't work. In fact, we *prefer* artifacts that don't work. They are less dangerous that way."

"My understanding is that dragons don't make many artifacts," Val said. "Their magic is so powerful that whatever they need done, they can wave their fingers—talons—and do."

"Yes, such artifacts are very scarce. Hence the lack—the *previous* lack—of gnomish devices incorporating dragon magic."

"I have a dark-elven artifact you can study if you'd like," Arwen told Imoshaun.

"Are you not still using that to seek the vampire?"

"I am." Arwen had told Imoshaun about Zoltan's disappearance when she'd dropped off the jumpsuit. "Ineffectively. Maybe you could—"

*Possible trouble approaches,* Sindari interrupted, his striped silver tail twitching as he looked toward a front window.

"The dragon is already addicted and coming back?" Val dropped a hand to the butt of her pistol.

*No. I sense many orcs in a fast-moving conveyance turning onto this street. It is possible they intend to engage in an ammunition unloading.*

"A drive-by shooting. Amber, take our gnome friend and hide in the back under the table." Val ran to the front, tucking her body behind the wall as she peered out a window. "Did that dragon send minions to do his dirty work?"

"Hide in the back?" Amber asked. "We just had a sword practice. You said I'm getting good."

"Not against bullets." Val jerked a thumb toward the hall.

Amber rolled her eyes but took Imoshaun's hand and led her

away. The gnome was so busy perusing the article about her work that she didn't seem to have heard them talking about a threat.

"At least this place is well-armored these days." Val waved at the windows. The rain had started and beaded on the glass.

Arwen, with unease creeping into her belly, nocked an arrow and joined Val. The van Sindari had sensed roared into view. With black paint and *Fiona's Flower Delivery* written on the side, it was familiar, and Arwen groaned.

"Those are the mercenaries that Harlik-van hired." Arwen tightened her grip on her bow, but the windows didn't open, so she couldn't shoot unless she stepped outside. Since the sliding van door opened, and orcs with rifles leaned out, that seemed like a bad idea. Why hadn't she stripped down and put her armored jumpsuit on right away? "I thought he'd killed them all. We found the cut-up bodies in the park."

"Harlik-van?" Val drew her pistol. "That's your dark-elf half-brother, right?"

"Yeah. You met him."

"When he tried to kill me, I remember. Funny that he didn't give me his name first."

"Dark elves can be rude."

"Among other things."

The van drew even with the Coffee Dragon, tires spraying water as they spun through puddles, and the orcs opened fire.

# 5

ARWEN SPRANG BACK FROM THE WINDOW AS THE ORCS FIRED AT THE Coffee Dragon. Val stayed put, looking through the glass of the closed door, her pistol out as she scowled at the black van rolling past. The driver and two orcs hanging out the open sliding door fired rifles, bullets striking the front of the shop.

They pinged off without doing damage. Even the bullets that hit the windows didn't so much as scratch the glass. More, evergreen shrubs growing in huge ceramic pots to either side of the front steps tilted sideways, and tiny cannons popped up from the dirt. They boomed, firing at the orcs.

A flaming cannonball just missed the van, spinning past it and over the roof of the building across the street. Where would it land? Lake Union? The other fiery cannonball struck the side of the van and tore into it, prompting the orcs to duck back inside.

"Nice," Val crooned.

Arwen had sensed the Coffee Dragon's magical defenses before but had never seen them in action.

As the van continued away, the driver unaffected by the attack, Val risked opening the door. She leaped out and opened fire.

Magic infused her bullets, and they glowed blue as they streaked through the rain, pounding into the back of the van. Just as the cannonball had, they pierced the metal frame.

The orcs in the back might have flattened to their bellies, but that didn't keep the driver from pulling a U-turn. The move was so sharp that when the van clipped a curb, it went up on two wheels. It came down with a thud and sped back toward the coffee shop.

This time, Val fired at the windshield. Arwen stepped out beside her, finding the room to aim her bow. But the windshield was more armored than the frame, and even Val's magical bullets bounced off. Arwen, afraid her arrows would do the same, aimed for a tire instead. It wasn't her first time targeting that van—or another identical to it.

Her arrow pierced the rubber, but the tire didn't blow.

"That thing's armored." Val stepped back into the cover of the shop, pulling Arwen with her. "Orcs in vans attack me so regularly that they know what to expect."

Sindari roared from behind them.

As the van passed again, an orc standing in the sliding door opening rose into view over the roof and fired at Val and Arwen. Prepared, Arwen erected a magical barrier. She didn't know if the shop's defenses would keep bullets from passing through an *open* door.

The orcs fired several more bullets. Again, none pierced the windows or siding of the shop. Two deflected off Arwen's barrier.

The orc driver yelled something to his buddies and pointed to the ice-cream shop next door.

"Shit," Val said. "They'd better not target mundanes."

The standing orc shifted his aim, rifle pointing across the roof of the van and toward a kid peering through the doorway of the ice-cream shop.

Arwen and Val fired at the same time. Arwen's arrow struck the orc in the chest, but he was armored. Val had aimed higher, and her bullet tore into his throat. Before he could shoot, the orc pitched backward and tumbled out of the van. The vehicle roared on, leaving him in the street.

Drawing her sword, Val ran out with rage in her eyes. Sindari tore after her, charging for the van as it sped down the street. Val pounced on the fallen orc, who was trying to get up.

"You'd shoot a kid, you asshole?" she demanded, sword raised.

Arwen drew another arrow and started to aim after the van, but a cry of, "Val!" came from the back of the coffee shop. Amber?

Black mist flowed out of the hall, and Arwen's gut knotted as she registered a hint of magic in it. Was that the same mist that she and Azerdash had encountered in the dark-elf lair? It couldn't be. Rain or not, it was broad daylight. Dark elves couldn't come above ground when the sun or even a bright moon was out.

Still, it had to indicate *some* kind of danger.

"Val!" Arwen yelled, in case Val hadn't heard, and ran inside and toward the hall.

Worried the mist would be dangerous, Arwen made herself pause to strengthen her barrier. As she entered the hall, the mist thickened, and malevolent energy lashed at her defenses. Hell, maybe this *was* the stuff the dark elves had summoned. Just because her mother's people couldn't walk in daylight didn't mean that their allies—or minions—couldn't have access to some of their magic.

Bow drawn, Arwen sprang into the back room. The table was empty, and Amber crouched behind it, her sword drawn.

"I'm sorry," she blurted. "I thought they were coming after *me*, so I was only worried about defending myself."

"What do you—" Abruptly, Arwen realized she didn't sense Imoshaun's gnomish aura. "No," she blurted and ran for the back door for the second time that day.

Weapons fire continued to ring out from the street out front, but when Arwen raced out the back door, she couldn't sense any orcs or anyone at all. She *did,* however, sense and see the mist. It filled the alley, keeping her from spotting anything else.

Fury surged into her. If another ally had been kidnapped out from under her nose...

More malevolent magic lashed at her barrier, trying to sap the power from it, trying to get to her.

"Leave me alone!" Her fury built, and she willed the mist to disappear, to go back to where it had come from.

A hint of red infused the formerly translucent barrier she'd formed around herself. Her anger affecting the type of magic she called upon?

Her tattoo throbbed, and a purple glow seeped out from under her sleeve.

*Yes,* a voice in the back of her mind whispered in Dark Elven. *Draw upon your power. Use it fully. The demons will reward you.*

"No," Arwen snarled, but she waved an arm, longing so badly for a target to unleash her frustration on. With a chopping motion, she summoned a whirlwind of power that batted away the mist, sweeping the alley clean.

She'd called upon dark-elven magic, nothing she'd twisted to be similar to a surface elf's magic, and when it worked, that only frustrated her more. She didn't want to use the power of her mother's people, didn't want to need it. But if dark elves had kidnapped Imoshaun...

Tattered by her power, the mist faded, leaving the damp alley in view. As her senses had told her, nobody was back there, but with the haze gone, she detected something that was. Another spider-shaped artifact rested on the pavement, precisely facing her. It was identical to the other, and she checked her pocket, at first thinking that the device had fallen out.

It hadn't. After pulling it out, Arwen stared numbly at both of them until voices in the hall made her stir.

The gunfire had stopped, as had the squeals of tires. Arwen

didn't know if the van had been destroyed or if the orcs had gotten away, but she hardly cared. They'd been a distraction for the kidnapping, nothing more.

Arwen slumped, failure making her tilt her head back, letting the rain hit her cheeks.

Val stepped into the alley, her weapons still in hand. "Is the gnome..." She trailed off when she spotted the spider-shaped artifact on the ground. "Hell, is that another one?" She answered her own question when she looked at the one in Arwen's hand. "They must want you to find them."

"A card with an address would ensure that more than these." Arwen was tempted to hurl the one in her hand to the ground, but it might blow up or do something awful.

"I doubt dark elves live somewhere you can look up with Google Street View."

Arwen returned her arrow to her quiver, hardly caring if the two she'd fired at the van were retrievable. Feeling defeated, she hunched forward, hands on her knees.

"I don't know what to do, Val," she whispered. "First Zoltan and now Imoshaun."

Even as the words came out, she stood. She had the power to track people, and she would. These prints would be fresh, *very* fresh.

"Maybe we should go back and check that cave where your brother was camping," Val suggested. "I doubt he left a forwarding address, but maybe there's a clue we overlooked."

Arwen doubted it. Willard's people had already been back to that cave behind the waterfall, looking for Harlik-van's body or evidence that he'd left behind. They'd found nothing.

Kneeling, Arwen rested a hand on the damp pavement. In the past, she'd hesitated to use her soul-tracking ability—a dark-elf talent—in front of others, but, at that moment, she didn't care if Val witnessed it. She closed her eyes and drew upon her power, willing her sight to change so that she could see the paranormal realm—and who had recently passed this way.

Dozens of whitish-green footprints came into view, the essences that people's souls left behind when they walked through an area. The prints were a confusing tangle, thanks to all the patrons who'd recently fled out the back way. Arwen could get a sense of who the owners had been, each person's soul being distinct, but only the faintest of traces were left behind, especially when a person didn't pass through an area frequently. She sifted through the prints, groping for patience, as she tried to pick out the malevolent essence of a dark elf in the mix.

But *would* the kidnapper have been a dark elf? In the middle of the day? More likely, it had been an orc who was working for her mother's people.

A twang plucked at her heart when she picked out Imoshaun's prints, her soul burbly and excited. But they didn't lead away from the area. After the prints went out the door, they disappeared. Someone might have picked her up—or formed a portal. During the shooting, Arwen hadn't sensed one forming, but she'd also been distracted.

A large print drew her eye, a series of them. They belonged to an orc, and the length of the strides promised the owner had been running. Perhaps with a gnome tucked under his or her arm?

Arwen started after the prints. They headed toward the same corner she'd run around to flee the dragon.

"Uhm, Arwen?" Val's forehead creased as she watched. "Whatcha doing?"

"Hunting a kidnapper." Arwen hadn't explained soul tracking to Val before and didn't now, only striding after the orc prints.

"Did you know your sleeve is glowing?" Val followed after her, waving for Sindari to stay behind, probably with a telepathic order to keep an eye on Amber.

Arwen glanced at her tattooed forearm and shook her head,

not caring if the dark-elven mark had something to say. It was probably happy she was using the power she'd inherited from her mother.

When she didn't respond, Val added, "We really need to find Zoltan so you can fix your arm. It's too bad the formula and all the ingredients disappeared along with him. If those had been left behind, we could have found an interim alchemist, though Zoltan would be the first to tell you how inferior all other alchemists in the Greater Seattle area are. Possibly the greater *Earth* area."

Concentrating on keeping her vision shifted so she could follow the trail, Arwen didn't answer. Val fell silent, walking at her side, trusting that she knew what she was doing. Arwen appreciated that.

The trail led to one of the still-open manhole covers. Arwen stared, wondering if she'd been mistaken. She'd assumed the dark elves had been behind the orc shooting, but was it possible Saruknorath was tied into this?

"They went down here." Arwen crouched to peer into the dark hole.

"After throwing the manhole cover like a frisbee into a pet store?" Val pointed at a shattered glass front door with a paw on the top half and the manhole cover embedded in the bottom, a dozen cracks radiating outward.

"The dragon did that."

"Rough day for the neighborhood. I'll lead."

Before Arwen could stop her, warning about possible dark elves, Val jumped through the hole. She landed with a splash below.

"Uh, can you track through water?" Val called up.

Opting to use the ladder rungs, Arwen climbed down. "Not usually, no."

A couple of white-green smudges on the rungs were the only signs that had survived the damp environment. Rainwater flowed through a channel in the middle of the passage. There were ledges on the sides that one could walk on, but the orc must have deliberately trod through the water. Knowing he would be tracked?

With her pistol back in hand, Val peered both ways down the tunnel. "Do we guess? Maybe I could call Sindari over, and his nose would guide him."

In the distance, magic swelled. A portal forming.

Val must have sensed it too, because she leaped onto a ledge and took off running. Arwen charged after her. The magic was too far away for her to tell what race had formed it, but she wouldn't have guessed any of the orcs had been strong practitioners of magic. None had seemed to have the auras to suggest the power to create portals.

A squeaky cry sounded in the distance. Imoshaun.

Arwen ran faster, sensing the gnome's aura for the first time. She also sensed an orc. For an instant, she thought she caught a third person's aura, but it disappeared before she could pin it down. Someone with camouflaging magic.

After they passed the other open manhole that the dragon had left, the tunnel grew dark, no light reaching them. It was dark enough down there for a dark elf.

The tunnel curved, and Arwen and Val ran around the bend in time to spot a silvery disc floating in the center ahead. Someone in a cloak with their back to them leaped through the portal. A second hulking figure stayed behind, turning to face them. The silver glow of the portal highlighted his tusks, broad face, and squat nose.

With a whisper of steel, the orc drew a sword. He shifted and stepped toward them, deliberately blocking the portal.

Val fired at his shoulder. Arwen loosed an arrow, only at the last second shifting her aim from his eye to his thigh. Both attacks landed, knocking the orc back.

Though he dropped to one knee, he lifted the sword, bracing to meet them. Val fired twice more.

"We need to question him," Arwen said, afraid Val would kill him.

"Orcs answer questions more freely when blood is leaking from a dozen holes in their body." Val sprang, stomping on the orc's sword arm as he pitched backward into the water. She pinned his weapon under a boot.

"Is that really true?" Arwen stopped a few paces away, aiming an arrow at the orc.

"No, they aren't cooperative with interrogations under any circumstances."

As if in agreement, the orc spat at them and cursed in his tongue. He tried to jerk his arm up and shift away from Val. She only planted her other boot on his chest. Mired in a foot of water and wounded, he couldn't find the leverage to knock her away.

"Who'd you give the gnome to?" As she stood on him, Val pointed her gun between his eyes.

He spat and cursed again. "Mogdok die before he tell the Ruin Bringer anything!"

In the fae realm, Arwen had successfully read minds. There had been more natural magic in the ground there, much more power that she could draw upon, but she tried to emulate what she'd done then, mentally cupping the orc's head.

"Mogdok will die if he doesn't." Val bent and pressed the cool metal muzzle of her gun to his forehead. "Where is she?"

The only thought Arwen received from the orc was one of utter hatred for Val.

Arwen attempted to comb through his mind, as the dragons did when they read hers, hoping to sift through his memories and learn what he'd seen recently.

For a heartbeat, she glimpsed Imoshaun in the orc's thoughts, the gnome held in his big hands as he gave her to the cloaked figure. A hood and the darkness of the tunnel hid the person's features, but Imoshaun writhed and twisted, and managed to pull something out of her pocket. A ring? Blue light seeped between her fingers, enough to highlight the albino skin on the hooded person's chin, as well as the lines of a masculine jaw.

The orc struck Imoshaun, and the ring she'd grabbed fell from her grip. The blue light disappeared as it sank into the water. Darkness filled the tunnel until the hooded figure—a dark elf—formed a portal. He slung Imoshaun over his shoulder, gave the orc a coin, then patted him on the shoulder. That gesture of camaraderie surprised Arwen, and the sense of confusion and suspicion that accompanied the orc's thoughts suggested he hadn't expected it either.

"What the—" Val said as the orc's thoughts scattered.

In the water, his legs twitched. He bucked, surprising Val and almost knocking her free.

"Knock it off," Val told the orc, keeping the gun to his forehead.

But his eyes had rolled back, and his arms and legs only twitched more violently.

Frowning, Val stepped back. "Do orcs have seizures?"

"They do if they're poisoned." Arwen remembered the shoulder touch. She hadn't seen a ring or anything the dark elf might have used to puncture his tusked employee's skin and deliver a dose but wouldn't be surprised if he had.

The orc's flailing grew more violent, his head cracking the cement ledge, water surging everywhere with his contortions.

"Hell." Val stepped back farther.

She lifted a hand, as if she might help somehow, but the seizure soon ended. The orc lay still in the water, his aura fading as death took him.

"I think..." Arwen licked her lips, the orc's memories imprinted in her mind. "I think that might have been Harlik-van."

If he'd taken Imoshaun and left that artifact, he must have been tied in with the kidnapping of Zoltan too.

"I guess that's another reason to visit his cave," Val said, "and see if he left any clues about his whereabouts."

Arwen would rather visit Azerdash and let him wrap a comforting arm around her shoulders while promising to help her find her friends. But he was on his own quest now, one far from Earth and those who lived here. Including her.

"Yes." Arwen attempted to sound more resolute than glum. "I'm ready."

# 6

As Val drove east out of Seattle, Arwen sat in the passenger seat of her Jeep and fingered the gnomish magical ring she'd fished out of the water after the orc died. She didn't know what it did, what Imoshaun had *hoped* to do when she'd dug it out of her pocket, but her presence clung to it. Maybe it would help Arwen find Imoshaun. *And* Zoltan.

Who would disappear next because the dark elves were irked with Arwen? And why couldn't they just come after her? Instead, they were targeting everyone around her.

Arwen groaned and leaned forward as far as the seat belt would allow, dropping her forehead into her lap. The armored jumpsuit, which she'd changed into before leaving, rustled with the movement.

"I would worry you're about to get carsick," Val said, "but you've survived riding with Amber, so my driving *can't* be bothering you."

"I'm depressed and guilt ridden, not sick." Arwen made herself sit up.

"That's a relief. Sindari always says my air fresheners nauseate him, so I did worry for a second that the piña colada was getting to you." Val flicked the tree-shaped, scented cardboard dangling from the rearview mirror.

"It is dreadful, but I have a hardy stomach."

"Air fresheners are a requirement when you drive around with tigers and occasionally your mom's wet dog in the car. It's not my favorite scent, but it irritates Sindari to no end, so I buy them in bulk."

"Is it wise to irritate a thousand-pound magical tiger?"

"Oh, not at all, but he threatens to gnaw my foot off all the time, so I assail his nostrils with air fresheners. Our relationship works for us." Val grinned over at Arwen. "Hey, don't sweat this stuff. I'm sure Zoltan and Imoshaun will be fine. I bet they were tossed naked into a cell together as bait for a trap for you."

"Comforting." Arwen hoped that *was* all that would happen to them. "Why do you think nudity is involved?"

"Well, it was the last time Zoltan was kidnapped, so I just assumed. Making people naked tends to take some of the fight out of them. Prisoners aren't as tough without their clothes. Even vampires."

"I don't think that's a dark-elf tactic. I assume they weren't Zoltan's kidnappers last time."

"No, mad scientists who wanted to figure out how to increase human longevity by studying the undead kidnapped some vampires. They also stole a dragon egg."

"How did that go for them?"

"It turned out to be a recipe for *decreasing* their mortality." Val pointed toward a freeway exit. "Are you sure you don't want to tell Imoshaun's husband?"

"I asked Amber to take Imoshaun's pamphlet back and let him know what happened." Arwen grimaced at her cowardliness. She would eventually have to go in person to apologize to Gruflen— maybe *he* could somehow use the ring to find Imoshaun—but...

Arwen couldn't help but hope she could find the kidnap victims right away and deliver Imoshaun along with her apology. "I'll go later."

Val looked over at her. In judgment?

Maybe that was Arwen projecting her own feelings on Val.

"I'm ashamed that I haven't been able to track Zoltan down yet," Arwen admitted. "And that my mother's people are... I'm not sure they're toying with me, but they're not being direct. They're..."

"Baiting a trap, like I said. They want you to find them. They wouldn't be leaving dark-elf doohickeys behind otherwise."

"The *doohickeys* aren't that helpful in locating their lair. At least not that I've been able to discover." And she'd asked Matti, Willard, Gondo, Amber, and everyone else she could think of with a reputation for researching magic.

"Those artifacts hold the secret," Val said with certainty.

"What makes you so sure?"

"Because the dark elves keep leaving them for you. An invitation."

"Nothing says come visit like ugly spider crystals," Arwen murmured.

"If you're a dark elf, I'm *positive* that's what ugly spiders say."

Arwen couldn't deny Val's assumption. She had the same suspicion and felt obtuse for not being able to figure out how to follow them to the prisoners—and her mother's kin. *Her* kin, whether she wanted to admit it or not. The evil kin that she wanted nothing to do with, but what choice did she have? What if she had to sacrifice herself to the dark elves to ensure the safety of those she cared about?

"I need to find them, Val," Arwen whispered. "And I need to make sure the dark elves won't take anyone else."

"We'll find them."

Arwen drew out one of the spider artifacts. When she'd found the first one, she hadn't touched it with her bare hands, but nothing had happened in the days she'd had it, so she'd stopped worrying it would kill her. Her mother's people had a use for her. Unfortunately. Thus far, they had struck all around but never at her.

"I wish Azerdash were here," Arwen said. "He might know something about this artifact. And he... I'd just like him here."

"You're really falling for him, huh?"

"I guess. He's nice."

"Kind of quirky."

"Yeah. Nicely so."

Val smiled at her, then squinted at something in the rearview mirror. "Company is on the way."

"Zavryd?"

"If only we were going to be that lucky. Camo yourself."

As Val changed lanes so she could take the next exit, Arwen sensed what she'd sensed—and groaned.

A dragon was coming but not the right one. It was Saruknorath again.

"I'll do the same, but it may be too late." Val rubbed a charm on the thong around her neck.

"Let's hope he has trouble sensing us with so many other people driving on the freeway," Arwen said but doubted that would be the case. Few of the other drivers had magical blood, so Saruknorath wouldn't register them at all.

As Val exited the freeway and drove into a gas station advertising showers and hot wings as well as the best prices, Arwen looked for the black-scaled dragon in the side mirror but couldn't yet see him. That didn't keep her from sensing that Saruknorath was flying straight toward them.

"I don't suppose we can open a manhole cover and trick him into looking for me in there," Arwen murmured.

"Probably not, but if you see one, I'm game to try." Val pulled around to the back of the gas station and parked, a weed-choked field dotted with garbage stretching away from them.

They sensed the dragon flying closer and grabbed their weapons and slid out of the Jeep.

Val fingered the cat-shaped charm on her thong. "Is it me, or is he flying straight at us, despite our camouflage?"

Arwen couldn't yet see the dragon past the gas station and other buildings blocking the sky, but she nodded, her senses telling her the same. "The Jeep isn't camouflaged, right?"

Their charms couldn't do that.

"No, but there are two other Jeeps just in the gas station. There's even another black one." Val waved toward one turning into the lot.

"But is it piña colada scented?"

"He's not tracking my Jeep by my *air freshener.*" Val frowned, perhaps rethinking her confidence in that assertion. "It *is* a strong scent."

"It is."

Val shook her head. "I missed his visit to the Coffee Dragon earlier. I arrived after he left. He shouldn't have seen—or *smelled*—my Jeep."

"After we *think* he left the coffee shop." Arwen lowered her voice, expecting to see the dragon at any second. He continued to fly closer.

Val didn't deny the possibility that Saruknorath could have been hidden and in the area during the shooting and kidnapping. For all they knew, he might be allied with Harlik-van. As if the dark elves needed any more advantages over Arwen.

The black dragon came into view, his wings outstretched as he glided in for a landing. A landing on the roof of the gas station, facing the Jeep.

"Shit," Val muttered.

By unspoken agreement, she and Arwen backed into the field.

Innocent people were fueling up their cars and getting sodas and Doritos. Arwen didn't want to risk anyone being caught in the crossfire if she and Val had to fight the dragon.

As Saruknorath's topaz eyes locked on the Jeep, Arwen raised her bow.

Val hadn't yet called for Sindari. Since he'd been on Earth earlier, maybe the magic of the charm wouldn't allow a return so soon. Instead, she drew her pistol and pointed it at the dragon.

Saruknorath hopped from the gas station to land on the roof of the Jeep, the vehicle a ridiculously tiny perch for such a large creature. Metal screeched as his talons dug into the frame to find purchase.

*Damn it,* Val spoke telepathically. *I just got the tiger-claw scratches buffed out after the* last *time a dragon attacked us on a road trip.*

That road trip had also been to the waterfall cave where Harlik-van had been staying. Maybe this was a sign that they should stop visiting that place. Arwen kept her focus on the dragon—and the thought to herself.

*He's not looking right at us, at least,* Val pointed out.

Once he settled into a spot he liked, talons gouging into the Jeep's frame, tail spilling onto the pavement—was it too much to hope someone with an oversized truck would drive over it?—Saruknorath gazed at the building, the parking lot, and out into the field.

A small spinning orange ball appeared in the air in front of him, as if it had popped into existence—or been extracted from another dimension. It emanated magic. Was it a grenade or something similar?

Arwen braced herself in case they needed to run and dive. Not that the open, trash-littered field offered any cover. Maybe they should have run into the gas station and hidden behind the ICEE machine.

With a slight flick of his snout, Saruknorath batted the orange ball up to the roof.

When it landed, its magic grew stronger, and it popped and flashed. Startled cries came from the people out front, and Arwen flinched, squinting at the brilliance, but the light soon faded. When her vision cleared, she could make out Saruknorath staring intently at the roof. But his gaze soon left it, and another ball appeared in the air in front of him. He tossed it into the parking lot near the Jeep.

Knowing what to expect this time, Arwen closed her eyes before the flash. It still turned the insides of her eyelids red with its brilliance.

*He's looking for us,* Val guessed. Or maybe she knew. *Back up. I'll wager those balls break camouflage when they blow up.*

Arwen obeyed, not taking her eyes from the dragon or lowering her bow but carefully creeping farther away. Should they turn and sprint across the field?

Before she'd decided, the dragon conjured another ball and tossed it in their direction.

As the light flashed, an unpleasant buzz rippled over Arwen's skin.

*Ah, there you are, my little mongrels,* Saruknorath spoke into their minds.

Arwen turned to sprint away, hoping she could reactivate her camouflage when she was farther from the dragon, but his power wrapped around her, stopping her before she'd gone three steps. Val also halted mid-step, caught in the same invisible grip.

She pointed her pistol at Saruknorath, finger tight on the trigger. Arwen lifted her bow again, wishing one of her arrows could pierce dragon defenses. She sensed his magical barrier up and doubted either her or Val's projectiles would slip through. Val's powerful dwarven-forged sword might, but she would have to get close to use that.

*We shall now have the conversation you rudely evaded earlier.* His gaze skewered Arwen as he ignored Val. He showed no concern about the weapons pointed at him.

*Little mongrels don't get that excited about the prospects of chatting up dragons,* Val told the dragon.

*You will tell me where Azerdash Starblade is hiding,* Saruknorath said, still focused on Arwen, *when he is not popping into existence to plan an insurrection with world leaders.*

*Sure, we'd love to tell you that.* Val holstered her pistol and drew her sword. *But answer a question for us first, will you? We were having a heated debate. Did you track us down by the scent of the air freshener in the Jeep or what?*

While Val attempted to distract Saruknorath, Arwen groped for something she could do to break his hold. She could form a magical barrier around herself, but it did nothing to push away the dragon's grip.

*Air* freshener? Saruknorath looked at Val for the first time. *Surely, you do not refer to the pungent, detestable odor wafting from the conveyance where I am perched.*

*I'm guessing you're not a fan of getting caught in the rain and making love at midnight in the dunes of a cape.*

Arwen glanced at her.

"What?" Val asked. "You're too young to know that song?"

"I guess."

"It's a classic."

The magical grip around them tightened, flexing Arwen's barrier inward and threatening pain.

*When a dragon speaks to you, you will attend him assiduously.* Saruknorath's eyes flared brilliant topaz, and his talons flexed, further gouging the frame of the Jeep. *Where is Starblade?*

Val snarled and crouched. If not for the dragon's grip, she might have charged in to defend her vehicle.

*I honestly don't know,* Arwen replied, not wanting the Jeep to be destroyed. Or worse. She had to speak with the dragon herself. As much as Arwen appreciated Val trying to help her, this was her problem, and she had to handle it. *You may read my mind, if you wish.*

Arwen was relieved she didn't know where Azerdash was so that she couldn't betray him.

*Of course I wish, mongrel. It is why I have come to this backward world and am perched on this odious-smelling ambulatory box.*

"It *was* the air freshener that he tracked," Val whispered.

Painful itching started under Arwen's skull, and she flinched. Her magical barrier might protect her from an enemy's blades, but it couldn't save her from this.

Her tattoo also itched. Itched and throbbed with indignation. Its power radiated from her arm, burning through her veins like venom.

The dragon's eyes flared brighter. *Your thoughts are inaccessible to me, little mongrel. You* dare *fight me.*

*It's not me,* Arwen said.

*I should slay you for your impudence.* But his gaze shifted to Val. *You have no dark-elf blood to protect you.*

*No, just surface-elf blood,* Val replied. *But it's not keen on being mind-scoured either.*

The itching in Arwen's skull disappeared as the dragon focused on Val.

She gasped, lifting a hand to the side of her head.

*She doesn't know either!* Arwen tried to step in front of Val, to draw Saruknorath's attention back to her.

Face contorting with pain, Val dropped to one knee. Arwen lifted her bow and fired, hardly caring if the dragon lashed out at her. She couldn't let a friend suffer.

Her arrow sailed toward the dragon's maw but struck his magical barrier and bounced off.

"I hate these guys," Arwen whispered, pulling out another

arrow.

"Tell me about it," Val bit out.

She rapid-fired her semi-automatic pistol at the dragon. As with the arrow, the bullets didn't pierce the dragon's defenses. They *did*, however, piss him off.

Saruknorath sprang into the air and flew toward them, death in his eyes, his talons extended.

*We're mates,* Arwen blurted telepathically. *Azerdash and I. You were right about that. He'll come to me three nights from now. We promised to have a sexual encounter.*

The dragon's eyes narrowed to slits. He flew over the field instead of diving for Arwen and Val. But he banked to come around again.

*Staging insurrections makes him randy,* Arwen added, hoping the dragon would believe her lie, that his inability to read her mind would force him to take her words at face value. *I'm going to make him tacos and cookies, and then we'll have sex.*

Val looked over at her.

Maybe Arwen should have made her telepathic words more pinpoint.

*Three Earth nights from now?* Saruknorath flew in a slow circle over them.

*Yes. We're meeting under the Aurora Bridge at the troll sculpture.* Arwen shared a telepathic image of the bridge and its location in the city.

*That is not a strange place for a sexual encounter?*

*No, it's very romantic.* Arwen sensed the dragon didn't believe her—nobody had ever accused her of being an accomplished liar—and sought inspiration. What could she say to make the story more plausible? *Just so you know, I'm going to tell him about you when he comes. I can't let you hurt my friend, but I don't want to betray Azerdash either. He'll be ready if you show up at our rendezvous spot.*

*I am not afraid to fight a lowly mongrel dragon. I have even slain my own kind—when the reward was sufficient enough.*

*What's the reward for Starblade?* Arwen wondered if Sarukno-rath would give her that information. *And who's offering it?*

*Multiple parties want the conspiring mongrel half-dragon dead and are willing to reward he who brings Starblade's head before the Dragon Council. Even my own apolitical clan wishes his demise.* After flying another slow circle around the field and pinning them once more with his hard glowing eyes, Saruknorath flapped his wings and headed back toward Seattle.

Val lowered her weapons. "Oysters are a more known aphrodisiac than tacos."

"You can dredge and fry oysters in a cornmeal mixture and use them *in* tacos."

"That's your plan to get your half-dragon in bed?" Val headed toward her Jeep.

"No." Arwen hurried after her. "I said that to get rid of that guy. As far as I know, Azerdash isn't coming to Earth anytime soon."

Unfortunately.

"If he *does* come, he's going to be in trouble since that dragon can break camouflage."

"Well, he wouldn't visit me at the troll bridge anyway."

"I assume not, especially now that you've got that elven hot springs in your backyard." Val fingered a deep gouge in the door of her Jeep. "Bastard."

"Sorry," Arwen said.

"I wish you'd come up with your ruse *before* he clawed the hell out of my ride."

"Me too. I hope he believed it and leaves me alone for three days." Arwen eyed the sky in the direction Saruknorath had gone. He'd already disappeared from her senses. "I need time to find Zoltan and Imoshaun."

"And get the ingredients for oyster tacos."

"No doubt."

---

## 7

CHECKING THE WATERFALL CAVE NEAR NORTH BEND TURNED OUT TO be a waste of time. There weren't any clues they'd missed about Arwen's brother. There wasn't any sign that he'd ever been there at all.

As Val drove her back to the farm, Arwen slumped against the door of the Jeep and brooded out the window at the darkening sky.

They'd stopped at Imoshaun's basement laboratory and found her husband there, goggles on as he worked fervently on a project. *Gotta help her, gotta help her,* he'd repeated as he hammered and welded, barely acknowledging Arwen when she'd apologized for losing his wife. Only when she'd given him Imoshaun's fallen ring had he paused, his eyes lighting. *This will be useful,* he'd assured her before ushering her out because he had *so very much* to do.

"It's amazing how much of a pain in the ass dark elves have been lately," Val said as she turned onto the gravel driveway, "considering nobody can find them."

"Will you ask Willard if she knows anyone who's an expert in magical artifacts? Or dark elves?" Arwen agreed with Val that the secret to finding her mother's people had to be in the spider-shaped crystals they were leaving her.

"*You're* her expert in dark elves. That's why she hired you."

"I may know less about them than she believes. I'm more of an expert on gardening and baking. And I know all about pickling and canning."

"As handy as those skills are, they're not why the Army is interested in you." Val stopped the Jeep in front of Father's home. The lights were on, and his truck was parked in the driveway. "Have you shown those spiders to your dad yet?"

"I told him about the first one, but he didn't ask to see it."

"You can't *wait* for people to ask to see dark-elven artifacts. You'll never get a taker for that. You have to clunk them down on their desks, whether they want them or not."

"I haven't been giving him all the details of my dark-elf encounters. He wouldn't want me saying this, but he was traumatized by being their prisoner, being trapped in those dark tunnels for so many years, and used by my mother to..." Arwen waved at herself. "Make me." She frowned bleakly.

"Well, he was an adult when all that happened, so he might remember more than you, right? Maybe he's seen the spider artifacts before. He could be a good resource for information. Better than a goblin and a teenager."

"Gondo and Amber have been helpful researchers."

"They have their uses, but dark elves don't publish their evils on the internet for people to Google." Val waved at the house. "Check with your dad. Maybe stack some of your cookies next to the artifact to make it seem less evil."

"I'll keep your suggestion in mind." Arwen slid out of the Jeep and waved. "Thanks for driving me around. You charge less than Amber does."

Val hadn't even accepted Arwen's offer of gas money.

"I ought to charge *more* since you're a magnet for crabby dragons." Val pointed at one of the deep gouges in the door.

"Sorry."

"Amber asked me to let you know she's available if you need rides this weekend, but I'd prefer you *not* take her up on that, given how many powerful magical beings are messing with you."

"I understand. But, uhm, why did you tell me if you don't want me to call her?"

"She made me promise to because you—or those who hang out in your orbit—pay so much better than anyone else willing to hire a teenager."

"Azerdash is a generous tipper," Arwen murmured.

"Gondo said if you were offering more gold coins, *he'd* also offer to drive you."

"He doesn't have a car, does he?"

"He knows goblins with steam-powered jalopies. The hubcaps fall off, and the goblins have to sit on a stack of phone books to drive, but they'll come if he calls."

"It's good to have such a bevy of transportation options." Arwen waved again, then headed inside.

As Val drove away, Arwen touched the pouch in her pack that held the artifacts. Maybe her father *would* have some useful information. She'd long suspected he knew more than he'd told her about why he'd been kidnapped, why her mother had wanted to birth a mongrel, and what the dark elves planned. Even though Harlik-van and Zyretha had hinted of some of what her mother wanted her for, Arwen doubted she had the whole story.

She found her father in the living room, sitting on the couch while whittling and watching *Jeopardy* reruns. Shavings from a stick he was turning into a bear scattered a cloth on the coffee table.

"That's looking good. I remember when all you made were hot dog prongs for the fire pit." Arwen pantomimed whittling pointy sticks.

"I've had a lot of time to practice."

She didn't mention the idea of him dating or otherwise looking for a companion, something she'd brought up before. He'd always shied away from such suggestions. Besides, she had something else on her mind.

"Was it a good day at the market?" Arwen asked while mulling a way to bring up dark elves.

The afternoon's and evening's events had distracted her from her guilt over not being there for him, but it returned when he fixed a sour look on her.

"Three people came up to the table at once, and I had to run off to make change."

"Because you needed change or you didn't want to handle that many people at once?"

"It was *crowded*." He scowled at his whittling project. "Made some decent money though. The vegetables did okay, and then I went through all your latest jams. That cream for skin scales too."

"Psoriasis," Arwen corrected.

He waved away the accurate term. "Been a dry summer. People are getting scaly."

"I'm glad we've got something to help them." Arwen touched her pack and stepped around the coffee table to sit on the faded recliner near the couch. "Can I show you something?"

Father glanced toward her hand. "Nothing good ever gets shared after asking something like that."

"That's probably true."

He sighed and set down his stick and knife. "What is it? Something to do with your dragon friend?"

"I wish it had to do with him. These are... things I'm wondering if you've seen before. Back when we were prisoners." Arwen reached for the artifacts but hesitated at the deep wariness that entered his eyes.

But he nodded resolutely. "Go ahead."

Before drawing the artifacts out, Arwen said, "Don't try to touch them. They'll defend themselves. So far, I've only seen them get uppity about magical probes, but..." She glanced at his bear stick, as if he might have used that, stabbing them like the hot dogs they'd cooked so many nights around a fire.

"I'm not a total ogre," Father said dryly. "I can resist the urge to thwack things across the room."

"Good." Arwen thought about mentioning that one of the artifacts had attacked Matti when she'd applied her enchanting power, but she didn't want to worry him. It wasn't as if he had magic to probe them with anyway.

She rested the two identical spider-shaped artifacts on the coffee table, well away from his work area.

The humor vanished from her father's eyes. Was that... recognition that replaced it?

Maybe Val had been right. Maybe he *was* a resource.

Arwen clasped her hands between her legs, waiting for his response. She wanted to be patient, but that only lasted a few silent seconds before she caught herself asking, "Have you seen anything like them before?"

Father blew out a long, slow breath. "Yup. Didn't ever want to see them again."

"Sorry, but I could use your help if you know anything about them. Two of my friends have been kidnapped." Maybe *friend* wasn't the right word for Zoltan, whom she barely knew, but he had been helping her. And he was Val's housemate. Imoshaun... She was definitely a friend. Arwen fingered the sleeve of her armored jumpsuit. Definitely.

"And one of these was left behind each time." Father said it like he knew for certain. It was a logical conclusion, but she suspected it was more than that.

"Yes. We—Matti, the half-dwarf enchanter, also took a look— think they're more than calling cards. Both times, the kidnappers took portals to escape, and I wasn't able to track them, but I'm hoping these might be a way to find them."

Father shook his head slowly. "They aren't calling cards, that's for sure. And I don't think they'll point the way to the rest of the souls, but I'm not certain about that. I suppose they could. All I know is that you need to be careful not to break them until you find your friends and get the spells reversed. *Very* careful."

"Uh, souls?"

"Yes. Dark-elf priests can take a piece of a person's soul and lock it away in a receptacle. It's not always spider-shaped, but that's a popular symbol with them." His mouth twisted, and he glanced toward her covered tattoo. "Those artifacts will be hollow in the middle. I saw receptacles like them in my time as a prisoner. The one who birthed you threatened me with—" He glanced at her face and changed what he'd been about to say. "She explained them and threatened to use one on somebody to ensure my compliance."

"She threatened to use one on me?" Arwen guessed.

Father sighed. "Yes. If the receptacle is broken, the entire soul is automatically sacrificed to the demon Zagorwalek, and the person dies."

Arwen's jaw dropped. God, the assassin dragon had flung the first one across the roof. The idea that it might have broken by accident and destroyed Zoltan horrified her.

"I didn't realize," she started, then paused. "Do vampires still have souls?"

Father blinked and looked at her. "You claim a vampire as a friend?"

"He's an alchemist. He was working on a formula for me." Arwen lifted her right forearm. She'd already explained to her father her quest to have the tattoo removed.

"Guess I'd consider anyone who could do that a friend too." He shook his head again. "I don't know how well it works with vampires, but I saw it work on a dark elf. That... woman *demonstrated* the process on an enemy of hers. Or maybe it was some water boy that she was peeved at that day. I saw the kid die when she broke the artifact."

As the new ramifications flowed through her, Arwen ran into the kitchen. She cut bubble wrap that she used when she shipped jars of jams to a handful of clients who'd moved out of the area, then snatched tape from a drawer and returned. While her father watched, she wrapped the artifacts as if they were priceless porcelain dolls that needed to be shipped. Once done, she leaned back and stared at the bubble wrap.

"I need to find them," Arwen whispered. "My friends and... the dark elves. I need to figure out how to get them to leave me alone. Or, if they won't, I'll have to trade myself for their lives. I can't let two people die for my sake."

Father closed his eyes.

"You understand, don't you?" she asked him.

"Yes, but I insist you find a way to rescue your friends while surviving yourself." His eyes opened, and he gave her a hard look. "Selfless sacrifice may be noble, but I refuse to allow it when it comes to my daughter."

"It won't be my first tactic to try."

"*Good.* Listen, Arwen. The dark elves have been pestering you all summer, but *she's* behind it all. I'm positive. She wants you back."

"I think so too."

No need to mention *who*.

"I should have killed her all those years ago. I should have realized she wouldn't abandon you. I... even had a chance once. Maybe. It was hard to know with all that magic she had access to, but she was sleeping, and I..." He lifted his hands in disgust. "I didn't even try. If she'd been a man, I would have done it. It wasn't as if I had any feelings besides loathing for her. But I couldn't. Because she was a woman. Does that make me sexist?"

"I don't know, Father, but you might not have survived. Even if you'd succeeded."

"I know. Getting out of those tunnels and away from all of them wasn't easy. When we finally did get away, I wondered if she'd *let* us go. If she *wanted* you to learn about the world above ground."

Arwen licked her lips. "That could be. They want to use me. Do you know... I mean, did you ever figure out why they picked you?"

"She picked a number of human men. In the beginning, I had cellmates." His lips thinned, his expression grim. "She wasn't that fertile—none of the dark elves were—and I gathered she got a bunch of us to see if any had seed that could germinate in that hellhole of a garden." He glanced at her, waving his fingers to apologize for the words.

Arwen had heard worse and nodded, appalled that lots of men had been imprisoned in those tunnels. She didn't remember any others. Was that because by the time she'd been born...?

Father nodded, as if he could guess her thoughts. "She kept me because for whatever reason—chance probably—I got through, and she became pregnant. She got rid of the other males. Let them go, she told me, but I doubted that." He looked warily at her. "Just so you know, she used magic to force me—to *compel* me. That's the term. She was attractive, I guess, if you're into red eyes, but I wouldn't have if not..." He shrugged. "I got you out of it, so I don't regret anything. Not even being captured, I guess."

Throat tight, Arwen shifted to sit beside him on the couch. "I'm sorry it was so rough on you."

"I'm sorry it's been rough on *you*." He wrapped an arm around her shoulders while looking at the bubble-wrapped artifacts, his eyes haunted.

"On both of us."

"Yeah."

"I don't want to lose you, Arwen."

"I don't want to be lost. I promise."

He squeezed her shoulder. "She needs to die this time." His gaze shifted to the rifle mounted over the fireplace and the gun safe that held more. "The brother too. I think that might be the only way to get them off your back forever."

Arwen leaned away, eyeing him warily. "You're not thinking of going Rambo on them, are you?"

"That would be suicidal."

That wasn't, she noted, a *no*.

"You don't know where they are these days, do you?" She'd asked before and didn't *think* he did, but she kept watching him, tempted to use her fledgling mind-reading ability to see what he was thinking. But this was her father, not an enemy. She couldn't intrude on his privacy that way. Besides, if he felt the itching, sensed it in any way, he would feel betrayed.

"Just where they were back then. That place burned and was fully buried. I doubt they ever returned." He looked at her. "Maybe you should stay here on the farm for a while. If they want you as badly as we think, they'll eventually come here for you. We could set some traps and get ready for them. A *lot* of traps."

Father glanced at his gun safe again, and Arwen recalled that he had grenades in there too. She didn't know where he got his munitions, but he'd stocked up after the aggressive yetis showed up in the area.

"I can't stay here, Father. I have to find Zoltan and Imoshaun. The dark elves might be torturing them as we speak."

"Or they might be holding them prisoner and lying in wait for you to come get them. Better to make them come here, a place we know and can defend."

"I'm surprised they haven't shown up here already."

If the dark elves wanted prisoners for the purpose of manipulating Arwen, her father would have been the best candidate. Not
that she wanted them to go after him. She had to keep him safe;
she couldn't lose him too.

Father looked sidelong at her. "Maybe I'll set a few traps in the
morning. The dragon's wards might help some, but so would land
mines."

"You don't *have* land mines, do you?" Arwen knew about the
grenades, but he didn't have a whole arsenal in that safe, did he?

"You keep the pantry stocked, and I keep the armory stocked.
Like I taught you, it pays to be prepared."

"Father, I'm positive land mines aren't legal." Arwen doubted
grenades were either, but out in these rural areas, booms weren't
that uncommon, so she wouldn't be surprised if some of the
neighbors had more than hunting rifles too.

"But effective on intruders." He swept his mess up, then stood.
"Don't host any more dinner parties until we get the dark-elf
problem under control." The look he gave her as he headed for
the door suggested he would prefer she *never* host any more
dinner parties.

"I wasn't planning on it."

Alas. Arwen would prefer if nothing crazy were going on in
her life, and she could invite Azerdash for the tacos she'd
promised him. Normal tacos, not oyster tacos. After all, shortly
after they'd met, he'd assured her that he didn't need any of her
herbal teas because his male areas were functioning optimally.

She smiled, a lump in her throat as she walked outside and
headed toward her cob house on the back half of the property.
The stars had come out, and she couldn't help but look up and
wish she would spot his winged form gliding in for a landing.

But the memory of Saruknorath returned, and she reluctantly
admitted it would be better if Azerdash stayed away from Earth for
now. Far, far away.

# 8

ARWEN HAD BRUSHED HER TEETH AND PUT ON HER NIGHTIE WHEN her phone rang. Hoping for an update that would help with finding Zoltan and Imoshaun, she sprang on it, hardly caring that it buzzed angrily at her touch.

Matti's name popped on the display.

"Matti!" Arwen answered promptly. "Do you have good news? Or any news?"

A long pause followed, and Arwen frowned at the display, worried her dark-elven blood had irked the phone, and it had turned off. But a baby squalled in the background, proving the connection remained.

"I would not have opened up this line of communication were there not news to share." That was Sarrlevi.

"Uh, hi. Is Matti okay?"

"She is nursing hungry babies. I have recently returned from Zokthoran, the world where the Assassins' Guild Headquarters is located, and Mataalii suggested that I use this device to relay information to you."

"Yes, it's good for that. Thank her, please. And thank you."

Arwen perched on the edge of her bed, drumming her heels on the floor. "What information?"

"I spoke to Nesheeva, the guild leader. As always, she was coy with me, and I am uncertain if everything she said is factual, but she informed me that the entire guild is not after Azerdash Starblade. He has not at this time been made the Prestige Hunt, and only Saruknorath has accepted an assignment to eliminate him. Many of the guild members may secretly approve of what Starblade seeks to accomplish, though few dared state that outright."

"I guess that's good. I don't suppose this Nesheeva shared Saruknorath's kryptonite?" As soon as the word came out, Arwen realized Sarrlevi would have no idea what she was talking about. If she hadn't been given a stack of superhero comics as a kid, she might not have known the term either.

"His what?"

"A hidden weakness that I can exploit. Did you hear that he pounced on Val's Jeep and made magical balls that could break camouflage and reveal innocent people standing in a field?"

"He is a dragon," Sarrlevi stated, as if that were the answer to her question.

"Yes, I noticed the scales. And the fangs."

"He is arrogant, though not as greatly as some. He's also crafty and not as obtuse as the Silverclaws. It would be unwise for you to battle him. I suggest you tell Starblade to avoid him."

"I'm sure he would prefer to do that. Do you know who hired Saruknorath?"

"Dragons claim that they would never stoop to hiring assassins, but I deem it likely that one of their kind is responsible. Or one of their *clans*. While it is true that many of the lesser species are lickspittles who wouldn't dare oppose the dragons, and pretend they are delighted by dragon rule, I doubt they would hire an assassin. More likely, they are calculating the odds and attempting to position themselves favorably, no matter how events turn out."

"Okay, thank you."

Another squall sounded in the background.

"Are the babies doing okay?" Arwen asked.

"They remain healthy and well, but their dwarven blood makes them strongly opinionated."

"They're only a quarter dwarven, right? You don't think the elven blood dominates?"

"Elven blood is polite and rarely raises a fuss. It may step aside and allow the dwarven blood to rear up most prominently."

"So, dwarves are pushier than elves?"

"Certainly so. Dwarves are also *very* stubborn." His voice had turned fond. Maybe he was gazing at Matti while he made these statements.

"Whose blood was responsible for waking me eight times during the night?" came her query.

"My knowledge of babies is limited," Sarrlevi replied, "but I believe *all* bloods encourage that."

"It figures. Say *hi* to Arwen for me."

Sarrlevi paused before speaking into the phone again. "Hi," he said, like he'd never spoken the word before.

Arwen managed a smile.

Sarrlevi, apparently no more familiar with saying *goodbye* than *hi*, hung up.

As Arwen lowered her phone, she caught the approach of a familiar aura, one she hadn't sensed in days—it had seemed like weeks.

Barefoot and in her nightie, she lurched to her feet. Azerdash.

Eager to see him, Arwen almost sprang outside without changing clothes, but he was flying fast. Worried that trouble might be chasing him, she hurried to dress. As she shoved her feet into her moccasins, he landed on her roof.

Arwen stepped onto her front patio and peered toward the top of her small home. Even though Azerdash was smaller than full-blooded dragons, he barely fit up there. His tail dangled past her window, and his snout was mashed against the chimney as his violet eyes gazed down at her. He didn't appear to be alarmed by pursuers or anything else.

Grinning, Arwen waved, but concern tinged her delight at seeing him. The assassin dragon was on her mind—and likely still on Earth.

"I have to warn you about something," she said.

Azerdash's outline blurred as he shifted into his elven form. He jumped down, landing lightly beside her, and clasped her hands.

"If it is that goblins have been leaving offerings on the aerial conveyance I was working on repairing, I am aware." His lip curl suggested they weren't *appealing* offerings.

"That's not it." Arwen returned his hand clasp and caught herself leaning into his chest. As always, she was drawn by his aura—by him. She wanted to reach up and trace the outline of his strong jaw, to touch the side of his face, to trace one of his pointed ears. "I haven't been up there since you left. There didn't seem to be any point in visiting."

"I should have requested that you stop by to ensure offerings made from lard, honey, and pitch didn't show up, leaking greasy residue onto my engine." Azerdash extracted one of his hands from her grip so he could wrap an arm around her and pull her closer, resting his face against her head. He breathed in her scent, as if he'd missed it—missed her—greatly this past week.

Arwen closed her eyes, loving that he appreciated her. Loving him? They hadn't spoken that charged word, but surely the ache in her chest and the tightening of her throat whenever she thought of him—and especially thought of him in danger—meant she felt that strongly.

"That does sound like a substandard offering," she murmured, "but goblins have different tastes than humans do. And elves. And dragons."

"Than *all* intelligent beings. Though I have seen yetis break into goblin larders to steal their desserts."

"Yetis are only quasi intelligent, aren't they?"

"Yes. Were they brighter, they would avoid goblin baked goods at all costs." Azerdash nuzzled the side of her head. "I have missed you. Are you well?"

"Uh." Technically, she was fine, but his question brought up all the frustration of the past week as she'd not only failed to track down Zoltan but had now lost Imoshaun as well.

She told him everything, the words burbling out so quickly that she switched to telepathy a few times so she could share everything faster and include imagery—imagery of the spider artifacts she'd placed on her dining table after bubble-wrapping them. If her father hadn't been pawing through his safe earlier, counting his bullets and grenades, she might have asked to store them in there.

"That is unfortunate, and not only because I'd hoped I would return and find that you had some of the tattoo-removal formula that I could use." Azerdash leaned back, smiling ruefully as he released her long enough to rest his hand on his pectoral, the spot where his commanders had once marked him with a tattoo so they could track him if he was in the area. Even with his magical camouflage, he couldn't completely escape those who sought him.

Arwen stared grimly at his chest, hoping Saruknorath didn't know about it but fearing he did. What if he could, even now, sense that Azerdash had returned to Earth?

"I also came to check on you. And... to see you."

Touched, Arwen met his gaze. "Not just for tacos?"

"No. I do not yet know if that is a food that will delight me."

"I have some pickled asparagus in the kitchen." Arwen waved

into the house and realized she'd never invited him into her home. "Can you stay? Would you like to come in?"

He glanced at the sky—did he know about Saruknorath?—but nodded. "Pickled, you say?"

"Yes. And there's even a mechanical contraption for you to tinker with if you grow bored with me."

Her father had dragged the gas-powered mulcher to her house from the barn the other day in the hope that one of her magically inclined friends would give it more oomph. She knew he'd meant Azerdash. For someone who thought she should date a normal, mundane human and not be involved with magical beings, he was taken by Azerdash.

"I'm certain I would never grow bored with you. I enjoy when you talk about your passions and listen when I talk about mine."

"I'm glad to hear it."

Azerdash gazed contemplatively at the door. "What *kind* of mechanical contraption?"

"I'll show you." Clasping his hand and smiling, Arwen opened the door.

His eyelids drooped as he followed her inside and surveyed her home. "Is it in the bedroom?"

"I don't have any of the kinds of mechanical contraptions that one might keep in there." Arwen had never even been to an adult store. "But I can drag the mulcher in and park it next to my night-stand if it would be more appealing to you there."

Arwen released her grip on him and walked to the table, pulling out the chair that had half-hidden the bulky piece of equipment. Only her father would consider it appropriate to bring such a thing into a house. Well, maybe her father and *Azerdash*.

His eyelids remained drooped, his expression making her think he might have romance on his mind. Whether that romance would be with her or the mulcher, she didn't know. The last time they'd discussed such matters, he'd admitted to not being over his deceased half-dragon-half-dark-elf companion, Gemlytha. Arwen kept hoping he would sort through that, realize he cared about her, and profess his love while leading her to the nearest bed.

"Interesting." Azerdash strolled over, brushing his shoulder against hers, and considered the machine. "What is it?"

"A mulcher."

"What does it do?"

"You put branches and other woody debris in there, and it cuts them up into tiny pieces that we can spread under trees and shrubs. It helps keep the soil moist by slowing the evaporation of water, and it can reduce weed growth." Arwen stopped herself, doubting he wanted that many details.

Azerdash touched the machine's funnel. "This is how you composted the yetis you spoke of?"

Arwen laughed. She had forgotten she'd shared that story with him. "No, Father did that by hand. I think he burned them and composted the ashes. Oddly, he didn't invite me for the dismemberment and cremation. He considers some things too garish for his little girl."

"He wishes to protect you from the horrors of the world." Azerdash nodded, as if he approved and would do the same.

"I suppose. There's something I need to tell you about. To protect *you*."

His expression grew grim. "You speak of the assassin dragon? Saruknorath?"

"You've already run into him?"

"He attempted to run into *me*. Violently and with powerful magic. We crossed flightpaths on the ogre home world. The great chieftain there was amenable to hearing me speak about the need to combine forces with other intelligent species to oust the dragons, but one of his advisors, I believe, tipped off the Dragon Council about my location there. Even though I camouflaged myself as soon as I sensed Saruknorath, he was able to hunt me down, which forced me to make a portal and leave prematurely. I believe the elves informed him about my tracking tattoo." Azerdash touched his chest, then grimaced, letting his hand stray to his side. Was that a fresh rip in his shirt? In *him*?

"I wish I could say I now have a formula capable of removing that, but it disappeared along with Zoltan." When she'd learned the vampire was missing, Arwen had focused on trying to track him and his kidnapper down, but Val had thought to see if the formula, or at least the ingredients that Arwen had worked so hard to gather, had been left behind. Neither had remained in the laboratory. The dark-elf who'd taken Zoltan had likely destroyed everything. A depressing thought.

"Zoltan? That is the vampire alchemist?"

"Yes."

"I feared you might be targeted as a result of my choices. I should have realized the dark elves might *also* continue to pester you."

"That's how my life goes these days." Arwen pointed to the rip in his shirt. "Are you injured? Do you want me to clean the wound and apply a bandage?"

"I have already done so." Azerdash lifted his shirt to show a green elven regeneration pad wrapped around his side, though it didn't entirely cover the wound, what looked like a couple of deep claw marks. Or *talon* marks.

"Do you want to sit in the rejuvenation pool?"

He gazed at the mulcher. When he said, "That would be wise, yes," it sounded a little reluctant.

"I don't think we should take that to the pool. Water tends to short out human machinery."

"Because of the reliance on electricity instead of magic." Azerdash shook his head as if the notion were primitive. "I will examine this later." He gave it a fond pat. "It is malfunctioning, I assume?"

"It's working, but it needs more horsepower. According to my father, that is. I think it's fine. Only loggers need to mulch entire trees."

"Hm." Azerdash patted it again before lowering his hand. "With a touch of magic, it *could* reduce entire trees into chips. This funnel and these blades would need to be enlarged, but... I will do this later. Also, once I am healed, I will assist you in locating the gnome inventor. Such a person should never have been snatched up into dark-elf clutches. Especially not *twice*."

"I agree." Arwen smiled at him, not surprised he'd prioritized Imoshaun. "I need to find Zoltan too."

"Yes. They will likely be together."

"But you can't stay here. Not with that assassin after you. I'll find them on my own."

"It has been an arduous task for you thus far." Azerdash gazed into her eyes.

The frustrations of the last few days threatened to bubble up again, and bring tears along with them, but she swallowed, not wanting him to risk sticking around. "Yes, but I'll handle it. I didn't think you'd be back and told the assassin to look for you in three days under a bridge in Fremont."

"Under a bridge?" He tilted his head. "Why would I go to such a place?"

"For romantic sexy times. That's what I tried to get him to believe, that we would meet there for a liaison. I didn't want him following me around—or showing up *here*."

"I see. Perhaps a dragon would believe such a story, one who does not know much of human mating habits. Or *is* the bridge a place where humans join in coital activities?"

"Uh, I really don't know. I was only there once, and some teenagers were smoking pot."

"Pot," he mouthed.

"A drug."

"Ah." Azerdash rested a hand on her shoulder for a pleasant moment before removing the back scabbard holding his blade. His shirt followed, leaving his bare torso on display—it captured her attention the way mechanical constructions captured his. After draping his shirt over a chair, he stepped outside. "Let us both enjoy the rejuvenation pool for a time. Yendral is attempting to obtain a promise of military assistance—archers with magical bows—from the fae queen. He will come here when he is done, and we will *both* assist you with the dark elves. Then I will return to... Ah, I'd best not tell you my full plans."

"Yeah." Arwen was glum that their enemies could read her mind, so he couldn't share everything, but it wasn't as if she could have assisted him with raising his armies regardless.

"You would be good—better than I—at negotiating with world leaders," Azerdash said softly. "Were your comrades not missing, I would ask to take you with me to do this work. Also, I could then make sure nobody slips in and scours your mind."

"While it might be interesting to see other worlds, I don't have any experience negotiating with even a car salesman much less a world leader." Arwen almost scoffed at the idea, but he seemed serious.

"You negotiated with the fae queen."

"I gave her cookies and asked her for cave-corn husk."

"And a rare dark-elven ingredient, which she also gave you."

"But she didn't give me the tour of her gardens that I asked for." Arwen, who'd been attacked by a lake serpent and locked in a rolling fertilizer machine, didn't feel that she'd gotten the best of the fae queen.

"True, but that is because she was irritated by the intrusion of a dragon in her court, not that she was unwilling. You got the ingredients you needed, *and* she didn't succeed in killing you."

"Yes, it takes a crafty diplomat to walk away from a negotiations table with her life."

"On some of these worlds, it does." Azerdash smiled at her. "Do not underestimate yourself. Come." He touched his side, then nodded toward the rejuvenation pool, its eucalyptus scent detectable from the house when the breeze came from the north. "You will join me in the water."

Though Arwen wasn't sure it was wise with Saruknorath still on Earth—especially if he could track Azerdash through his tattoo —she grabbed a couple of towels and stepped outside with him. It was hard to resist a shirtless half-dragon, especially when he lowered his eyelids halfway and gazed at her with the same appreciation he gave to machines. Was there any chance that he wanted a nude soak in the pool to lead to... something else?

On the one hand, Arwen would feel guilty enjoying herself when Zoltan and Imoshaun were missing. On the other, how many opportunities did they get for private time together? And those looks he was giving her... She couldn't help but feel something had changed. Maybe, after she'd helped him find his sword, he had decided his feelings were clearer, that he cared for her and had gotten over Gemlytha.

"Come," Azerdash repeated softly.

He left his shirt in her house, but he carried the sword in its scabbard. As valuable as it was, he probably slept with it.

As Arwen trailed him down the path, she imagined him in bed with the sword on one side and the mulcher on the other, a hand draped across each. Would there be room for a woman? For her?

Azerdash slanted an amused look over his shoulder. Like with other dragons, he'd admitted he struggled to read her mind, thanks to the protective dark-elven magic of her tattoo, but maybe he'd caught that image.

"I would allow you to use the mulching contraption as a pillow," he said.

Yup, he'd definitely caught it.

"Comfy. Not the sword, huh?"

"It is a prized possession, and being sentient, it might object to someone using it such." His lips twisted wryly. "It objected to being laid on the floor *next* to the hammock I slept in on the orc home world."

"It sounds snarky. Like Matti's hammer."

"Yes, that word may be accurate."

When they reached the pool's edge, Azerdash rested the sword on the wooden bench he'd crafted, the legs formed from vines that grew up between gaps in the flagstone deck that surrounded the water. Before withdrawing his hand, he raised his eyebrows. Communicating with the sword? A hint of light seeped out of the top of the scabbard, and he released it.

"The bench is acceptable."

"I'm so glad." Arwen wondered if the sword would have comments if she and Azerdash grew intimate in the water. She decided she didn't care. If he kissed her, she would forget all about their strange witness.

"I did offer to construct it a special rack."

"Having an intelligent sword sounds like a lot of work."

"Yes, but it is worth it." Azerdash glanced toward the night sky before removing his boots and the rest of his clothing.

Arwen bit her lip and looked away as he slipped into the steaming water. Maybe he wouldn't have minded her gaze, but it seemed polite not to gawk at his naked body, even though she would have liked to openly peruse it. Instead, she looked toward the pumpkin patch and breathed in the eucalyptus scent. It was stronger here, stronger and enticing. Even though she wasn't injured, the pool beckoned to her, promising to soothe her muscles if she climbed in.

"You will join me," Azerdash said, the water lapping around his hips as he watched her.

The command and his intent gaze sent a zing of anticipation through her, but she told herself that as a strong modern woman, she shouldn't leap to a man's orders. Even those of a half-dragon whose aura emanated great power, *appealing* power.

"Still giving orders like I'm one of your troops, huh?" she asked.

Azerdash started to nod, then seemed to get that she didn't approve. "I *request* that you join me naked in the pool. I have been thinking about you."

"Oh?" Arwen touched her chest, delighted that she might have wandered into his thoughts. He had to have been busy visiting all those worlds and dodging an assassin dragon.

"Yes. Nightly." His gaze tracked her hand and lingered on her chest. That attention sent a hot flush through her, one that intensified in her core. "Days, too. I did not get to properly express my appreciation for you after you were integral in retrieving my sword."

"And you wish to do so now? With me... naked?" Feeling brazen, she shifted her hand to trace the outline of her breasts before lowering it to the hem of her shirt.

His eyes flared with violet light. "*Yes.*"

That sent another flush through her, stirring arousal deep within. He hadn't even touched her, physically or with magic, and she was turned on.

"Okay," she whispered, a squeak to her voice.

It sounded silly, not sexy, to her ear, but his gaze intensified, and a rumble came from his chest. A rumble that sounded more like a dragon's growl than that of an elf or man. It excited her. *He* excited her.

As she tugged her shirt over her head, the button on her jeans unfastened of its own accord, and they sagged off her hips.

"Are you using your magic on me, Azerdash?"

"I am." Watching her as if she were the hottest, sexiest woman he'd ever seen, he sent a whisper of his power to unfasten her bra, the straps slipping from her shoulders, and a gentle caress whispered across her skin, cupping her breasts. Pleasure swept through her, gooseflesh arising on her skin.

She hurried to remove her moccasins and jeans, wanting to jump into the water with Azerdash and mold herself to him. A voice in the back of her mind wondered if she should ask if he'd sorted through his feelings, but the front of her mind didn't care. His caresses and the steamy look in his eyes promised he wanted her. And she wanted him.

As soon as she'd set her clothes aside, careful not to disturb the snarky sword, another whisper of magic swept around her. This time, it lifted her into the air as it stroked her skin. In the scant seconds it took for him to levitate her over the water to him, she was trembling with arousal.

She stretched her arms toward him as he lowered her into his grasp, his hands joining his magic in stroking her body. Her legs dipped into the water, but he caught her hips, holding her up so he could nuzzle her bare breasts. A groan escaped her as she pressed her body toward him and gripped the back of his head.

*I have wanted you,* he spoke into her mind as his mouth explored her, his tongue sweeping over sensitive flesh that had never been touched by a man before, *since you stood naked in my rejuvenation pool. Many nights, I've awoken aroused from dreams of you.*

The words, as much as his touch, made her passion flare, and she squirmed under his delicious ministrations. She dug her fingers into his soft hair, scraping her nails along his scalp and locking her legs around him as he licked and kissed her breasts, hungry, as if he'd wanted to see and touch them all along and had barely restrained himself. The thought that she might excite him that much made her feel sexy and beautiful.

*For weeks, I've let my mind get in the way of what my body has longed for. You.*

His hands drifted lower, exploring more of her as his magic

held her aloft, keeping her from dropping fully into the water. A little brush between her legs made her gasp and arch into him.

"I've wanted you too," she blurted.

"Yes," he agreed.

It wasn't a revelation to him, and she blushed with embarrassment.

"Not because of my power," he said, lowering her into the pool, the warm water a caress in and of itself. When their eyes were level, he added, "Perhaps at first, that attracted you, but I believe you desire me now because of who I am."

"Yeah," she said, though at that moment, with his hands and magic making her tremble with growing need as he settled her against his hard body, she might have gone to his bed even if he'd been a stranger who only wanted to use her for sex. Never had she felt so turned on, so alive.

He smiled, maybe tracking those thoughts, and kissed her.

The sound of her father's truck starting up reached Arwen's ears, but it was on the other end of the property. He wouldn't see them. She didn't know where he would be going this late—to get some beer, maybe—but the thought that she and Azerdash would be completely alone for a while was appealing. If she cried out—would she?—nobody would overhear.

*You* will *cry out,* he stated into her mind.

*You're not having much trouble following my thoughts tonight.*

*You're broadcasting them to me. Deep down, you want me to know your desires so that I will fulfill them.*

Was that true? She hadn't intended that, but maybe it was happening. She kissed him back and wrapped her arms around his shoulders.

The memory of their first kiss not far from here came to mind, of how she'd wanted it to be real, for him to crave her, but he'd only been putting on a show for Yendral, wanting his comrade to believe they were a couple so he would stay away.

*I wanted you then as well,* Azerdash stated into her mind, deepening his kiss as he cupped her ass, pulling her tight against him. *It incensed me that Yendral wouldn't stay away from you. He is fortunate I did not turn into the dragon and tear his head off.*

*Stay with me tonight, Azerdash. We'll sleep on the multitool with the camouflaging magic activated so nobody can find us—nobody will interrupt us or know you're here.*

*That sounds even more appealing than sleeping on a mulcher.*

*Your multitool is a lot less poky, as long as the blades are tucked away.*

*And the bottle opener.* He shared the memory of her using it in their battle in the fae queen's court.

Arwen might have been embarrassed, but he also shared how much he had appreciated her coming to his aid, that she'd blasted her magic into the enemy dragon's backside.

*You have helped me many times,* he stated, his kisses growing harder, more full of need. *I will help you before I return to my quest.*

*After tonight,* she thought, wriggling her body against him. She wanted him to slide into her, to fulfill the need intensifying within her.

*Yes. Tonight, we will—*

He broke their kiss and looked toward the sky.

"No," she groaned, afraid one of their enemies had already found him.

"Saruknorath comes." Arms still wrapped around her, Azerdash let his head fall back and groaned in frustration. "I thought it would take him more than an hour to find me here."

Arwen, hot and aching for him, shared that frustration. She gripped his arms and leaned her forehead against his shoulder, longing to keep her legs wrapped around him, longing to finish what they'd started. Would she *ever* get to be with a man who cared about her? With Azerdash?

# 9

---

*ANY CHANCE YOU CAN CAMOUFLAGE US, AND HE WON'T SENSE YOU?*
Arwen asked silently.

Azerdash sighed and released her. *I did have us camouflaged, and he's flying straight toward this pool.*

Saruknorath came within range of her senses. Arwen slumped and let Azerdash go, realizing they would have to face the dragon naked if they didn't hurry and get out. Such a powerful being would have no trouble barreling through the magical defenses around her property.

Azerdash reached the patio first, pushing himself effortlessly out of the water, the steam wafting off his damp skin. The appealing view made Arwen wish they'd had far more time together naked.

She'd no sooner gotten out than the black-scaled dragon came into view over the trees. Topaz eyes flaring, he looked down as he flew over her father's house.

Arwen cursed, realizing she hadn't brought her bow or even the multitool down to the pool.

At least Azerdash had his sword. He drew the blade from its

scabbard as it flared with power, the stars shining brilliantly from the magical metal. "I will not flee from him again."

Though naked and dripping water on the flagstones, Azerdash looked deadly as he crouched in a fighting stance, the sword raised toward Saruknorath. Not only did his usual strong aura emanate from him, but the magic of the galaxy blade accentuated it. Its power radiated outward while mingling with his and somehow enhancing Azerdash, as if the weapon fed extra energy into him.

Even so, Arwen didn't know if it would be enough to survive against a full-blooded dragon. Azerdash's magical defenses were up, wrapping around her as well as himself, but a barrier also protected Saruknorath. And he'd already proven himself clever. What if he'd brought more magical devices to aid in defeating Azerdash?

"I'll get my weapons," Arwen blurted, intending to grab her bow and pepper the dragon with every arrow in her quiver if needed.

"Stay," Azerdash ordered, his magic ensnaring her before she'd run more than two steps toward the house.

His power drew her back into the protective sphere of his barrier as Saruknorath soared overhead. Even though Arwen appreciated Azerdash wanting to defend her—and he could conjure a barrier far stronger than hers—she wanted to do something, not stand helplessly beside him and hope for the best.

"I request that you stay," he added, his gaze locked on the dragon overhead.

Arwen snorted. "It's not a request if your magic is enforcing it."

"I thought you might find the order less odious if it were phrased politely." Azerdash squinted at Saruknorath.

Had the dragon said something telepathically?

Saruknorath banked and circled the property. He glanced a few times at the glowing blade—here, on the otherwise dark half of the property, it had to be hard to miss—but didn't appear cowed by it. Of course, he didn't dismiss it and Azerdash fully. He kept his distance as he flew about. Studying his enemy?

*I knew you would not mate with your female under a moldy bridge with a troll looking on,* Saruknorath stated, glancing at Arwen.

She thought about pointing out again that it was a *cement* troll, but it hardly mattered.

*But I did sense your aura all over this female. I knew you would come to mate with her again. Your elf blood makes you weak and prone to primitive mammalian urges.*

Azerdash said nothing, at least not that Arwen could hear, merely standing like a statue with his sword raised. Only his eyes moved, tracking the dragon as he circled their area.

*You will not succeed at your quest,* Saruknorath stated. *Your mongrel blood will ensure you lack the power to defeat even one dragon, much less all the clans invested in keeping their rule over the Cosmic Realms.*

*Do you talk this much before attacking all your prey?* Azerdash asked.

*Certainly. I am from the Starsinger Clan. Sometimes, I even croon dragon songs to my targets.*

*A more harrowing weapon than your talons and fangs, I have no doubt.*

Saruknorath's jaw parted, and he showed his fangs. It *might* have been a smile, but Arwen didn't know if dragons did that. Maybe he was just showing off those fangs.

Saruknorath flew past, banked, and then flapped his wings hard as he arrowed toward them.

Again, Arwen wanted to run for her weapons, but Azerdash hadn't released her. All she could do was clench her fists as he pointed the sword at Saruknorath, and a beam of brilliant starlight streaked toward the dragon. Arwen's senses told her that great power traveled with that beam. She willed it to be enough to hurt the dragon.

It struck Saruknorath's invisible barrier and was deflected into the sky. Her first thought was that it wasn't strong enough to do anything, but the dragon's wingbeats faltered, and he banked and flew behind tall evergreens to the side of the property. Even though the beam hadn't appeared to breach his barrier, the scent of something burning mingled with the eucalyptus from the pool.

"Did that hurt him?" she whispered.

"Unlikely. But if he comes close enough for me to strike with the blade…"

Saruknorath flew around the trees and over their heads again. Before, he'd been diving, as if to come straight at them. This time, though he swooped lower, he didn't commit to an attack. He watched Azerdash *and* the galaxy blade.

The beam didn't lance out again. Did Azerdash control that, or was it the sword?

Arwen glanced toward her house. She was glad her father had left, wherever he had gone, so the dragon couldn't snatch him and make him a hostage.

But as Saruknorath banked again, it occurred to her to wonder *where* her father had gone. If it had been to the store where he picked up drinks now and then, wouldn't he have returned by now? Why had he gone out so late anyway?

"Saruknorath wishes to test the blade," Azerdash guessed. "To see what attacks it is capable of. Since most of the galaxy blades disappeared centuries ago, he's likely not encountered one before. He is being wary. That's surprising in a dragon. Usually, their arrogance leads them to believe nothing can stand up to them."

"*Can* it defeat him?" Arwen asked.

"If he comes in close, we will find out."

Arwen didn't know if that meant *yes, probably not,* or *I haven't tried battling a dragon with it before.* When he'd been embroiled in war centuries before, his opponents had been dwarves.

Saruknorath roared and flew toward him.

Once again, the beam shot from the galaxy blade. This time, it pulsed as well as striking at Saruknorath.

Instead of being deflected, it streamed straight into his barrier. The sword's magic mingled with that of the dragon, and what had been a translucent shield glowed, brightening with each second. Absorbing the power? Or trying? Given enough time, might the blade burn through and make a hole?

A wave of mental power crashed into Azerdash and Arwen. She gasped and stumbled back as tremendous pain bored into her brain.

Azerdash also grunted. His barrier remained around them, but this attack on their minds circumvented it.

Arwen grabbed her temples, again wishing she had a weapon. She wanted nothing more than to prong that dragon in the ass.

Saruknorath landed on the bench, not ten feet from them. His talons curled around Azerdash's pile of clothes as he turned to cast a gout of fire at them.

Again, Azerdash's barrier held, but it wavered under the conflagration that burned all around. It was so bright that Arwen couldn't see the dragon through the flames.

She willed her own power into Azerdash, hoping it could help him strengthen the barrier even more. If it dropped, they would both be incinerated.

While maintaining the barrier, Azerdash used her power and his, not to add to the defenses but to channel into the galaxy blade. The beam shooting from its tip intensified.

Saruknorath roared and sprang away from the bench. The mental attack disappeared, and Arwen gasped in relief.

Flapping his wings hard, the dragon flew upward and behind trees again. Something dangled from his talons, but Arwen couldn't tell what. The beam followed Saruknorath, slicing off several branches as it sought to maintain contact with their enemy.

The dragon perched in a hemlock at the edge of the property, the needles and trunk hiding him from view.

Azerdash quashed the beam. "My apologies for damaging those trees."

"It's okay. We'll need some branches to test the mulcher with once you tinker with it."

"I fear I won't be able to stay long enough to improve it." Azerdash looked sadly at her. "Or sexually satisfy you."

The blunt terminology made her blush—or maybe the fact that their enemy was close enough to hear the words. Not that a dragon would care about sexual satisfaction.

"Do both things distress you equally?" Arwen asked lightly before she sensed Saruknorath springing into the air. No doubt to charge them and test the blade again.

"Not equally, no. As enjoyable as it is to tinker with machinery, I am certain that relations with you would be even more pleasurable."

"I do hope you'll find them so."

Saruknorath started flying at top speed, but he didn't come toward them. A dark winged beast against the starry night sky, he flew eastward, toward the mountains. Something still dangled from his talons. Clothing?

"Did that dragon steal your pants?" Arwen asked in puzzlement.

Azerdash groaned again and bent over.

Surprised by the reaction, since Azerdash never seemed to care much about his wardrobe, Arwen rested a hand on his back. "Are you okay?"

Before he answered, she sensed the auras of two more dragons. Zavryd and was that his Uncle Ston'tareknor?

At first, Arwen was pleased, glad they'd chosen a timely moment for a visit. But then she remembered Val's warning that the dragon queen, Zavryd's mother, had ordered Azerdash incarcerated. The Stormforges as well as the Silverclaws—and probably every dragon in the Cosmic Realms—knew about Azerdash's quest, and, as Saruknorath had said, none were happy about it. What if, in the week that had passed, the queen had decided she wanted Azerdash dead instead of captured?

"You should go," Arwen said.

As much as she wanted Azerdash to stay and spend the night with her—many nights with her—it would be better for him to go somewhere safe.

"I must help you find your comrades." Azerdash straightened, sword still in hand, and shifted his stance to face west, the direction Zavryd and Ston were coming from.

"That's going to be hard to do if you're in a dungeon on the dragon home world."

"I will not allow them to take me. I must assist you."

"Azerdash." Arwen gripped his shoulder. "Make a portal, and get out of here. Please. I... I love you. I want you to live."

He gazed over his shoulder at her. "Your words mean much to me."

She'd hoped he would say *I love you* back but told herself that didn't matter now.

"I'm glad. Your *living* would mean a lot to me. Please. I'll find Zoltan and Imoshaun. I'm capable." Even though she hadn't capably done *anything* yet, Arwen wanted him to believe her, so she held his gaze and attempted to look certain of herself. In case it mattered, she tried to genuinely believe the words. She *would* find them.

"You *are* capable."

The two black dragons came into view. They weren't flying that quickly. Maybe they *wanted* Azerdash to escape before they were forced to apprehend him. Was it delusional to hope that?

"Go," Arwen said.

"You are giving me an order." His eyebrow twitched.

"I *request* that you go."

"Ah, better."

"They won't hurt me, and they'll protect me if Saruknorath comes back." Arwen thought that was true, if only because she was, as Zavryd always put it, a friend of his mate's.

"Yes, I believe they will. Very well."

Azerdash glanced at them, sheathed his sword, grabbed his remaining clothing, and formed a portal. He kissed Arwen before leaving, such longing in the gentle gesture that she wanted to rescind her words, to wrap her arms around him and make him stay.

She made herself release him and step back, lifting a hand in farewell as he leaped through the portal and disappeared.

# 10

ARWEN DIDN'T HAVE TIME TO PUT HER CLOTHES ON BEFORE THE dragons landed. Zavryd alighted in the pumpkin patch and his uncle on the flagstone patio, his tail almost knocking her over as she hurried to wrap a towel around herself. It was more than she'd worn to face the assassin. Not that any of her visitors likely cared about human nudity when they were in their dragon forms.

*Is this a* yavasheva? Ston asked the question telepathically, looking to Zavryd instead of Arwen.

*Yes, Uncle. The half-dragon made it for the mongrel female. As I told you, he clearly intends to claim her as a mate.* Zavryd's nostrils flexed as he gazed at Arwen from the garden, the vines curling over his talons. The pumpkins weren't yet ripe and looked ridiculously small under him. *It is possible he has already done so.*

*Indeed. It is a great gift.* Ston dipped a taloned foot into the water, then leaned his snout over the pool to inhale the steamy eucalyptus-scented vapors. *Ah, my old bones do so love an elven yavasheva. This is a result of the half-dragon experiment that I had not anticipated.*

*What is that?*

*Offspring capable of creating hedonistic elven pleasures.*

*We came here for a reason, Uncle.*

*Indeed. While you question the female, I will test the efficacy of this pool. My old bones ache despite the many magical rejuvenation treatments I've endured. I blame it on the dastardly Silverclaw illness that afflicted me while I was in their stasis chamber for ages.*

*Your bones are not so old that you cannot cavort like a juvenile with your fae female.*

*I only need one bone for that.* Though in dragon form, Ston had an impressive leer when he looked back at Zavryd.

*I do not know what that means.*

*Has your mongrel elf female not taught you about sexual innuendos?*

*We enjoy our time in the nest together and speak plainly of our desires. There is no need for innuendo.*

*Hm.*

Just as Arwen was thinking she might not need to worry about this visit—had Azerdash even needed to leave?—Ston startled her by roaring and springing into the air.

Arwen scurried back, bumping the bench and almost landing on her butt. Her towel flapped and fell to the ground.

Ston's spring took him not toward her but into the water. He landed like a sumo wrestler cannonballing into a wading pool. Eucalyptus-scented droplets sprayed everywhere, spattering Arwen and even Zavryd in the pumpkin patch.

Arwen gaped as the dragon rolled onto his back like a golden retriever. He lay his head on the damp patio, stuck his hind legs and tail out on the other side, and swished his body back and forth, creating waves and sighing in vast contentment as the warm water lapped at his scales.

*Uncle, are you truly a full-fledged member of the Stormforge Clan? If I did not know better, I would believe you a Starsinger.* Zavryd shook his body to flick water droplets off.

*If you delve far enough back in our bloodlines, you will find that the clan boundaries blur. At one time, we all came from one world where we mated with abandon, scattering eggs in nests all over the clifftops.*

*The heresies you speak. It is amazing the queen has not cast you out.*

Not sure what to make of their conversation—or Ston's undragonly antics—Arwen took the opportunity to towel herself off and dress. She didn't know why the dragons had come, unless they'd hoped to find Azerdash here and capture him, but she wouldn't bring him up.

*Oh, she has a few times,* Ston said. *That is how I ended up ruling the gnome home world. They adored me, you are aware.*

*They appreciated your leniency—that is what the historical records say—and they are most resentful now that a Silverclaw dragon rules there. If the spies can be believed, the gnomes were the first to invite your insurrectionist mongrel offspring to speak.*

Ston harrumphed and sat up, though his tail remained sticking out of the pool. *I do not appreciate that I am being blamed for the actions of that one. A moon ago, nobody knew he was created from my genetic material.*

With those words, both dragons turned their gazes upon Arwen.

"Uhm." Under this new scrutiny, she was glad she'd had a chance to dress. Mostly. One moccasin still dangled from her fingers. "Can I help the two of you?"

*We will not mind-scour you, as some have threatened to do,* Zavryd said, *to learn Starblade's destination and plans.*

"Good. I appreciate that. And there have been more than threats." Arwen slipped the moccasin on, then touched the top of her head at the memory of the painful magical scraping under her skull.

Not showing sympathy—dragons weren't good at that—Zavryd continued. *We have come to give you a message to deliver to your mate.*

"We're not, uhm. I mean, nothing is official. He hasn't claimed me, and we haven't said we're..." What was a term a dragon would understand? Arwen wasn't even up on modern human terminology for relationships. She almost said *going steady*, but she didn't think teenagers had said that even when she'd been a kid. She was fairly certain she'd heard her *father* use it.

*He has made you a* yavasheva, Ston said, as if that confirmed their dedication to each other.

Maybe it did. Weeks earlier, Zavryd had implied something similar. Azerdash hadn't said he loved her, but he *had* admitted that he cared. And he wanted her. If only they hadn't been interrupted...

*A most excellent pool.* Ston sank back down as low as his bulk would allow. *I'd heard all the tools for making them were lost. Perhaps Starblade's possession of one is the true reason Saruknorath seeks him. He does not need coin.*

*Reputedly, he likes a challenge.* Zavryd flicked a wing toward his uncle and focused on Arwen again. *You are prepared for the message?*

Did he expect her to pull a pen and pad of paper out of her pocket? "I don't know when I'll see him again, but I can relay your message when I do."

That earned another wing flick. Acceptance?

Arwen nodded, glad they didn't want to mind scour her.

*I hope this will be sufficient,* Zavryd said. *The queen has suggested that you be brought before the Dragon Council for questioning, to learn what you know of the wayward mongrel's plans.*

"But... you're not going to take me because you loved the meats at the dinner I hosted a few weeks ago? And you believe my ability as a chef means I should be left on Earth to fulfill my true purpose?"

Zavryd gazed at her with unblinking violet eyes.

Val had once said that her mate had a sense of humor. It was, however, possible that he didn't find Arwen funny.

*If the queen switches from suggesting to ordering, I will have no choice but to bring you to her. But I do not believe that Starblade would have told you any crucial information about his current base of operations or his plans. A dragon can acknowledge the capabilities and competence of a mate while still wishing to protect her, and I believe that for his sake, as well as yours, he has not spoken of these things to you.*

"That's right."

*The message I require you to deliver to him is thus: by the queen's words, Azerdash Starblade must stop his efforts to rally world and military leaders to join forces against dragondom in an insurrection that would result in great carnage for the lesser species, not to mention the razing of ancient cities. Such a war would be futile for beings so much weaker than dragons. Further, the aftermath would require a tedious changing out of rulers to ensure compliance going forward. If Starblade comes to the queen and the Dragon Council and promises on his sword to cease his incendiary activities, she will allow him to live.*

Arwen tamped down her initial irritation that Zavryd was *requiring* her to deliver a message and reminded herself that all dragons were full of themselves. She also didn't point out that it was possible the dragons themselves would lose in Azerdash's war. Her fear all along had been that an insurrection *would* be futile, fancy sword with glowing stars or not.

*Afterward,* Zavryd added, *Starblade may even return to this world to enjoy his mate and produce offspring.*

Arwen's mouth drooped. Did Azerdash *want* that? Despite his interest in learning about the natives and fiddling with engineering contraptions on Earth, he'd sounded restless being a refugee here. And he'd never mentioned a desire for children with her or anyone else.

Did *she* want children? She didn't know. For so long, it had seemed too much to even hope for a romantic partner.

*In truth, we do not know if that latter is possible for their kind. In nature, dragons cannot produce viable offspring with any of the lesser species, only with other dragons. That is why we've always considered the existence of half-dragons an abomination and an affront against nature.* Zavryd, perhaps reminded that Ston was the reason Azerdash existed, looked over at him, but the other dragon had his head and long neck back on the flagstones, the part of his body that would fit still contently soaking in the pool. *Whether a half-dragon born in a laboratory can have offspring with lesser species is not known.*

Arwen shook away the distraction of children. "Don't take this the wrong way, please, but as a concerned party, I have to ask... if Azerdash were to voluntarily go to the Dragon Council, wouldn't the queen, who wants him incarcerated, the last I heard, take the opportunity to lock him up?"

Zavryd's head jerked upward, his long neck stiffening. *The queen is my mother. She is honorable, as all Stormforge dragons are honorable.*

Ston, whose eyes were closed, sighed with contentment in the pool. Was he paying attention to the conversation?

Zavryd turned exasperated eyes on him. *Even dragons who might have Starsinger ancestors are honorable.*

*Did your mother not teach you to be polite to your elders, Zavryd'nokquetal?* Ston asked without opening his eyes. *I do not remember you being this pompous in your youth when you used to dive and play among the aeries.*

*I am not a youth any longer. And after my brother passed—was slain by an elven assassin—it was my duty to rise up and serve as my mother's law enforcer and her eyes where she could not be.*

*Ah, yes. I was imprisoned in my magical slumber and missed the event. Unfortunate.* Ston sat up, though he didn't leave the pool.

*Yes. The Stormforges have suffered losses at the hands of insurrectionists before.*

Arwen hadn't heard that Zavryd had lost a brother and lifted a hand in sympathy, but wasn't that all the more reason to suspect the queen was setting a trap? Because she wanted to get rid of Azerdash before he could start a war?

*The queen is honorable,* Zavryd repeated. Maybe he'd caught her thought. *Also, since you uncovered the truth of his heritage and that there is a link to our clan... she would prefer not to kill him. She* will, *however, incarcerate him for his own good and the good of our kind if he doesn't cease his errant ways. She has had a gnomish stasis chamber brought to the dragon home world, and it waits for him. Should he continue on the flightpath he's started on... she will do all within her power—* Zavryd lifted a taloned forelimb to his chest, to indicate he might be the one executing the queen's desires, *—to capture him and lock him in it forever.*

A chill went through Arwen. Azerdash had spoken of the nightmares he'd suffered during the centuries he'd been interred in the last stasis chamber. She believed he would choose death over returning to that fate.

*As you can see,* Zavryd continued, *it is better for all if he puts a stop to his revolution before the egg is truly hatched. You will deliver this message to him.*

Arwen nodded. "I don't know when I'll see him again, but I will."

*Do so. Uncle Ston'tareknor, if you are ready, we will return to the queen.*

Ston stretched his wings out over the flagstones, letting water drip from them. *You will not enjoy the pool first?*

*It has been occupied by someone else the entire time I was here.*

*My offspring should have made it larger.*

*Undoubtedly.* Zavryd sprang into the air, wingbeats stirring the branches on trees as he gained elevation.

After sighing, Ston climbed out of the pool, leaving the water level noticeably lower than before he'd gotten in. Arwen wondered how she was supposed to fill it. With a garden hose? Azerdash had said the magic would keep it clean, but they hadn't discussed extra maintenance that might be required if a dragon used it.

*Why, mate of my offspring, does Azerdash Starblade wish death and destruction of dragons?* Ston gazed at Arwen with solemn eyes.

That gaze made her feel guilty, even if she had nothing to do with Azerdash's plans. She liked Ston though—for a dragon, he almost seemed decent—and wished there were a way he and Azerdash could have a relationship, not be at odds.

"Well, he's part elven too and was raised by them. I gather he wants dragons to leave the worlds they rule to the natives."

*Dragons, thanks to their power, make ideal rulers who maintain law and order on the worlds where they have a presence.*

"They do more than have a *presence*, though, right? They're in charge. Some people want to rule themselves."

*And that is ideal? On this wild world, where dragons are uninterested in imposing rule, there is anarchy.*

"I wouldn't say we have *anarchy*. Just different governments that work, admittedly to varying degrees, in different countries." Arwen shrugged, hardly feeling she was the right person to discuss the geopolitical situation of Earth, not when she spent as much time as she could in the woods, ignoring what humanity as a whole did.

*To this dragon observing from the outside, it looks like anarchy. Crime is rampant. Wars are frequent. Poverty and despair are easy to find.*

Arwen spread a hand. "When it comes to humans, we'll give up safety and security for the freedom to choose our own fate."

*Illogical. Perhaps I will mention to the queen that this world would be vastly improved by dragon rule.*

"Uhm, that's not necessary."

*We shall see.* Ston flicked the last of the water off his wings and sprang into the air, flying off in the same direction that Zavryd had gone.

Great, the dragon she'd decided she liked might now be the biggest threat to Earth. Arwen hoped he would soon forget that musing and that the queen, too worried about what Azerdash was stirring up, wouldn't think to turn her eye toward this world.

# 11

AFTER THE DRAGONS LEFT, ARWEN TOOK HER TOWELS AND WALKED up the path toward her home. She realized she hadn't heard her father return. A light was on in his house, but unless he'd stealth-driven his truck down the driveway, he wasn't home.

Their earlier conversation floated through her mind. Had he gone out to buy booby traps for the property? It was too late for that, wasn't it?

Arwen rounded his house, confirmed his truck was gone, and stepped inside, wondering if he'd left a note.

As soon as she entered the living room, the open door of his gun safe caught her eye. Strange that he would leave it ajar. Even though she was long past the age when he'd had to worry about her accidentally shooting herself, he always put his guns away after using them and locked the door.

When she turned on a table lamp for a better look, she realized why he hadn't bothered to secure the safe. It was empty, as if a robber had swept through.

No, as if he'd taken the guns and grenades and whatever else he had in there to assault a stronghold.

Her stomach sank into her moccasins as she looked out the window at the empty driveway. Where could he have gone? After the dark elves? To protect her? Unless he'd been lying to her, he didn't have any more idea than she where they lived now.

"Would he have gone to their old lair?" she wondered aloud.

They'd both been back years before and confirmed that it was abandoned. Maybe Father thought he would find a clue from the past that would lead him to their location in the present. Or maybe he had a reason to think they'd returned.

That thought distressed her more than any other. No matter how many guns and grenades he'd taken, he wouldn't be a match for dark-elven magic. They would kill him. Or worse.

Arwen dug out her phone. She remembered where the old lair was, but it would be a long walk. Besides, if he'd driven up there, she needed to follow as soon as possible. Before he ran into trouble. The thought of a third spider artifact being delivered to her doorstep made her wince.

Val's phone rang a number of times before she picked up. "Hey, Arwen. What's up?"

"My father disappeared. I think I know where he went. Is there any chance you can give me a ride?"

"I'm following a lead that Willard dug up about dark elves in Mill Creek. Or *under* it more specifically. I'm up there now. Since there are so few dark-elf encampments around, we figure if we find one, it might be the one where Zoltan is being kept. Unless your father found some other new lair?"

"I think he's going to an old lair. It should be abandoned, but I'm not positive. He may know something he didn't tell me. To protect me."

"Why don't you check with my mom?" Val suggested. "She's not like a normal old person. She's probably still up and can drive you."

"Does she like it when you call her an *old* person?"

"Nope. She calls me a pain in the ass though. Let me check out Mill Creek, and then I'll head out that way if you don't get a ride from her."

"All right. Thanks." Under other circumstances, Arwen would have joined Val to follow a dark-elf lead, but she had to find her father before he did... whatever he thought he was going to do with all those weapons.

When she dialed Sigrid's number, the only response came from her old-fashioned answering machine. Sigrid might not stay up as late as Val thought. Or she could be having a romantic interlude with her werewolf friend across the street. Arwen left a message, then paced, urgency making her steps agitated.

Maybe it was time for her to learn to drive. Even if technological things hated her—or her blood—she *had* successfully taken Frodo around the property. A car might not overheat and stop that often with her at the wheel.

As if to mock her thoughts, her phone warmed painfully in her hand, flashed twice, then turned off.

"You're lucky I don't shoot you full of arrows," she told it, then pressed the power button. Maybe she could call Willard for a ride. Or... someone who wouldn't ask questions if Arwen paid her?

After a moment's hesitation, during which she remembered that Amber had been *kidnapped* the last time she'd been doing research for Arwen, Arwen called her. She only needed a ride up to the pass. If her father was parked along the forest service road where they'd accessed the wilderness that led to the old lair before, Arwen could track him down and get a ride back with him. After she convinced him not to take on any dark elves by himself.

"Hey, Arwen," Amber answered. "Do you have work for me? I'm about to start school shopping. It's my senior year. That means it's *super* important to look good."

"I could use a ride, yes. You haven't spent the money you got from exchanging Azerdash's gold coins already, have you? That was a lot."

"Don't forget that I had to cut *Gondo* in. And it's not my fault that school clothes are expensive. Inflation is a bitch, Arwen."

Arwen suspected Amber shopped at much pricier stores than she did. She could have replaced her entire wardrobe with one of those coins *and* gotten new canning equipment for the kitchen.

"You need a ride up to the pass in the dark?" Amber asked after Arwen explained their destination. Keys rattled in the background. Hopefully that meant she would come right away. "Why don't you ever need to go anywhere normal?"

"I'm... a tracker. Visiting a forest service road is normal for me."

"In the dark?"

"Sometimes."

"You're so weird."

Arwen smiled. "As we've established."

"I'll be there as soon as I can get over to the Davy Crocket savageness where you live." A door thudded in the background. "Wait. Do I need like... emergency gear or anything? Climbing rope? Shovels in case of rockslides or avalanches?"

"It's August, so avalanches are rare, and I-90 will take us almost all the way to the service road. You won't even lose cell service."

"Okay, but I should bring my sword, right?"

Arwen hesitated, wanting to say Amber wouldn't be in any trouble, but with the way her life had gone lately, could she absolutely ensure that? "Probably."

"I knew it. You'll have snacks, right? Like pickled cherries and some of those caramel apples you're making now? Those are straight fire. And it's important to have emergency rations on road trips."

"I'll pack a few things while you're on the way, and you can raid my pantry after we're done." Arwen resisted the urge to tell

Amber to hurry, but it was hard. Her father had left more than an hour ago, while she'd been busy... kissing Azerdash in the pool. She had nobody to blame but herself for not noticing he'd left with all his gear. "Thank you for coming to help, Amber."

"Naturally. I'll be right there."

# CHAPTER12

Because of the distance between Edmonds and rural Carnation, *I'll be right there,* unfortunately meant it took Amber an hour to arrive, even at night.

After Arwen had packed a few supplies, and the food she'd promised to bring, she'd spent most of the time pacing. She'd also left a message for Val, belatedly realizing she should ask Amber's mother if it was okay to get a ride from her. After the kidnapping incident, Arwen felt uneasy even standing close to Amber for any length of time and wouldn't have called her if she weren't desperate. Even so, if Val called back and forbade her from getting a ride with her daughter, Arwen would have to look for another way to get out to the wilderness.

But Val hadn't called back. Was it possible she'd found previously undiscovered dark-elf tunnels? Under Mill Creek?

The sleepy suburb well north of Seattle seemed an unlikely hotbed for magical-being activity, but, a few weeks ago, Arwen would have said the same of Edmonds, and it had recently hosted a dragon battle and housed a magical sword guarded by a golem.

She'd called Willard to try to get more details about Val's lead, but the colonel also hadn't answered.

It didn't seem fair that Arwen's father was in danger and everyone she could reach out to for help was busy doing something else. But she reminded herself that Zoltan and Imoshaun had been in danger first. Her acquaintances had to prioritize hunting for *them*.

On a whim, Arwen called Matti. She didn't expect the new mother to pile her babies in the car and come give Arwen a ride, but it crossed her mind that Sarrlevi might be available to assist. He probably didn't know how to drive, but, as a powerful elf mage, he could make portals.

"What's up, Arwen?" Matti answered as a text came in from Amber, saying she'd passed through Carnation and would be there in a few minutes.

"My father may be in danger."

"He wasn't kidnapped too, was he?"

"No, not yet. Hopefully not at all, but he... He took all his guns and left, I think to look for dark elves." The whir of a power screwdriver on Matti's end almost drowned out the last sentence, and Arwen debated repeating it.

"Does he know where to *find* dark elves?" Matti answered, having no trouble hearing over whatever she was doing. "Despite their propensity to fling their artifacts everywhere, they're kind of elusive."

"I didn't think he did, but do you empty your gun safe and take every bullet and grenade if you aren't positive you're heading into trouble?"

"I don't own guns or grenades, so I couldn't say. I take my hammer everywhere though."

The screwdriver whirred again.

"Are you certain that will be sufficient to deter our offspring from gaining entry?" came Sarrlevi's voice from the background.

Arwen straightened, glad Sarrlevi was home. Maybe he *would* be willing to help her.

"They keep out human babies fine," Matti said.

"*Human* babies." Sarrlevi didn't scoff, but his tone effectively conveyed how inferior he believed such children to be. "Our babies have magical blood. They may even have the ability to employ magic at a young age."

"Dude, they're only a week old. Babies don't crawl until they're like nine months. It was *not* necessary for me to do this tonight."

"Dude?" Arwen mouthed. Was she still talking to Sarrlevi?

"It is likely our babies will be superior to human babies in all aspects including development," Sarrlevi said. "My mother informs me that I was a precocious child."

"Are you sure the words she used weren't *huge pain in the ass*?"

"Elves do not have such a term."

"I'm sure your people have a word that conveys something similar and that she used it. Anyway, even if our kids turn out to be precocious, they still won't be crawling anywhere next week. Why don't you go check the wards and booby traps around the house again? Maybe beef them up a bit to deter your friend?"

"The dragon assassin is *not* a friend," Sarrlevi said. "I do not know why he is circling the area. I have no knowledge of Starblade's whereabouts."

"Tell him that, will you? Dragons flying over my roof make me nervous." Matti's screwdriver whirred again. "Maybe I'll add some childproof locks to the front door to protect against intrusion."

"Such weak devices will not deter a powerful being."

"The one on the toothpaste drawer deterred you," Matti said.

"Only because you withheld the information about the magnet required to gain entrance, and I did not wish to destroy that which you'd recently installed."

"I do appreciate that. Sorry, Arwen. My mate has too much time on his hands this week. For some reason, he told Willard and

King Eireth that he needs paternity leave so he can hover over me and the babies this summer." Matti lowered her voice. "I love him, but he's driving me batshit. He needs work to keep him busy."

"I have work," Arwen said, glad for the opening. She described her dilemma. "You could send him out to help, just in case there *are* dark elves."

"I was thinking of asking him to help with the hunt for Zoltan, but, like you, I wouldn't know where to tell him to start."

"I think my father might have more of an idea about where the dark elves are than he's admitted in the past."

"Let me run it by him. With the dragon assassin loitering like a stalker, he may not be willing to leave, but if I can talk him into it, I'll send him your way. Where are you?"

"The farm, but I'm leaving soon and heading up to Snoqualmie Pass. Well, not all the way. There's a turnoff before you get up there." Arwen started to describe it but glimpsed headlights through the brush and trees and heard music. Was that Amber?

"I'll talk to him," Matti said and hung up.

Arwen didn't know whether to get her hopes up or not. Maybe this was overkill. Her father could be going up to the old tunnels on a whim and wouldn't find anything. But if he'd believed there was nothing there, why would he have gone?

The red hatchback rolled down the gravel driveway, the windows down and blasting pop music that might raise Mrs. Zuber's eyebrows, especially given the late hour. The properties down this road were spaced far apart but not *that* far.

Fortunately, Amber turned the music off when Arwen stepped outside with her pack and her weapons.

After stopping the car, Amber called, "Hop in."

Arwen opened the passenger door and noticed a stack of gear and Amber's sword in the back when she looked for room for her bow and pack.

"I brought my dad's camping stuff, just in case. But only the things that don't smell like mildew. Or body odor." Amber wrinkled her nose and shoved a pack over to make room.

"I wouldn't have guessed your father owned camping gear," Arwen said as she slid into the seat.

When she'd last seen Thad, he'd been in a Dungeons and Dragons T-shirt. And he drove a BMW. He seemed like someone who would stay, if not in a luxury hotel, at least a clean and practical chain.

"Oh, he camps at the Midsummer Renaissance Faire every year. I don't know if you noticed, but he's a total geek." Amber managed to turn around in the driveway without hitting anything but did peel out fast enough that gravel flew.

Since Arwen was in a hurry, she didn't complain when a rock *thunked* off a beehive.

"He did mention his appreciation for Lord of the Rings," she said.

"Uh-huh. *Daily.* I'm lucky he didn't name me after a character. Talk about being set up to be a nerd for life."

Arwen looked over at Amber, surprised by the dig. Usually, if Amber insulted her, it involved helpful-in-her-eyes criticism. But Amber didn't return the glance or notice her reaction, and Arwen realized she might not have read the books herself and met Arwen, the half-elf.

"Val named me, I think," Amber added as she drove, hitting potholes in the dark. "I'm lucky I didn't get a really screwed-up name."

"From her? Val is normal, isn't it?"

"Val, short for Valmeyjar—which means *corpse maiden* in some Viking language—is definitely not normal. I'm surprised you didn't call her about this."

"I did. She's got a lead and is checking it out tonight."

"So, I'm your backup plan? I'm wounded that I'm not your Number One."

"Sorry. If Val drives me, it's free."

"That's because she's independently wealthy since she got all that gnome gold. She doesn't *need* to charge to drive. Also, she doesn't need new school clothes. Have you *seen* her wardrobe? She has like three outfits, and they're all loathsome." At a stop sign, Amber glanced in the rearview mirror. "No dragons are going to show up this time, are they?"

As if on cue, a flare of power came from behind them, back by the farm. A portal opening. Dread swept into Arwen. Had the assassin dragon returned?

# 12

ARWEN STARTED TO REACH FOR HER MULTITOOL TO ACTIVATE THE camouflaging element but paused. The portal felt like it had been made by elven magic.

The engine vroomed as Amber applied the gas, but the car didn't move past the stop sign.

"Uh." She looked at the dashboard. "What happened? We're not going anywhere."

Sensing elven power wrapped around the vehicle, Arwen lifted a hand. "Hang on. I'm hoping that's someone coming to help. There's only one elf I invited to come help us."

The magical signature from the portal disappeared, and she didn't sense Sarrlevi, but, as a former assassin, he probably skulked around camouflaged by habit.

"I've noticed that a lot of magical bad guys who you *don't* invite to help you show up anyway," Amber said.

"That's unfortunately true."

Between one eye blink and the next, Sarrlevi appeared in the dark street in front of the car, the headlights shining on his brown trousers, forest-green tunic, short blond hair, and twin longswords, the hilts poking above his shoulder from their scabbard on his back.

"Shit," Amber blurted in surprise.

Had elven power not continued to keep the car from moving, she might have accidentally run him over.

Sarrlevi nodded as he walked up to the passenger-side door. "There is indeed excrement in the street." He pointed to where he'd probably almost stepped in a pile as he'd approached. "From one of your bovines, I believe."

"Yeah, they don't put cattle guards on all the streets out here," Arwen said. "Will you come with us?"

"Apparently." Sarrlevi pressed his lips together. "My good-intentioned but perhaps overly frequent advice on the proper way to secure a home from talented half-elven babies has been exasperating my mate."

Arwen took that to mean he hadn't wanted to come but Matti had insisted. Bless her.

"I will require the seat with more leg room," Sarrlevi stated.

Arwen glanced at the hatchback's small rear seat, which was already brimming with gear, but agreed that he was taller than she, so it made sense for her to stuff herself back there. Especially if he was coming along as a favor to her.

"Okay." As Arwen got out to let him in, she glanced at Amber, surprised she hadn't mentioned extra fare or being put out at having another magical being in her car. She always had numerous comments about Azerdash riding with them.

But Amber gazed dreamily at Sarrlevi as he folded himself into the front seat. When Arwen squeezed into the back, finding room between the camping gear, her own pack, and the bow and sword, she caught Amber looking back and mouthing, "Isn't he *hot*?"

"This conveyance lacks the room of Mataalii's truck." Sarrlevi, knees against the glove compartment, peered around, his gaze lingering on a smear on the dashboard. "Also, it is begrimed."

Arwen arched her eyebrows, wondering if his pickiness would alter Amber's assessment of his appeal. She merely sighed, perhaps thinking of the lack of students in her high school who were as handsome as elves—a lament she'd voiced to Arwen before—and put the car in gear. Sarrlevi had removed his magic, so it turned onto the paved road without trouble.

While Amber drove them to the freeway, Sarrlevi withdrew a folded, clean white kerchief that emanated slight magic and wiped away the smear—and then polished the rest of the dashboard.

If Arwen hadn't sensed the power of his aura, and seen him fight in the past, she might doubt that he would be sufficient *help* if they ran into dark elves, but she knew he was deadly. And fearless. He thought nothing of springing into battle with dragons.

"Do you both have your seat belts on?" Amber flicked her finger at a light on her console.

Arwen thought Sarrlevi would have a baleful comment about Earth safety devices, since he could cocoon himself inside a magical barrier, but he said, "Yes. Mataalii's new truck beeps incessantly if one does not strap oneself to the seat. I have observed to her that magic would do far more to protect her than such a crude and primitive method."

"I bet she appreciated your observation like extra homework dished out by a teacher." Amber glanced in the rearview mirror at Arwen.

"Let me see if I can reach it." Arwen dug under the camping gear, groping for a seat belt. She bumped something hard hooked to the pack and drew it out. "Is this a flashlight?"

Since the light had gone out inside the car, she flicked the switch. A little illumination might help her locate the seat belt.

But whatever she'd pulled out was much longer than a flashlight, and the tip bumped against the door. Some light *did* come on, a soft blue glow from a long clear stick.

"That's Dad's plastic lightsaber. Sorry, I didn't take the time to toss away the unnecessary stuff."

The illumination wasn't ideal, but Arwen used it to assist in her search and finally located both halves of the seat belt.

"Is that a weapon?" Sarrlevi looked back, frowned at the toy, and then cleaned something on the ceiling near the dome lamp. Despite his tackling dust, grime, and suspicious stains, the magical kerchief remained as pristinely white as if he'd taken it out of the laundry.

"Only in a Hollywood movie." Amber lowered her voice as she took the ramp onto the freeway. "Dad has more toys than I ever did. I can't *believe* he implies I'm spoiled."

Once belted in and wedged between the gear, Arwen clasped her hands between her legs and willed them to reach their destination. There had already been so many delays. By now, her father could have found all kinds of trouble. At least they were heading out of town late enough that there wasn't much traffic on I-90.

"Before I left, Saruknorath formed a portal over Green Lake and departed." Sarrlevi must have deemed the car clean enough, because he returned his kerchief to his pocket.

"I hope that means he's given up on finding Azerdash here—and harassing those who care about him—and won't be back." Arwen also hoped Saruknorath had no idea where Azerdash had gone and wasn't, even now, tracking him down on another planet.

"Saruknorath does not give up," Sarrlevi said. "Few professional assassins do."

"When a woman is upset, you're supposed to say something reassuring," Amber told him, "not confirm that her worst fears might come true."

Sarrlevi gazed blandly at her. "Arwen Forester's voice did not connote that she is upset."

"Because she's *hiding* it. If a woman's boyfriend is being hunted by an assassin, you can be sure she's upset."

Sarrlevi shifted his gaze to Arwen. Was he trying to decide if that was an accurate assessment? Or thinking of using his kerchief on her?

"She has dark-elven blood," he stated.

"*So?*" Amber gave him an incredulous look. "She has feelings. She's half-human and a woman and cares about people. Even that weirdo half-dragon who can't visit my house without *tinkering* with something."

Though a little surprised and even touched that Amber was sticking up for her, Arwen lifted a hand to indicate she was fine.

"I see." Sarrlevi didn't sound offended. He also didn't apologize or say anything to soften his earlier words. Which was fine. Arwen preferred the truth, no matter how distressing.

"I'm going to assume nothing will come up if I say *dark-elf lair* to my GPS." Amber waved at her phone plugged into a port, a map app open on the display. "Which exit do I take?"

"I'm not sure," Arwen said. "I've only been up here once, but I'll know it when I see it."

"Great." Amber glanced at Sarrlevi. "This is why I charge by the hour instead of the mile."

"There is a fee for this taxi service?" he asked.

"Don't worry. Arwen's covering your half. I trust she brought the goods."

"Numerous jars," Arwen said.

They drove past an exit for North Bend, the one she and Val had taken earlier to check on her brother's former cave hideout. For the first time, Arwen realized it wasn't that many miles from where the old lair had been. Was that a coincidence? Or were those tunnels not as abandoned as everyone had thought?

"Jars of food items you've prepared in your kitchen and which Mataalii enjoys?" Sarrlevi peered toward Arwen's pack with interest.

"Yes." Arwen was about to add that she would share a couple

of jars with him, since he'd come out of his way to help, but Amber was quick to interrupt.

"Matti can make her own deal with Arwen. Those are mine."

"You are unwisely abrasive with those who are your elders and superiors," Sarrlevi told her.

"I get that a lot."

"I believe the next exit is the one we need to take," Arwen said, hoping to stave off an argument—or what might be a building need within Sarrlevi to discipline Val's daughter.

After eyeing the tree-filled darkness on either side of the freeway that had replaced all evidence of civilization, Amber glanced at the map on her phone. "An exit that leads to some hiking trails and a bunch of nothing?"

"That sounds right," Arwen said.

"Of course it does. I hope there are a *lot* of jars in that pack."

"Don't forget my offer for you to raid my pantry when we're done. You can take whatever you believe is a fair trade for this outing."

"Oh, I will." Amber drove onto the exit and turned on her high beams as the road headed into darkness.

Towering trees to either side blocked the view of the night sky, but they occasionally glimpsed brake lights through the branches. The map showed the road following the freeway until a river forced it farther away.

By night, the area looked different from what Arwen remembered, but she nodded to herself, certain they were going in the right direction. The first of what would be many dirt roads cut away from the pavement and up slopes dense with vegetation.

Amber glanced back.

"Keep going," Arwen said.

Their road grew rougher as it headed uphill. All traffic noise from the freeway faded.

"Turn there." Arwen pointed to another dirt road, grasping branches and encroaching ferns making it narrow and uninviting.

Amber slowed down but didn't turn. "You know this isn't an off-road vehicle, right?"

Arwen debated if she and Sarrlevi should get out and walk. In Val's Jeep, an ascent up a steep dirt road would have been simple, but she didn't want Amber's car to get stuck and need a tow. Who knew how much that would cost if someone had to come way out here?

"Should the conveyance become mired," Sarrlevi said, "I can levitate it."

"Nobody's levitating my car," Amber said.

"Should it lose traction and fall off a cliff, such magic might be necessary."

"To keep us from plummeting off a cliff, I'll allow levitation." Amber frowned back at Arwen. "There *aren't* any cliffs, are there?"

"The road does cut across a steep slope at one point, but I don't remember any sheer drops." Arwen rolled down her window to peer out, hoping for sign that her father had driven this way. Was that a recently crushed fern frond?

"When were you last here?"

"About twenty years ago." Arwen unfastened her seat belt and slipped out.

"Oh, I'm sure your memory about every rock and turn and *cliff* is totally to be trusted then."

Since the lighting was poor—Arwen left the dimly glowing toy in the car—she used her magic to examine the earth, trickling it into nearby trees in the hope that they had noted the recent passing of her father's truck. She would like to know that they were on the right track before sending Amber back and traipsing into the woods with Sarrlevi.

One of the trees responded right away, a narrow fir with the vigor of youth. Though this area was close enough to Seattle that random people came out to explore often, it had noted that a truck *had* come through that night. It had been in a hurry and had rolled across one of the fir's roots at the edge of the road.

Though trees lacked eyes and could share only what they sensed, nothing like what a person saw, Arwen got enough to believe it *had* been her father's truck. She apologized to the fir for the root rolling and used her magic to delve into the soil and extract extra nutrients to share with it. Its needle-filled branches seemed to sigh with contentment.

"You turn your dark-elven magic into that of a surface elf," Sarrlevi observed when Arwen returned to the car.

"I try, yes." Ignoring his speculative—maybe slightly approving?—look, Arwen added, "My father came this way."

She pointed up the road, intending to say she would walk, but Amber waved to the back seat.

"Get in. It doesn't look that bad as long as nobody's coming from the other direction. I'll go as far as I can before dropping you off."

"Does that mean it hasn't been a full hour yet?" Arwen smiled as she slid into the back. "I know you don't feel comfortable taking my twenty dollars if we come in under an hour."

"I want to be a good employee and fully earn the right to peruse your pantry with my grocery tote." Amber headed up the dirt road. "And, FYI, it's been two hours. I started charging when I left Edmonds."

"You have a unique method of billing."

"Yup." As she drove along the rough road, Amber added, "Remind me to help you fill out a 1099 for me at the end of the year. Of all the troubles in my life, *that's* the one that disturbs my father most."

"Your tax standing with the IRS is more important than the fact that you were kidnapped by orcs, tied and gagged in an oubliette, and abandoned in the face of an encroaching petroleum fire?" Arwen asked.

"Yes, but mostly because he doesn't know about any of that." Amber held a finger to her lips. "Val kept her mouth shut when I told him I'd been caught up in my research, forgot my phone was on mute, and hadn't meant to make him worry. I'm a little lucky he was out looking for me when I got home, because I was able to change out of my soggy clothes before he got back."

"Val and your father don't share everything?"

"Of course not. They're divorced."

Amber glanced to the left as the road meandered across the side of the hill that Arwen remembered, the slope in that direction steep but not a cliff. Even so, they wouldn't want to test driving near the edge. The last time Arwen had passed this way, there'd been a lot fewer trees, but the forest had largely recovered from the fire of twenty-three years before.

Amber added, "Their shared guilt over me having to grow up in a single-parent household makes it easy for me to get what I want from them."

"Didn't you say your dad refused to buy you a Mercedes?" Arwen leaned forward in the seat, looking out the windshield for more evidence of her father's passing.

"Well, not *everything* I want. But if I need one of them to keep a secret from the other, that's easy to finagle."

"I sense magic," Sarrlevi said, not commenting on any of the rest.

"Uh, do I stop?" Amber asked.

"Is it in the road ahead of us?" Arwen didn't yet sense whatever it was. "A trap?"

"Ahead, no." Sarrlevi pointed out his window and up the slope in the distance. "Whether it's a trap is unknown. It is a magical device, its power not of great significance."

Now that he was pointing at it, Arwen also detected something. The magical telescope that Harlik-van had used to spy on her came to mind, but that had been a powerful artifact. This felt like something that might have been left behind long ago, buried under leaves and needles.

"My question is not being answered." Amber had slowed down, but her headlights glinted on something farther up the road.

"That's my father's truck," Arwen blurted.

"I'll park behind it, and you two can go look at the magical doohickey if you want." Amber peered toward the left, the descending slope concerning her more than whatever was higher up the mountainside. "Meanwhile, I'll figure out how the heck I'm going to turn around and get back down this road. I hope there's a pull out up there."

"You might have to back down," Arwen said.

"*Back* down a windy dirt road overhanging a cliff? That was *not* on my driver's licensing test."

"It's just a slope," Arwen said, though she had so little experience driving that she acknowledged it could be more difficult than she realized. Her father could back down anything, anywhere, even with a trailer attached, but she'd seen Amber run over bushes just turning around in Arwen's driveway. "And don't forget that Sarrlevi can levitate us if needed."

"He's more useful than the half-dragon." Amber stopped her car behind the truck.

Arwen was on the verge of objecting—Azerdash would have no trouble levitating them, after all—but Sarrlevi issued a pleased, "Yes," and nodded at Amber, so Arwen kept her mouth shut. He was there helping them. It was best to appease his ego.

As soon as Amber applied the parking brake, Arwen jumped out and ran to her father's truck. The darkness made it hard to tell, but it seemed to sag to the left. Had he parked in a hole?

No, she realized when she stopped by the back. One of the tires was flat.

That was strange. He always kept his truck in tip-top shape, and they hadn't driven over glass or anything that she'd noticed.

As she crouched to touch the tire, a faint hint of magic warned her that she would encounter a foreign object before her finger found the source. Dark-elven magic.

She swore, and her gut churned. Why hadn't her father told her he was coming up here? And that there would be dark elves? What had he been thinking?

When Arwen brushed whatever it was, a sharp edge made her jerk back. She shined the light of her phone onto it, and her gut twisted further. It was a slender throwing star identical to the ones she'd seen her brother hurl.

There was one in the front tire too. Maybe in all four. The truck had been parked here long enough for the tires to fully deflate.

Arwen pushed shaking hands through her hair, hardly noticing when she knocked her bun free and her locks tumbled about her shoulders.

"Amber, you better go home." The concern that it had been a mistake to bring her out here reared into the forefront of Arwen's mind again. She started back to the car. "I'm sure Sarrlevi won't mind helping you get back to the pavement if you need it."

Sarrlevi, who'd stepped out of the car, was gazing back in the direction where they'd sensed something else magical.

"Is that—" Arwen started, but light flashed, magic swelled, and a boom came from the slope above the road. "Look out, Amber!" she yelled, afraid the explosion would start a rockslide that would bury the car.

Before she'd taken two steps, Arwen remembered that she could create barriers now. As boulders flew, dirt tumbled free, and trees were uprooted, Arwen struggled to concentrate, to draw upon her own power as well as that in the earth to form a magical defense.

After two failed attempts, she managed to focus enough to achieve her goal. She needn't have bothered, because Sarrlevi formed a larger and more powerful barrier that protected the three of them as well as Amber's car.

Only a few pebbles struck it. Most of the rocks—and uprooted trees—tumbled down the mountainside they'd passed over a couple of minutes earlier. Had the magical trap misfired? Or been delayed?

As rocks continued to clunk and clatter down the slope, dust filled the air, blotting out the sky and reducing the already poor visibility. It wasn't until it settled that Arwen realized the trap hadn't been ineffective after all. It might not have smashed the car, but the rockfall had blocked the road.

"Shit," Amber said, sounding exactly like her mother. She opened the car door to dig something out.

From their elevated perch, the distant roar of freeway traffic was audible again, but Arwen doubted anyone driving below had noted the rockfall.

"We *are* going to need levitation magic to get out of here," Arwen murmured, though she had no intention of departing before she found her father.

"I sense a dark elf." Sarrlevi drew his swords. He wasn't looking toward the landslide but in the opposite direction, up the mountainside beyond the truck.

"I don't." Arwen squinted into the gloom.

"Your human blood dulls your senses. He is there."

*He*? Could it be her brother? Arwen had never believed that she'd killed him.

"I will capture him to question." Sarrlevi ran up the road with his swords in hand.

Arwen took a step after, but he added telepathically, *Stay and guard Thorvald's offspring.*

Though she always bristled at being given orders, Arwen looked at Amber and realized she had no choice. As badly as she needed to find the dark elves, she couldn't abandon Amber, and Amber couldn't leave until Sarrlevi returned and used his magic to unblock the road or levitate the car past the rocks.

*Okay,* Arwen replied. *Keep me updated.*

Sarrlevi didn't respond. He'd camouflaged himself and already disappeared to her eyes.

As one would expect from the assassin he'd once been, he didn't make a sound as he ran, so she couldn't tell which way he'd gone. She still couldn't sense the dark elf and hoped Sarrlevi wasn't being lured into a trap.

# 13

AMBER LEANED OUT OF HER CAR WITH HER SWORD IN ONE HAND AND her father's lightsaber in the other. With a fierce expression on her face and her blonde ponytail hanging over one shoulder, she appeared ready for battle.

"That won't be effective against dark elves, I'm afraid." Arwen managed a smile as she waved at the toy.

"I was just moving it out of the way so I could grab my sword." Amber tossed it back into the car. "And you'll want your bow."

"Yes. Thank you." Arwen slid it and the quiver out along with her pack, but she only went as far as her father's truck.

The rockfall had distracted her before she could search it, and she realized he might have been inside when those throwing stars hurtled out of the darkness to incapacitate the vehicle. What if the dark elf had killed him before he'd gotten out?

The front door wasn't locked, and she opened it warily. He wasn't inside. Nor were any of his belongings. Given how many guns he'd brought, that surprised her. Unless... Ah, there was his mobile vault in the back of the truck, and it was locked. He'd probably left some stuff in there. And headed up the road on foot?

After so many years, her memory was fuzzy, but there was a switchback ahead, and she thought one found the tunnels by walking off the road at that point. Since he'd been an adult, he probably remembered this area better. She would use her magic to track him once Sarrlevi returned.

A rock shifted behind her as Amber walked up to join her. "I'll go with you if you want to look for him. I get that you're worried, and Sarrlevi thinks you should stay and babysit me."

"He included you in that message?"

"No, but he's an adult. I assumed that backward look he gave you came with presumptuous elf orders about me. He probably also told you not to let me get my car dirty after he wiped everything."

"He didn't mention the car."

"But the rest is right." Amber nodded, not making it a question. "I like that you don't try to boss me around like most adults."

"I probably should." Since Amber was giving her a rare appreciative look completely devoid of sarcasm, Arwen didn't mention that her lack of transportation options might make her more flexible about employing a teenager than other adults. "I can't believe Val hasn't forbidden you from seeing me yet."

"She can't forbid me from working. There are laws." Amber waved airily.

Arwen didn't think that was true.

"He went that way?" Amber pointed her sword up the road. "I'm ready. Though if another thing blows up and crushes my car while we're gone, I'm going to be seriously salty. I *just* got it fixed up to my standards. And does insurance even cover magical booby traps? I know from the story Val has told fifty million times that it doesn't cover dragons throwing your car into a tree."

"If it helps, I don't sense any more magic on the slope." Arwen wished she'd ordered Amber to stop when they'd first sensed it, though... maybe not. They might have ended up parking in the path of what had turned into the rockfall. Even if they'd gotten a protective barrier up around the car in time, being caught in the middle of it wouldn't have been pleasant.

Falling rocks in the distance made Arwen spin, lifting her bow before she realized the noise had been too far away to provide a target. That was the direction Sarrlevi had gone. Had he encountered the dark elf?

*Sarrlevi?* Arwen asked telepathically.

He didn't respond.

"He might be fighting," she murmured.

"What?" Amber asked.

"We should wait here." Arwen closed the truck door, though she itched to follow her father's path. "Hopefully, Sarrlevi will finish up soon."

She had little doubt that he was the equal of a single dark elf, but what if there were a lot of them out there? Their people might have let him sense one of them while the rest waited camouflaged. The thought of having to return to Matti's home with a spider-shaped artifact that held a piece of Sarrlevi's soul almost made Arwen sprint off to help.

But a gunshot from the woods beyond the switchback made her jump. It had been muffled, as if there were rocks in the way. No, as if it had been underground.

"Are there *hunters* out here?" Amber asked.

"I suspect there are," Arwen said grimly, "*dark-elven* hunters, but I bet that was my father."

She leaned forward, wanting to go find him, but she remained rooted in place, torn. She couldn't leave Amber here alone. But the thought of taking her into danger made Arwen's stomach churn.

"I don't suppose you have your camouflaging charm with you?" Arwen could risk leaving Amber if she would be invisible.

"Of course I do." Amber withdrew a cute beaded purse from the car and opened the coin section to extract the charm she'd once lent to Arwen. Amber twirled it in the air on its chain. "Do you want to rent it again?"

"No. I want you to use it and stay here while I see if that was my father." Arwen waved in the direction of the gunshot.

"Stay here? Alone in the dark on a mountainside full of bad guys?"

"Alone in the dark but invisible."

"Arwen, it's creepy as hell out here. And I'm not—" Amber waved expansively around and pointed at herself. "I'm not like Val. I'm *normal*."

"You have a magical sword, a camouflaging charm, and the knowledge of how to use both." Arwen tried to smile encouragingly, but she couldn't help but look off into the distance. There hadn't been a second shot. She didn't know what to make of the single firing but worried. "*And* you've got a lightsaber."

"Ha ha. Just let me come with you, all right? I'll camo up. You won't even know I'm with you."

Arwen hesitated.

"The *bad guys* won't know I'm with you. But if you get in trouble, I'll take my sword and pounce on them like a cat obliterating a mouse."

"All right." Arwen didn't want to delay any longer and waved for Amber to follow her. "For the record, cats usually catch mice and play with them a while rather than obliterating them."

Amber activated her camouflage. "I'm not playing with a yeti or sasquatch or whatever is out there."

"Dark elves."

"I don't want to play with them either."

"I wouldn't recommend it. They don't play nice." Arwen withdrew Azerdash's multitool and activated her own camouflage. If Sarrlevi returned and couldn't find them, he could reach out telepathically. She would also prefer to sneak up and pounce. "Stay close," she whispered, wanting to make sure Amber wouldn't lose sight of her. The darkness already made this a challenge.

"No kidding." After stumbling and kicking a rock off the road, Amber produced a flashlight—or maybe that was her phone—and beamed it on the ground ahead of them.

She groaned when Arwen reached the switchback and headed off the road and into the undergrowth. Arwen was tempted to run straight in the direction of the gunshot, but following noise could be confusing in the mountains. She made herself pause and touch the ground, using her magic to ask the trees what they'd sensed earlier in the night.

An image of a cloaked figure came from one. That wasn't her father. It had to be Sarrlevi's dark elf.

Light flashed high on the mountainside, followed by a faint boom. A grenade? Or a magical weapon?

*Sarrlevi?* Arwen tried again. *Is that you?*

*The dark elf seeks to engage me in what the people of this world call a game of cat and mouse.*

*To keep you distracted? While others come after us?*

*That is possible. I shall attempt to deal with him swiftly and return to join you.*

*Don't play with him if you catch him.*

*What?*

*Like a cat plays with a mouse.*

*Does not a feline consume rodentia that it catches?*

*Yes, eventually, but never mind.*

"I think Sarrlevi is okay for now," Arwen whispered to Amber.

Hand still on the ground, she frowned, realizing the tree hadn't shared anything to indicate her father had passed through. She moved a few paces forward and rested her hand on the trunk of a pine, hoping for proof that he had come this way. She was on the verge of using her soul-tracking magic but worried that would break her camouflage.

"We should have brought Rocket and Grandma," Amber said.

The pine showed her an image of a hunter in Army camouflage with a gun. *That* was her father.

"We're on the right track," Arwen whispered.

"If you say so."

Not concerned about Amber's skepticism, Arwen hurried on.

More rocks clattered higher up the mountainside. Though Arwen worried that the dark elf was indeed trying to keep Sarrlevi busy instead of engaging him directly, she continued with determination after her father.

Even by night, she could tell the forest had changed a great deal since her last visit. Trees had grown to full maturity, and the undergrowth burned away in the fire had filled in. Now and then, the flashlight played over a rock cairn or jumble of boulders from long-past landslides that pinged her memory. She was getting closer to the old lair.

Between one step and the next, she sensed magic ahead. Dark-elven magic.

She walked faster until Amber grunted and urged her to slow down.

Arwen did but mostly because the scent of spent chemical explosives reached her nose. It mingled with recently churned dirt and broken vegetation. She might have thought another of those magical explosives had gone off, but dark-elf devices wouldn't have been made with chemicals. Her father's weapons would have. If he'd been attacked, he would have thrown everything he had at his enemies.

Arwen believed they were near where the gunshot had originated when they reached a cave-in, a yawning hole in the ground. Rubble filled the bottom but wasn't enough to hide the mouth of a tunnel down there. Maybe multiple tunnels.

Her father must have blown his way into the remains of the compound. When they'd visited before, the old entrance had been destroyed in the fire, leaving no ways in that they'd known about.

The magic that Arwen sensed came from below and somewhere down the tunnel. It felt more like an artifact than a person.

"What is that?" Amber brushed past Arwen and crept surprisingly close to the edge of the hole.

Arwen reached out to keep her from stepping farther forward. "The edge may crumble easily."

"Yeah," Amber said but didn't take her gaze from the hole. No, she was looking at the tunnel in the direction of the artifact, even though they couldn't yet see it. And were her eyes glazed?

"Let's check it out." Amber crouched to jump down.

"No." Arwen grabbed her arm.

But Amber had shifted her weight close enough to the edge that it *did* crumble. Roots gave way, and the ground under both of them collapsed.

Arwen flailed, almost losing her bow as they fell. Between her grips on the weapon and Amber, and the rock piled below, Arwen couldn't make her landing graceful. She clipped a boulder with her heel, and jarring pain shot up her leg. Further, she lost her grip on Amber, who tumbled away, landing hard in the darkness. Her phone—and flashlight app—flew from her grip. Surprisingly, Amber didn't cry out.

Ignoring the pain in her ankle, Arwen scrambled to her feet.

"It's beautiful." Amber was already up, shambling toward a purple glow on the ground in the tunnel.

She left her phone behind—that alone would have told Arwen that she was ensnared by a magical compulsion—but she still had her sword.

The artifact was an intricate purple knot made from what looked like glass. It was nothing so innocuous.

Arwen, who'd seen an identical device the year before when Matti had been cursed, ran to cut off Amber.

Not acknowledging her, Amber continued toward the artifact. She stumbled over rocks but barely noticed, her hands outstretched toward it, her eyes glazed.

Arwen didn't feel a similar pull. She sprinted, leaped over a boulder, and reached the glowing knot first. Though she wouldn't normally have snatched up a magical artifact with her bare hands, she knew what this one did. Fortunately, it didn't affect her.

After grabbing it, Arwen stepped on something small and hard among the dirt and rocks. It rolled, glinting in the purple glow of the artifact. A spent bullet. One of her father's, she had no doubt.

A rock shifted behind Arwen. Amber had caught up and grasped at the artifact.

Arwen pulled it away from her.

"No!" Amber raised her sword. "Give it to me. I *need* it."

Arwen backed away from her, clipping another boulder. Even in the tunnel, rubble covered the ground. Her agility kept her upright as Amber sprang after her, swinging the sword with competence. The compulsion didn't affect the skills she'd learned from her mother.

Arwen danced back out of Amber's range. With only her bow and the multitool, she didn't have a good weapon for parrying sword blows. And she couldn't *shoot* her driver.

She raised a magical barrier, hoping that sword wasn't powerful enough to slice through it.

"Give it to me," Amber repeated.

Arwen threw the artifact over Amber's head toward the collapsed ceiling where they'd come in. Before Amber could spin and run after it, Arwen drew one of her magical arrows and aimed at it. She willed her own power to aid the arrow, to be enough to destroy the dark-elven device. Her tattoo itched, but she couldn't tell if it was helping her draw power or objecting to what she wanted to do.

Amber started toward the artifact. Arwen fired.

Afraid there would be backlash, Arwen shifted her barrier and lunged at Amber to pull her inside. Her arrow struck as she gripped Amber's shoulder. Coiled magical energy burst outward from the artifact, like a grenade going off, and white light blinded them as the power struck the sides of the tunnel.

The tremendous energy that battered Arwen's barrier almost overcame her ability to maintain it, especially around two people. Her muscles weakened, as if this were taking physical exertion, and she sank to one knee and jammed the tip of her bow down for support.

Rocks shattered and collapsed, including the ceiling over their section of the tunnel. Boulders and dirt tumbled down, and Arwen groaned, afraid they would be buried alive.

With the artifact destroyed, its pull on Amber disappeared in time for her to return to the awareness of their predicament. Eyes round with fear, she threw up her arms as tons of dirt dropped all around them. An uprooted tree tumbled through the ceiling, angling straight toward their heads.

# 14

"OH, SHIT," AMBER SWORE, EYES SQUINTED SHUT AS SHE HELD HER hands over her head, as if they would keep the huge cedar from smashing through the barrier and crushing them. "Shit, shit, shit."

Arwen might have echoed the sentiment, but she was too busy using every ounce of her power to maintain that barrier. Dirt and rocks smashed up against it from all sides, and the massive trunk lay across the top, not two feet above their heads. Her muscles quivered from the effort, as if she were using them to physically hold up the weight.

Amber opened a single eye, peered up, and looked over at Arwen. If not for a faint glow from her sword, Amber wouldn't have been able to see how much trouble they were in. Maybe it would have been better if they were in darkness.

"Are you holding that up?" she asked.

"Yes, but I don't know how long I can." Breathless, Arwen dropped a hand to Azerdash's multitool.

"That's a concerning thing to hear when there's an entire redwood forest poised to fall on us."

"It's a western red cedar, and there's only one."

"It's big enough to drive a *car* through," Amber said, an understandable squeak to her voice.

"It is substantial. Centuries old, I'd bet."

It must have survived the fire twenty years earlier. What a shame to have inadvertently destroyed it.

"The natives used them to build houses and canoes with," Arwen added.

She pulled out one of the multitool knives and pressed it to the edge of her barrier, remembering Azerdash's lesson on molding the magic to slip a weapon through it. She'd done it before but not from so perilous a position.

"A real fun factoid, I'm sure." Amber watched her. "Is there anything I can do to help?"

Arwen shook her head and concentrated, keeping her barrier up as she poked the knife through it. Assuming she hadn't lost her bearings, the tunnel lay in the direction she was facing. As long as the rest of it hadn't collapsed. She hoped the rockfall didn't extend that far.

*If you are attempting a clandestine entrance into the dark-elf stronghold,* Sarrlevi spoke into her mind from a distance, *you may wish to make less noise.*

*I'll keep that in mind. I don't suppose you're close enough to help?* Arwen doubted it.

*At the moment, I am—* A long pause broke up his sentence. *—Engaged,* he finished.

Sweat dripped down the sides of Arwen's face as she struggled to split her focus—and her power—willing some of it to activate the multitool's ability to discharge magic. When she'd battled the lake serpent in the fae realm, it had shot lightning. She needed something like that now, something that could blow away the collapsed rubble.

"What I need is a gnomish tunnel borer," Arwen whispered.

"I can't help you with that. You should have brought the half-dragon. He could have souped up a lawn mower to get us out of here."

Despite her intense fatigue, Arwen managed a smile. She wished Azerdash *were* with them.

As if it understood her desire, magic swelled in the multitool, and an orange beam shot out of the dagger, burrowing into the rock and dirt. Though its versatility encouraged her, it was such a narrow beam that Arwen worried it would take all night to free them. And she could not hold that tree up there all night.

Even as she tried to direct some of her power into the tool, wanting to broaden the beam, her shift of focus caused the barrier to flex and weaken. The great cedar fell several inches before Arwen was able to switch her power and concentration back to their defense.

"Uh." Amber lifted her hands again and waved her sword at the tree.

"Sorry." Arwen dashed sweat out of her eyes. How the hell was she going to accomplish this?

While keeping a wary eye upward, Amber came over and rested a hand on her shoulder. "Can you use some of my power? I know I don't have much as a quarter-blood, but Matti's talked about doing that, drawing on the energy of other magical beings."

"I'm not sure how to use what you could offer."

"You should work on that."

Arwen wiped her eyes again. "There's a lot I should work on."

Her legs shook. Doing her best, Arwen split her concentration between the beam and the barrier while silently asking the multitool if it could do any more to help. But, as handy as it was, it wasn't sapient, not like Val's sword or Matti's hammer. It was her tattoo that itched and throbbed, sending heat up her arm to her shoulder where Amber gripped it.

Amber gasped. Could she feel its power?

The tattoo took what she offered, feeding more power into

Arwen and splitting it, strengthening the barrier and widening the beam. The scent of burning earth reached their nostrils as the orange energy bored its way through the dirt. Rocks exploded. The loose earth above crumbled downward as the hole grew, but the beam burned that away too.

"It's working," Amber said, her voice strained.

Because the tattoo was siphoning off her power. Arwen didn't like the way it throbbed, as if pleased by the task. Pleased to be vampiric.

"This won't take much longer," Arwen said.

It had better not. Her muscles kept trembling, and Amber's pale face suggested she might collapse if the tattoo took much more of her energy.

The hole widened, the beam creating a tunnel two feet wide, enough to crawl through.

After pulling out the knife and extinguishing the beam, Arwen crouched to peer into the new tunnel. Heat radiated out of it. The darkness was too complete for her to see what lay beyond, but a slight draft stirred the warm air and brushed her cheeks. It wasn't a dead end.

"You go first," Arwen said.

Amber looked like she might object to climbing into a narrow pitch-black tunnel, but she glanced at the cedar hanging over their heads, and didn't say anything. Sword in hand, she crawled into the tight passageway.

As she navigated the tunnel, Arwen leaned her forehead against the dirt beside it, the magic of her barrier rippling against her skin. Such weariness filled her that she didn't know if she had the energy to crawl after Amber. But she had to. And she had to keep the barrier up behind her as she did. But... she didn't know how to do that. She'd learned to form a ball of energy at her core and thrust it outward with her body at the center.

"Arwen?" came a muffled and uncertain call from the distance.

She lifted her head. Was that her father's voice? Relief sent a surge of fresh energy into her.

"She's back there," Amber told him before Arwen could answer, "holding a tree up with her brain."

Arwen managed an exhausted snort. Not quite.

"I'm through, Arwen," Amber called back. "But it's really dark. And I lost my phone."

"I lost an arrow," Arwen offered. A far greater prize than a phone, she thought. But it had been worth it to destroy the artifact.

"What the hell happened with that glowing knot thing? I kind of blacked out and don't know how we got down here."

"I'll explain later." Arwen slid her bow into the tunnel ahead of her.

After a few failed attempts to leave her barrier intact and in place while she departed, Arwen lunged into the tunnel and released her magic. She managed to get inside before the tree and everything else near it fell.

A whoosh of dust flowed into her newly excavated tunnel, and the ground shivered. On hands and knees, Arwen hustled through the darkness, her shoulders brushing rocks. If not for her ability to sense magical beings, she would have run into Amber, who was crouching and peering in her direction. Thuds behind Arwen announced the spot where her barrier had been filling in with rubble.

"Arwen?" came her father's more alarmed cry, closer this time.

"I'm here," she rasped, her mouth thick with dust. As the dirt and rocks settled, she collapsed on her side at Amber's feet, exhaustion forcing the move. "But I need to rest a minute."

A brilliant flashlight beam streaked out of the portion of the tunnel that hadn't been damaged by the rockfalls and swept across Arwen's face. She groaned and flung an arm over her eyes.

"Hi, Mr. Forester," Amber said.

Arwen had never heard Amber call anyone mister or missus. Maybe it had to do with the two rifles her father carried while wearing camo fatigues and a tactical vest decorated with grenades and ammo pouches. An armory's worth of weapons tended to inspire politeness in people.

"Sigrid's granddaughter, right?" Father shifted the beam of his flashlight aside as he approached.

"Amber. I was at your place for the dinner with the dragons, remember? And, if we all survive tonight, I have permission to raid your pantry tomorrow."

"Is that right?" he asked gruffly, kneeling and resting a hand on Arwen.

"I don't believe we specified a time for the pantry perusal," she murmured.

"It was assumed it would be promptly upon completion of the job," Amber said.

"Are you hurt?" Father set a big camo-patterned flashlight down and patted her, looking for broken bones. "I've got a first-aid kit along."

"I'm fine." Her ankle twinged, as if to remind her of her initial hard landing. "Mostly. I used magic. It was hard." Arwen made herself sit up. "Are *you* okay?"

"Better than you, I think." He squinted at her.

"Are you sure? I heard gunshots and saw one of your spent rounds."

"There's a dark elf out here. I didn't expect that. He's thrown a few blades at me from a distance. And then there are artifacts down here. The security knots are for those with magical blood and didn't bother me, but the dark elves left other stuff behind to defend this place." He grimaced and touched a bloody gash in his temple.

"Security knots?" Amber looked thoughtfully back toward the

collapsed tunnel, though the cedar and a lot of boulders blocked the view.

If they couldn't find another exit, they would have to dig out when they wanted to leave.

"Is that what made me black out?" Amber added.

"It would have branded you if you'd succeeded in touching it," Arwen said. "Remember Matti's curse last winter?"

"I remember the glowing purple *thing* on her hand and that she was dying from it." Amber groaned. "I almost walked up to it like a dumbass and did the same thing? I'd assumed I was, uhm, a little brighter than her."

"Don't underestimate Matti because she likes to pound things with a hammer." Arwen patted her father's hand, then shifted so she could stand. "And it's not about how smart you are. People with magical blood are drawn to those artifacts. Like my father said, dark elves put them out or leave them behind to curse any powerful enemies who invade their territory."

"Among other things." Father rotated a shoulder. He must have been caught in a rockfall of his own. Or some other booby trap.

Glad he was still walking and that she'd found him, Arwen hugged him. He stiffened, probably on edge from everything, but soon hugged her back.

"The question is *do* they still consider this their territory?" Arwen mulled over the ramifications of artifacts in these tunnels and a dark elf skulking around outside. "I thought they'd abandoned it ages ago. After the fire. Why did you come up here? And why didn't you *tell* me?"

"You were busy." Father waved vaguely.

Arwen opened her mouth to say she wouldn't have been too busy to come with him to keep him safe but realized he might have seen her smooching with Azerdash. She blushed.

"Besides," he continued, "safe on the farm was a better place for you than up here. I thought I was just coming up to check an old map I remembered."

"If you thought that, why'd you take everything from your gun safe?"

"Gotta be prepared." He patted his favorite rifle, Aragorn. "And I remembered everything had been sealed up—all the entrances—when I showed you the place before. Thought I'd have to blow my way in, and I did. I—"

A soft scrape followed by rocks shifting sounded near the collapsed ceiling.

Nocking an arrow, Arwen spun toward the noise. Her father raised his rifle to his shoulder while using his foot to nudge his flashlight to point in the right direction. Amber lifted her sword.

Arwen didn't sense anyone, but that dark elf could be camouflaged. Was he alone? Had he been left behind all these years to keep an eye on the place? Or had Arwen's mother recently decided these tunnels needed a guard again?

Boulders stirred, then rolled aside. Magic whispered through the area as a draft swept in from the forest above, the scents of moss and pine cones replacing some of the dusty air.

Her father's finger tightened on the trigger of his rifle as a shadow stirred.

"Wait," Arwen blurted, realizing that was *elven* magic and not dark-elven magic. She was so weary she hadn't noticed. Raising her voice, she asked, "Sarrlevi?"

Maybe calling out when enemies were around wasn't a good idea, but considering how much noise they'd recently made, the whole forest knew they were here.

"Yes," he said dryly. "Your light is a more fearsome deterrent than your weapons."

"Aragorn is plenty fierce," her father said.

"That's his rifle." Arwen doubted Sarrlevi was familiar with the Lord of the Rings.

"A simple weapon to deter. The light, however..." Sarrlevi stepped forward, allowing his camouflage to drop so they could see him. A few fresh dirt smudges on his shirt were the only signs that he'd been scuffling in the forest. That and...

"Is that a head?" Arwen stared, the flashlight showing him holding the albino-skinned profile of... Yes, that was a dark-elf head.

Sarrlevi carried it at his side by the hair, as if he gripped the handle of a shopping bag.

Amber screamed.

The head might not have startled Father, but *that* did. He leaped several steps away from Amber, alarm flashing in his eyes. Arwen recognized his reaction. Unease in crowds, fear of people in general.

Sarrlevi stopped and regarded them as if they were the odd ones. For assassins, even former assassins, decapitated heads were probably a commonplace thing.

Striving for casualness, since her twitchy father and the hyperventilating Amber both needed that, Arwen said, "I thought you were going to question the dark elf."

Sarrlevi regarded the head. "I did have that intent, but he was unwilling to cooperate."

"So you killed him?" Amber asked in a high-pitched voice.

"He was attempting to kill us and, I believe, responsible for the explosion that almost buried your conveyance."

At the reminder of her car's peril, Amber recovered some of her equilibrium. Though she pointedly looked at one of the tunnel walls instead of Sarrlevi's booty. "You couldn't have left the body in the woods? When I picked up Arwen tonight, I wasn't looking to have any canon events."

Sarrlevi gazed blandly at her. Or maybe *blankly*. Arwen didn't know what that meant either.

"The body *is* in the woods." Sarrlevi didn't respond further, instead shifting his gaze to Arwen. "I removed the head to bring to Colonel Willard. If this dark elf was known to have committed crimes against the magical community, she may have desired his death. She has not mentioned bounties, in the way that I am familiar with them, but she has, on occasion, given me a combat bonus, as she calls it, for dispatching more criminals than her mission originally required."

"And she likes it when you bring in the heads to show her you got them?" Arwen asked.

"She does not. I am not willing, however, to acquire and carry one of your world's *smart phones* merely to take images of the deceased. Thus, I provide other means of proof."

"I didn't know refusing her order to get a phone was optional," Arwen murmured.

"One does not give an *order* to an elf noble, certainly not when one is from the inferior species that populates this planet."

Father scowled, probably thinking of testing Sarrlevi's ability to *deter* Aragorn's bullets.

"You can get cameras that aren't phones," was all he said, touching his pack. He pointed to Arwen and then down the tunnel, a wide black-stone passageway that had survived the fire twenty-three years ago—and tonight's cave-ins. "I'll show you the map. I already took pictures of it for your colonel or whoever else you know that researches such things—"

Amber perked up but, after an uneasy glance at the head, didn't point out her knack for research. Maybe she was done taking on gigs offered by Arwen and her friends.

"—but there were some magical bits," Father continued. "They might mean something to you." He looked at Sarrlevi. "Or you."

Sarrlevi stepped forward and held something out to Arwen. Distracted by his grisly trophy, she hadn't noticed him holding her arrow, the one she'd fired at the artifact. He must have spotted or sensed it under the rubble when he jumped down.

"Thank you."

He also produced Amber's phone and held it out toward her.

Again, she eyed the head, but for such a prize, she was willing to get close enough to snatch it from his grip. Like a wild animal, she immediately scurried back.

Arwen looked at her father. "I'm ready. I'll look at what you found."

She didn't remember a map and was curious.

Father hesitated, giving her a long look before nodding and leading the way into the tunnel. Amber and Sarrlevi followed them.

"Would you like to leave that here?" Amber asked Sarrlevi without looking directly at him.

"I would not."

"Fine, but, FYI, you're not putting it in my car."

Arwen expected Sarrlevi to say that he didn't care or that he could form a portal and didn't need a ride from her. Instead, he nodded.

"Mataalii has informed me that human custom decrees that there are places where it is inappropriate to store a decapitated head, even one sealed inside a magical backpack."

"No kidding," Amber muttered.

Curious, despite the grisly subject, Arwen asked, "Where did you try to store one that prompted Matti to make that comment?"

"In the bedroom."

"She must think you're dope,'" Amber said.

Sarrlevi scrutinized her. Trying to decipher that? "We are fused and inseparable like trees that have grown together in the forest."

Amber scrutinized *him*. Maybe she hadn't seen that before.

"Your word for it is inosculation," Sarrlevi informed her. "The elven term is far more romantic."

"*Super* dope."

# 15

MANY OF THE TUNNELS IN THE LAIR HAD COLLAPSED. THOSE THAT remained stable had long ago been plucked free of the furnishings, books, laboratory equipment, demon statues, and other dark-elven items that Arwen remembered from the first seven years of her life.

So much had changed since her youth that their group had been walking for some time before they passed places that stirred memories for her. At that point, they must have reached chambers and tunnels she'd traveled back then, because more spots, however abandoned, were familiar.

As a girl, Arwen hadn't had the freedom to roam, to explore. Her life had been strict. Eating, learning, attending religious ceremonies, praying to demons who'd demanded everyone's obedience.

She shivered as the memories came to life, and she wrapped her hand around the cross she now wore, a gift from her father who'd introduced her to his faith as soon as they'd escaped. Sometimes, she still felt guilty about her childhood, the words she'd been indoctrinated to utter, the promises she'd been made to obey.

Rebelling hadn't been permitted. Proper behavior had been enforced with punishment.

Her imagination created a shadow that made her gasp and jump. Sarrlevi and Amber, following behind, might not have noticed, but her father looked over at her, his face grim. He glanced at her hand wrapped around the cross.

Arwen lowered it and attempted to look brave, not afraid. She should have realized this place would bother her.

Father said nothing, but he nodded. Maybe it hadn't been her busyness with Azerdash that had kept him from asking her to come along with him tonight. Maybe he'd wanted to spare her this.

"It's fine," she told him, forcing a smile. "They're all gone now. Nothing is that disturbing."

"Except the guy carrying a head," Amber muttered, proving she was paying attention.

"I have wrapped it and placed it in my pack," Sarrlevi said calmly. "It was only the cacophonous rockfall that prompted me to rush directly to your location with it in my grip."

"Which we appreciate." Arwen knew he'd only come along as a favor to Matti and nodded over her shoulder at him. "Thank you for your assistance tonight."

Arwen liked to think she would have been a match for a dark elf, but she didn't know that. It had taken Sarrlevi a while to get that guy, and he was a badass.

He inclined his head once in acknowledgment.

Amber rolled her eyes. Sarrlevi might have lost some of his appeal to her when he'd wandered in with a head. Well, he wouldn't lose sleep over it.

"Down this way." Father pointed his flashlight into a wide tunnel.

Arwen shivered in anticipation, or maybe anxiety, as they turned down it. Only his footprints were visible on the smooth dusty floor, nothing else. The whole place must have been well-sealed before tonight, because Arwen hadn't seen any signs that animals had gotten in. Maybe a hint of the old magic had kept them away. Or maybe the forest life had some collective memory of who had once lived here, and they hadn't wanted anything to do with the place.

"There is dark-elven magic ahead," Sarrlevi said.

"I assumed there would be." Arwen hoped it wasn't another artifact capable of cursing intruders.

"There are things in the map room," Father said, "besides the map."

"What does the map show?" Arwen asked.

"Maybe nothing. Maybe something." Father picked up his pace.

He'd never been a man of many words.

*Arwen,* Azerdash's telepathic voice sounded in her mind. *I am nearby and camouflaged.*

After recovering from her surprise, Arwen asked, *I'm glad you're here and okay, but what about the assassin?*

*I am certain he will appear shortly and unpleasantly, like pervasive scale rot spreading swiftly along one's back, defying all attempts at removal.*

*I take it you're in your dragon form.*

*The better to swiftly assist you should you need it. I do not sense dark elves, but you are near some of their artifacts.*

*I know. I already blew one up.* Arwen didn't mention that her action had prompted the ceiling to collapse and a cedar tree to almost squish her and Amber.

*That is rarely the safest course of action with dark-elven artifacts.*

*Oh, I know, but it was an emergency. Matti and Sarrlevi saw the assassin dragon in Green Lake earlier. They said he took a portal.*

*Yes, to seek me out, but I hope I've stymied him for a time.*

*Stymied?* Since Saruknorath knew she and Azerdash were

connected, Arwen imagined the assassin would always have a good idea of where Azerdash would show up eventually. It crossed her mind that she might protect him by asking him to stay away from her, but the thought made her heart ache. She appreciated that he'd come to check on her. If something happened, and she needed help, she liked having him there.

*Yendral and I visited the Assassins' Guild headquarters on Zoktho-ran. We spoke to the guild leader, ostensibly to recruit for the joint forces we are forming, but also in an attempt to learn who hired Saruknorath.*

*Were the assassins open to joining your army?*

*They were not. As you might imagine from self-centered beings such as assassins, they were not eager to risk their lives when the odds were stacked against them.*

Arwen glanced at Sarrlevi, thinking that not all assassins were self-centered, but maybe he was a rarity.

*I expected such,* Azerdash continued, *but we did learn that there was no love for dragons among the guild members and that most would be pleased to see them fall. In the past, dragons have attempted to force the assassins to work for them, often without pay. It's supposed to be an honor to serve their kind. Even though we did not secure any allies, we did convince Guild Leader Nesheeva to instruct her people not to work against us while we undertake our mission. Yendral especially convinced her.*

*In the same way he convinced the fae queen?*

*Yes. Nesheeva also sent a messenger to ask Saruknorath to return to the guild for a meeting. She admitted it is unlikely he will obey her if she tells him not to hunt me, but she said she will attempt to make it a long meeting with a feast of rotisserie* hyoklorth.

*Meat?* Arwen guessed.

*Fowl.* Azerdash shared an image of a bird the size of Amber's hatchback rotating on a spit.

*Tasty.*

*Yes. Your conveyances appear to be blocked from escaping.*

*Yeah, we accidentally set off a trap.*

*I will clear the rubble.*

*Thank you. We'd greatly appreciate that.*

*Or...* His telepathic tone grew thoughtful. *Perhaps some improvements to the conveyances would allow them to more easily navigate such challenging terrain.*

*Gnomish improvements? Fueled by half-dragon magic?*

Azerdash smiled into her mind. *Square 97 contains information on altering wagons and horseless carriages.*

*Square 97?* It took Arwen a moment to guess what he was referencing. *Are you still carrying around that toilet-paper roll?*

*Full of gnomish notes from the scientist Gruflen, yes. If you do not need my assistance in the tunnels, perhaps I will work on this project while I wait. What is your wish?*

"Uh," Arwen said aloud.

Her father slowed and looked at her.

"How would you feel about your truck having a sentience and some improvements?"

"A *sentience?*" he mouthed.

"Like the lawn mower that went crazy?" the more experienced Amber asked. "Hell, no."

Her father caught on and looked a little wistful.

*The owners of the vehicles have mixed feelings,* Arwen reported. *Maybe to be safe, you could just clear the road. Oh, and you could repair the tires on my father's truck. There are dark-elf throwing stars in them.*

*Hm.* Did Azerdash sound disappointed? Those tasks probably wouldn't require him to consult the toilet-paper roll. Naturally, that *would* disappoint him.

The tunnel turned a bend, and Father's flashlight shone into a cavernous, empty chamber. The tips of roots dangled down through cracks in the stone ceiling.

"There's the map." Father swept his beam over a wall filled by a drawing of the Puget Sound area done in white paint.

Even after decades, the lines stood out starkly against the smooth dark rock behind them. A spider symbol in the bottom corner glowed faintly like an artist's signature.

"It doesn't include cities or roads or anything that would be useful to us in identifying exact locations—and even the terrain details have inaccuracies—but I believe those circles represent dark-elven outposts. I remembered seeing this place long ago—" Father glanced toward a corner of the chamber, though it was devoid of furniture or anything else that might have once been there. "But not the details of the map."

Arwen couldn't remember ever having been in this chamber. She walked inside, wanting a closer look at the map, but paused when a glowing stone basin in a corner drew her eye. The size of a bathroom sink, it looked like a waist-high chalice, and memories washed over her as she recalled what such an artifact—a *yadrayku* —would hold at a ceremony. The blood of the sacrificed. A gift to the demons, it had also been used for adorning pale dark-elven faces with ritual lines and squiggles.

"Beware the artifacts," Sarrlevi said from the entrance of the chamber. He hadn't stepped inside, and he held an arm out to keep Amber back as well. "I do not recognize them all, but if that map holds important information, the dark elves may have left devices behind to guard their secrets."

"I got close enough to take a couple of photos." Father withdrew an old-fashioned camera from his pack. "We probably don't need anything else, but I wasn't sure if there might be some magic here, something Arwen could detect that could give us more clues."

Heeding Sarrlevi's advice, Arwen stopped well away from the map. Father ran his flashlight over it for her.

She did her best to ignore the sacrifice chalice, but its glow remained in her peripheral vision, refusing to be forgotten. She focused on the map.

Despite the inaccuracies Father had mentioned, she could tell it represented Western Washington between Puget Sound to the west and the Cascade Mountains to the east. It showed as far south as Mt. Rainier and as far north as Bellingham, though he was right. Cities weren't marked. Only terrain features. And six filled-in circles. One looked to indicate their current location.

Arwen's first thought was that the map, if it had been made twenty-five or more years ago, when the dark elves occupied this lair, might no longer be accurate. Whatever had been in the marked locations might be long gone. But the northernmost one drew her eye.

"I think that's Azerdash's sanctuary," she said.

Neither the Stillaguamish nor any other rivers were marked, but the circle was in the right spot for the timberlands near Arlington.

Father arched his eyebrows.

"Which originally belonged to a dark-elf priest with some magical artifacts and a plot to turn other species into his kind," Arwen clarified. "Matti found it last year, and I—" She almost said she'd met the priest earlier and had been the one to direct Matti to the location, but she hadn't told her father about that. "I heard things from her."

Sarrlevi issued a rumble that sounded like a dragon growling. Had he been there too? Arwen wouldn't have guessed full-blooded elves could make such an animalistic noise.

"Mt. Rainier is marked," Father said. "There was trouble up there a couple of years ago with dark elves."

Arwen hadn't realized he'd heard about that but nodded. "Val and Zavryd were in the thick of things, stopping a plot to destroy the southern Puget Sound area with a premature volcano eruption."

"I remember that," Amber said.

From what Arwen had heard, the plot had involved more than

a simple plan to bury part of the metro area under lava, but she didn't go into details. As with the priest's laboratory, the dark elves had been displaced—or killed—and weren't using the tunnels up there anymore. The tunnels under Seattle near Lake Union were also abandoned, again as a result of Val's work.

Arwen looked at two other circles. It was possible this map was outdated enough that all of the locations had been abandoned, but the unfamiliar ones would be worth checking out. One was on a peninsula near Olympia. The other was between Seattle and Everett.

Wait, where had Val said she was researching a lead? Mill Creek. South of Everett.

If dark-elf tunnels there hadn't been abandoned, Val might run into trouble. And she might not have Zavryd with her. *He* was busy delivering messages for the dragon queen.

"We can share your imagery with Colonel Willard," Sarrlevi said, not aware of her thoughts. "She may wish to send operatives to investigate those locations."

"I think she already has," Arwen whispered.

The chalice glowed a brighter red. Arwen frowned, the urge to fire an arrow into it sweeping through her. But she didn't need to cave in another chamber on top of their heads.

*You remain safe?* Azerdash asked into her mind. *If needed, I can switch forms and enter those tunnels to join and protect you.*

*I'm fine. Nothing has changed.* She glanced at the chalice. Nothing major. *Why do you ask?*

*I sensed dark-elven magic near you intensifying, as if being woken from a hibernation state.*

*We're about to leave.* Even as Arwen sent the words to him, red mist flowed over the lip of the chalice, down its stone pedestal, and across the floor. Was it her imagination, or was it heading toward her?

"What *Friday the Thirteenth* ghoulish crap is that?" Amber asked.

"The mist is magical." Sarrlevi stepped forward with his swords in his hands.

Arwen raised her bow, but she couldn't shoot mist. She eyed the chalice, again thinking of targeting it.

Her tattoo cooled abruptly, sending an icy chill through her nerves. A warning?

"Don't shoot anything." Father stepped forward and gripped her arm. "There are always consequences for destroying their stuff, whether they're here to see it or not. Like I said, I've got a photo of the map. Let's get out of here."

He pointed toward the tunnel, and Arwen turned to follow, agreeing with the sentiment. But the mist flowed faster, covering the floor all around them and between them and the exit.

Amber had already backed into the tunnel, but Sarrlevi remained, eyeing the mist and the chalice with the same speculation as Arwen had. With his magical swords in hand, he had to be thinking about destruction too.

Waving for him to lead the way out, Arwen took two steps toward the exit, but she met resistance. It was as if the mist had the density of water—or maybe gelatin. She only made it three more steps before she couldn't push farther against it.

Strangely, her father wasn't impeded in any way. He neared the exit before realizing she wasn't following him.

"Arwen?" He glanced at the mist as he stretched a hand toward her. "You don't want to linger."

"Oh, I know." Arwen licked her lips, again trying to walk toward him—no, to sprint from the chamber. But the resistance grew even greater.

She could move her foot backward without trouble—when she tried, her leg almost sprang in that direction, wanting to take her toward the map. But forward was out of the question. The mist didn't want her to go sideways either.

*We have waited for you,* a raspy voice whispered into Arwen's mind. It didn't sound like one of her mother's people, but it spoke Dark Elven. It seemed to originate at the chalice. That thing couldn't be intelligent, could it? *You will not depart. You will take the test to prove that you are loyal to the collective, that She Who Leads can trust you.*

*No, thanks. I don't like tests.* Arwen imagined Azerdash's face and called telepathically to him. *If you're still nearby, I might need help after all.*

Her father came back for her and reached out. "Take my hand. We'll carry you out if we have to."

As he reached for her, the cold emanating from her tattoo flared with heat and power. As it had in the Bellevue building where she'd first encountered the dark elves, it sent energy through her limbs, energy that took over her body. She caught herself lunging for her father, grabbing his arm before he could grip hers.

*Yes,* the voice spoke into her mind as more mist flowed into the room, rising above the floor, turning into a fog that made Sarrlevi and Amber hazy. *Long have we kept this one alive so he could be used in your test.*

Dread thudded into Arwen's gut. *That* was why neither Harlik-van nor the others had targeted her father when they'd been trying to get her to cooperate?

Surprise flickered in his eyes at Arwen's grip, but he didn't appear alarmed. He nodded and tried to pull her toward the exit.

With strength that came from her tattoo, and might have been enhanced by the chalice, Arwen pulled him instead.

The sentient *thing,* enchanted who knew how long ago by some powerful minion of her mother's, wanted Arwen to sacrifice him. Horrifying imagery sprang into her mind, so vibrant that she stopped seeing the chamber and the mist and her companions. All she saw was herself standing beside the chalice with Azerdash's multitool raised in the air, the knife extended, as she prepared to slice it into her father's veins.

Panic grasped her, and she panted, fighting to let go of him, fighting to keep from striding toward the chalice. But she kept walking backward to it. As she drew closer, its grip on her became stronger, its power to force her to do its bidding harder to resist.

To make things worse, her father didn't fight her, only frowning as she drew him toward the corner with the chalice.

Why would he fight? He *trusted* her.

"Pull away," Arwen tried to order him, but only a strangled gasp came out.

"I believe the dark-elf artifact is compelling her," Sarrlevi stated from the exit.

*Yes!* Arwen wanted to cry. Nothing came out.

Her tattoo flared, heating her arm up like a branding iron, and her hand jerked to her belt, to the multitool.

*Yes,* the chalice spoke into her mind. *You will prove yourself useful, the experiment of She Who Leads worthwhile. After you pass the test, you will go among the natives, finding the sacrifices and resources we need to repopulate our dwindling kind. Take his blood. Take his life. Prove your loyalty, your value.*

Against her wishes, Arwen jerked the multitool from its holder and thumbed open a knife.

For the first time, concern entered her father's eyes. "What are you doing?"

A great wrenching came from the root-dotted ceiling, and Arwen sensed Azerdash landing above them. A muffled roar floated to them before dirt and rocks tumbled downward, magical power ripping the earth away to open the chamber to the night sky.

Before Arwen could feel relief, the chalice said, *Do not fail the test, or the lives of the others you care about will be sacrificed.* An image of the two crystalline spider artifacts popped into her mind.

Azerdash's great head lowered through the hole. His eyes glowed violet as he gazed at her and the chalice.

*Help me,* she tried to beg him, even as her muscles worked against her. Her grip tightened on her father's arm, her other hand still wrapped around the multitool.

Azerdash met her gaze. *You have the power to defy your mother's people.*

If only that were true. But she'd dragged her father all the way to the chalice and couldn't release him, no matter how much she wanted to.

*You have the power to fight the compulsion. That you desire nothing of their ways is one of the reasons I care for you.*

As much as the words meant to her, in that moment they only frustrated her. Why wouldn't he use his power—put a compulsion of his own on her—to help her break away from the chalice's magic?

He only held her gaze, watching her expectantly.

Damn it, if he wouldn't help her, she would *have* to do this on her own.

Even as the chalice and her tattoo worked together, forcing her knife toward her father, she attempted to draw power not only from her own reserves but from the ground under her feet and from the trees growing above. She pulled in everything she could until a ball of energy formed in her chest and grew so intense that it hurt.

From there, she tried to use it to knock away all the dark-elven magic around her. Since the tattoo was a part of her, that wasn't easy, but she unleashed everything she had in an attempt to gain her freedom.

Her hands spasmed, and she released her father and the multitool, letting it fall. She sprang away, willing the damn mist to evaporate so that it wouldn't impede her. Angry, she batted power at the chalice itself, making the heavy stone wobble, the glow fluctuating.

*You've done it,* Azerdash told her, sounding pleased. His long neck flexed, whipping his head toward the chalice, and he snatched it up in his maw. He lifted it out of the chamber, and Arwen sensed it flying away. No, he'd *hurled* it away.

Her tattoo throbbed, and irritation smacked her in the back of the head like a whip.

Arwen stumbled, as if physically struck. Her legs were weak after the great effort she'd put forth, and her knees collapsed, startling her with their betrayal. Too exhausted to react quickly, she fell, her head passing through the mist and thudding hard against the stone floor. She lost consciousness.

# 16

ARWEN WOKE WITH A HEADACHE STABBING BEHIND HER EYES AND drizzle falling through the destroyed ceiling and onto her face. She lay on her back with Azerdash kneeling to her right and her father to her left, both frowning down at her with concern.

She blinked slowly, relieved to see them alive—especially her father. She hadn't succeeded in hurting him. Thank God. And damn those demons and the dark elves and all the horrible things they wanted.

"You alive in there?" Father asked. "It'll be light soon. We've got to get back to feed the chickens."

Arwen licked her lips, her mouth drought dry. "That *is* what I was most worried about when the magic held me," she rasped, then fought the urge to cry. She hadn't done anything that chalice had shown her. It was fine. Everything was—

Azerdash rested his hand on her forehead, as if to check her temperature—she *did* feel hot—then stroked his fingers through her hair. Healing magic flowed from them, cooling and soothing the lump on her head she'd received when she fell.

Azerdash gazed earnestly into her eyes. "I regretfully inform you that I did not have time to finish altering your father's conveyance to give it a sentience."

Arwen snorted, moved to smile despite the dreadful moments she'd experienced before losing consciousness.

Father returned her smile and met Azerdash's eyes. If he minded Azerdash stroking his daughter's hair, he didn't do anything to indicate it. If anything, they seemed to be sharing a moment. Maybe they'd agreed to be light and not let her dwell upon the seriousness of the night's events.

"There's enough sentience around here already." Arwen glanced toward the corner of the chamber, afraid she had misremembered Azerdash destroying the chalice, or that its magic had somehow reassembled it, and it was still glowing red, oozing mist at her. But it was gone. So was the mist.

"Malevolent sentience," Azerdash said. "That is not the kind I would imbue in a mechanical device."

"Our neighbors' dogs disagree," came Amber's voice from the tunnel.

She and Sarrlevi were still by the exit, their stances implying they were more than ready to get out of the place. Arwen didn't blame them and shared the sentiment. She wanted to go home and—

A memory swept over her, and alarm propelled her into a sitting position.

"Val." Arwen looked at Amber. "Have you heard from your mother?"

"No. She doesn't usually call me in the middle of the night."

"We need to check on her." Arwen patted around until she found her phone.

As she dialed Val's number, Azerdash finished applying his healing magic. Not wanting him to leave, she gripped his hand before he pulled it fully away. The call dropped immediately to voice mail, and Arwen hung up.

*Thank you for coming to help me, Azerdash, to tell me to get my ass in gear and push that thing away.* Arwen liked to think that she would have found a way to do that even without him encouraging her—and reminding her that he cared, which had made her not want to disappoint him. She was sure Sarrlevi would have stopped her if she hadn't found a way on her own, but this had been a better outcome.

*Certainly. If I am able, I will always come for you.*

Emotion thickened in her throat.

His gaze lowered to her midsection. *Your ass has gears?*

Arwen snorted again. *Like a gnomish locomotive.*

She didn't know if gnomes had trains, but it seemed reasonable to believe they would.

*Fascinating.*

*Damn straight, it is. If we ever get back in the pool together, I'll show you.*

*I'll look forward to it.*

Her father grunted and rose to his feet. He couldn't have heard their telepathic words, but he might have guessed from their goofy expressions that they were communicating. Maybe he thought it was gooey love stuff, because he put on a serious face and pointed to the exit.

"We need to get out of here," he said. "The chickens."

"You don't think Horus could break into the feed bin to liberate breakfast?" Arwen asked.

"Last time that happened, he only liberated enough for himself."

"True." Arwen put away her phone. She would try Val again soon, but it worried her that she hadn't answered. If Val *had* found dark elves, a whole lair of them, she could be in serious trouble.

"I'm more than ready to go." Amber yawned. "Arwen's pantry is calling to me."

"It looks like your bed is calling to you." The yawn made *Arwen* yawn. The night had been exhausting, and she longed for her own bed, but if Val was in danger, she couldn't rest.

The words the chalice had spoken about her other friends being sacrificed haunted her. It hadn't been sharing a recorded message. It had known what was going on in real-time with Arwen and the dark elves.

"I'd like snacks to take to bed. Assuming I can drive off this mountain." Amber frowned at the hole in the ceiling and the tunnels they'd walked through on the way inside.

Azerdash twitched two fingers, and he, Amber, Arwen, and her father levitated through the hole. He must have trusted that Sarrlevi could levitate himself out, because he didn't presume to lift the elf.

*I cleared the road so that you may more easily drive your conveyances away,* Azerdash said.

"Oh, good. Thanks." Amber looked around after he lowered them to solid earth. "Uhm, which way *is* the car?"

The first hint of dawn brightening the sky showed nothing but trees looming around them, though the distant freeway noise still reached their ears. Using it and the slope as a guide, Arwen pointed. Her father pointed in the same direction at the same time.

"I guess you Davy Crockets would know," Amber said.

"I will take Arwen to her destination," Azerdash stated.

Since Arwen wanted to check on Val as soon as possible, she didn't object, but she did say, "Let's wait and make sure they get off the mountain safely."

Though Sarrlevi had defeated the only dark elf they'd seen, that didn't mean there couldn't be another one out there spying on them. It was also possible that disturbing the chalice and the map chamber had alerted her mother or another dark elf that this place had been invaded, and they would send others to check on it.

"Especially since Sarrlevi probably won't be getting a ride back with Amber," Arwen added, reminded of what he carried in his pack. Sooner or later, Amber would remember the head and deny him entrance to her car.

Father took the lead, guiding the group through the trees.

*I came back because I'm considering kidnapping you,* Azerdash told Arwen as they walked.

*Oh?*

*For your own good.*

*Kidnapping people is illegal on Earth.*

*I will take you with me to other worlds, as we discussed.*

*Thus skirting the Earth-legality problem?*

*While employing you as my assistant negotiator and, more importantly, keeping you safe.* Azerdash gave her a worried look.

Maybe Saruknorath had said something to him to imply he would come after her again. As if having dark elves gunning for her wasn't bad enough.

If not for the danger to Zoltan and Imoshaun, Arwen might have been tempted to disappear for a while. She would feel guilty about leaving Father with the harvest season kicking into high gear, but the desire to escape her dark-elf woes for a time was real. Maybe they could hire a farmhand, and Azerdash could kidnap Father too.

She shook her head at the implausibility. *Even if I would agree to being kidnapped, I'd need to find my friends first.*

*Yes, I am aware. That is why I have returned to help you with that and also thwarting the dark elves. Then you will not need to worry about your kin while I've stolen you away.*

*You're a polite kidnapper.*

*I am.*

*Will you give me a ride to Mill Creek?*

*Yes.*

*Do you know where that is?*

*No.*

She bumped arms with him. *It's sort of on the way to Edmonds. A bit off to the north. I'll direct you.*

*Very well.*

The car and truck came into view, the rockfall magically swept off the road behind them. The flat tires had even been repaired. Dragon magic was quite handy.

Arwen's phone rang. Hoping for Val, she hurried to answer, but Willard's number popped up.

"Hello?" Arwen said with unease.

A call at this early an hour couldn't mean anything good. Something might have happened to Val.

"Get to my office now, Forester." Willard hung up.

Arwen stared at the phone. Willard could be terse, but that had been abrupt even for her. With her ongoing worries plaguing her, Arwen imagined a dark elf standing behind Willard, a dagger to her throat while ordering her to get Arwen to come.

Except that it was getting light out, so the dark elves wouldn't be stirring. The dragon *assassin* might have a dagger to Willard's throat.

Arwen sighed and told Azerdash, *I actually need a ride to Willard's office in Seattle.*

*New trouble?*

*Probably. It's finding me left and right lately.*

# 17

Arwen's father hadn't objected to her flying off with Azerdash instead of riding home with him or Amber, but he had given her a concerned look, a hug, and told her to be careful. Neither of them had spoken about what that chalice had been trying to get her to do, and she definitely hadn't brought up the words it had spoken to her, the revelation that the dark elves had kept Father alive all this time so she could prove herself to them by sacrificing him. Such a notion was too horrifying to voice. It was possible he already knew, or that he had an inkling, but it didn't matter. She would never tell him.

*You did well in the dark-elf lair,* Azerdash spoke into her mind as they flew.

Arwen stirred, wondering if he had been monitoring her dark thoughts and wanted to distract her from them. Though she wasn't an overall fan of having her mind read, she appreciated the sentiment.

*Thank you, but I was so close to failing, to letting that magic guide my hand. Even now that I've resisted it and the moment has passed, it's very unsettling.*

*Being compelled against one's will always is.*

Azerdash sounded like he spoke from experience. With his great power, it was hard to imagine someone forcing him to do anything, but a full-blooded dragon had even greater power.

*Yeah. How did you know that I— Well, you seemed certain that I could resist it. I wasn't. I thought...* Arwen shrugged.

*Back when we battled Darvanylar at the sanctuary, you resisted his compulsion to force you to shoot me. A dragon is equally or even more than equally as powerful as a dark-elf artifact. And you care for your father even more than you care for me. I knew you would find the strength.*

Arwen hadn't considered that. She *had* resisted the dragon. Of course, her tattoo had helped her then. This time, it had worked against her. It had wanted her to fulfill that awful destiny.

Not wanting to dwell on that, Arwen focused on the other part of his statement. She didn't wish Azerdash to believe he was at the bottom of some hierarchy of people she loved. *I care about you a lot. Not less than I care about my father.*

*You have known him far longer than I. It makes sense that you would care more for him. I am not offended.*

*Caring isn't logical though. You are both important to me. Equally important.*

*At the time, you had only recently shot an arrow through my thigh. I am certain your caring was at a lower level than it is now.*

*I was* compelled *to shoot you. Because I lost the battle with the dark elves. It had nothing to do with caring.*

*I know this. But you are now powerful enough to resist their compulsion. I am pleased.* Azerdash beamed his pride into her.

Arwen blushed. Why was she arguing with him about caring? *I hope I can continue to resist them. I... The tattoo makes things difficult.*

*Yes. Mine has also impeded me.*

Arwen patted his back again, wishing she hadn't complained.

His tattoo made it easy for assassin dragons and everyone else to hunt him down.

*I want to find my friends, so they'll be safe, but I also look forward to having Zoltan make a formula so we can both get our awful tattoos removed.* Arwen didn't voice her concern that the dark-elf kidnapper had destroyed the formula and the ingredients, and they would be forced to undertake a quest to get them again. Even if they had to, it would be worth it in the end.

*As do I. But in the meantime, we must endure. Challenges must be won, despite obstacles, not set aside because of them.*

*Did a dead general say that?*

*I am saying that.*

*Maybe someone will quote you one day.*

*That would be acceptable.*

Drizzle and rain alternated on the way back, so they didn't see the sun rising, but the gray sky lightened in proof of its existence. Arwen saw rather than sensed the silver glow of a portal forming against the cloudy backdrop and grimaced. Only a dragon would open a portal high above the ground.

*It is Yendral,* Azerdash said, his wingbeats not faltering.

*You were expecting him?*

*I was not. I thought his interlude with the female assassin would take longer. He may have news.*

Arwen touched Azerdash's back again. He'd just gotten here. She hoped he didn't need to leave. Finding Val and Imoshaun and Zoltan would be less daunting with his help.

*I guess I'd rather see him than the assassin,* she said.

*He has been a staunch ally in seeking out and speaking to various leaders. He's a good troop.*

*I guess. He hasn't nuzzled my ear and tried to talk me into sex for a while, so that's a perk.*

*If he does that again, I will kill him.*

*Even though he's a good troop and staunch ally?*

*Yes. You are...* Azerdash hesitated. Still working it out, was he? *Important. And not his female.*

Arwen smiled sadly, but all she said was, *True on both counts.*

The silver-scaled Yendral flew toward them, then banked and fell in beside Azerdash, matching his pace as they continued toward Willard's Seattle office.

*Greetings, Chef Arwen,* Yendral said. *Have you any snacks for a brave and mighty dragon who's been sent to fulfill many arduous tasks of late?*

*Didn't I leave you about to have sex with the Assassins' Guild leader?* Azerdash asked.

*Arduously, yes. She is a demanding female.*

*I gave my snacks to Amber,* Arwen said, *but I can get you some later.*

*Very well. In the meantime, let us hope the piteous whining of my stomach is not so loud that Azerdash cannot hear my report.*

*Indeed,* Azerdash said.

*I regret to inform you that Saruknorath is peeved with you.*

*He is not merely professionally stalking me?*

*No, he's peeved,* Yendral said. *Remember your plan to have the guild leader hold a days-long meeting?*

*Yes. I told Arwen about it.*

Yendral glanced at her, and she nodded.

*Hopefully, you didn't tell her because you were bragging about your brilliance, because Saruknorath saw right through it. He knew the guild members were trying to delay him and lit their meeting building on fire. Not only is he probably on his way back to Earth right now, but I believe you're now banned from visiting the Assassins' Guild hall. What's left of it.*

*I did not expect the meeting to delay him long. And I only informed Arwen of the event to keep her apprised of non-mission-critical events in my life.*

*Are you certain bragging wasn't involved?* Yendral asked. *Was your tone smug when you told her?*

*Would you like to see if your tail is as flammable as the guild hall?*

*It's not.* Yendral flicked said tail as they descended toward the block that held the Army office building. *You know dragons are fire-retardant.*

Arwen bent and rested her cheek on Azerdash's scales. Though the news was worrying, and likely meant he would have to leave again soon, she was glad he was attempting to do something about the assassin. They both had enough troubles in their lives without worrying about a deadly stalker.

Yendral and Azerdash landed on the lawn and transformed into elves. When Arwen headed for the front door, they walked to either side of her. She didn't know how thrilled Willard would be to have them invade the office with her. Judging by that terse message, she was already in a dour mood.

Despite the early hour, they found the door to the outer office open and Gondo on the desk, alternately using a pen to itch his eardrum and to make notes on a map sprawled under him. He must have been distracted enough by the project not to notice the half-dragons approaching, because he squawked in surprise when they walked in. He fell backward over the edge of the desk, bounced off the chair, and landed with a thump on the floor.

"Sorry to startle you, Gondo." Arwen remembered when he'd reacted that way to her. "Willard called for us."

"She only called for *you,* Tracker Arwen, you who bring fine food and *never* threaten to incinerate goblins."

"Yendral and Azerdash won't incinerate you either." Arwen was about to ask if they could go in but noticed a header written on a graph next to the map. *Dark-elf sightings.* Scraps of paper, napkins, and a piece of wood stacked on the edge of the desk held writing that had been penned by different hands. One on top said,

*Dogs disappearing, maybe sacrificed by dark elves, in Mountlake Terrace by recreation pavilion. Mugruk.* "Who's Mugruk?" she asked.

"An orc who wants to disassociate from the ways of his violence-loving people and become a spy to help our office protect magical beings." Gondo lowered his voice as he waved the note and said, "He's not very good though. He reports dumb things. Everyone knows dark elves don't sacrifice dogs."

"That is true."

"Because of their intelligence and killer instincts, cats are more appealing to demons."

Arwen scratched her jaw, wondering if Gondo believed that or was pulling her leg.

"The half-troll bard who sent a note about Mill Creek is more reputable." Gondo pointed at the napkin. "That's what led Work Leader Willard to send the Ruin Bringer up there."

Arwen withdrew her phone and brought up the photo she'd taken of the dark-elf map before leaving, the circles marking possible lairs. "You may want to add these data points to your, uh, graph."

Gondo proudly held up his paper. "It's called a dot plot. Work Leader Willard showed me how to make it. She *loves* when I collate data in a way that humans can understand." He glanced at the door and whispered, "Humans are a little limited in what they can grasp. Even the work leader, who is relatively wise in the ways of goblins, was flummoxed when I presented my findings using the Banana Peel Method."

"Strange." Arwen left the phone display on so Gondo could study the map while they met with Willard. "You might want to put more weight on these circles than the input from your orc informant. They came from a former dark-elf lair."

"Oh, excellent. Hm, there is no legend? Very primitive, but I shall use my intuitive reasoning to grasp the nuances."

"Good luck." As Arwen turned toward the inner office, Azerdash and Yendral silently observing Gondo's dot-plot creation with bemused expressions, the door opened.

Willard opened her mouth when she spotted Arwen, then noticed Azerdash and Yendral. Whatever greeting she'd been about to voice turned into, "Hell."

"Uhm, good morning, Colonel Willard," Arwen said.

"No, it is not. Get in here." Willard backed into her office, snatching a large coffee tumbler from her desk and taking a long bracing swallow.

"Your human employer does not treat you with the respect you deserve," Azerdash said.

"I agree," Yendral said. "Chef Arwen has impressive power for a mongrel and makes sublime desserts and meat dishes. Her abilities should result in others, especially lowly mundane humans, treating her with deference."

"It's okay," Arwen whispered. "I've heard Willard is a little cranky in the morning before her coffee kicks in."

Admittedly, she was quaffing that coffee now. How long would it be until the effects took hold?

"If I'm cranky, it's with reason," Willard said as Arwen walked in, flanked by Azerdash and Yendral. "And I'm already on my second cup."

Arwen stopped in front of her desk, standing instead of presuming to take a seat. "Does that mean the first cup didn't have enough caffeine to affect your mood?"

"It means this is as good as it gets." Willard thunked her mug down and opened a drawer.

A magical device inside emanated power, *dark-elven* power. The near constant feeling of dread that Arwen had experienced lately reared up. That felt like another—

Willard extracted a spider-shaped crystalline artifact and carefully set it on her desk. It glowed purple, the same as the others.

Eyes locked on it, Arwen shook her head slowly.

"You reported that these have pieces of people's *souls* in them?" Willard asked.

Arwen had shared that information in her voice mail the night before when she'd been trying to arrange a ride.

"That's what my father said," she whispered. "He's seen them before."

"And he said that if this is destroyed the owner of the soul could be killed?" Willard asked.

"I'm not positive but maybe. Uhm, where did it come from?" So far, the devices had been left as messages for *Arwen*. Why would the dark elves care about Willard? Other than the fact that she had her people trying to hunt them down and thwart their plans...

"It was on the steps leading to the front door of the building when I got here before dawn. I'm trying to figure out who's missing so I'll know whose soul it is. I've called all my troops to report in, even if they're not coming in to work today, but a number haven't responded yet." She glanced at the time on her watch, lips pursed in disapproval for anyone who wasn't up by seven.

"Have you heard from Val?" Arwen whispered.

"Not since last night." Judging by the grim set to Willard's eyes, she'd already considered that Val might be the missing person. "The dark elves do have many reasons to hate her."

"Yes." Arwen almost pointed out that they might kill Val outright instead of kidnapping her and performing whatever ritual stored a piece of her soul in the device, but that wouldn't make Willard feel better.

"Forester, you were supposed to track down these dark elves by now and get Zoltan back." Exasperation had crept into Willard's usually calm Southern drawl. "What's taking so long? This is what you're good at, isn't it?"

A rumble—a growl?—emanated from Azerdash's chest.

Arwen lifted a hand. "Yes, ma'am. I'm frustrated myself that I haven't been able to find Zoltan and Imoshaun yet."

"Arwen has been distracted," Azerdash stated. "A dragon assassin has been visiting Earth and attempting to question and capture her."

"Yes, I heard all about Drive-By Number 63 at the coffee shop," Willard said.

Azerdash frowned at her. "He seeks to mind-scour Arwen to learn *my* whereabouts."

"Maybe you should stay out of her life for a while."

"I have decided to kidnap her and take her with me on a quest so that I may protect her from the assassin and all other threats."

"Oh, good. Women *love* it when men kidnap them." Willard looked at Arwen.

"I told him I couldn't go until I found Zoltan and Imoshaun. And..." Arwen stretched a helpless hand toward the crystal spider glowing malevolently at them. "Whoever that is."

"But after that, you're fine with it."

"I don't know. I'm... feeling stressed by my life. It might not be so bad to take a vacation from Earth." Arwen smiled wistfully.

Willard's scowl only deepened. She opened her mouth, but an eager knock at the door interrupted her answer.

"Work Leader Willard!" Gondo squeaked, sticking his head in. "The information that Tracker Arwen gave me has provided another data point for the human village known as Mill Creek."

"That's where I sent Thorvald yesterday."

"It must have been the right decision!"

Willard eyed the spider. "I'm not sure it was."

"Many instances of dark elves have been reported there, and, this morning, there is news that a great sinkhole opened in McCollum Park." Gondo waved his arms expansively.

"Isn't that in Everett?" Willard pulled out her phone.

"In Everett *adjacent* to Mill Creek." Gondo nodded firmly, as if he'd provided irrefutable evidence.

"A sinkhole *is* odd," Willard murmured as she looked at a map.

"Unless one's father has hurled a few grenades at the ground," Arwen said.

Willard looked darkly at her, and Arwen fought the urge to shrink back and maybe hide under the desk. It looked like she was on Willard's shit list. And she couldn't say it wasn't deserved. Maybe not all of this was her fault, but the kidnappings—and soul imprisonments—were happening because of her, because the dark elves wanted to force her back into their cult.

Azerdash rested a hand on her shoulder. He looked like he would speak again, maybe coming to her defense, but his head jerked toward the north. Frowning, Yendral also looked in that direction, though both of their eyes were unfocused. They were using their magical senses, not their sight.

"A dragon?" Arwen guessed.

"Saruknorath." Azerdash sighed.

"I told you." Yendral pointed at him. "He's coming for you." His finger shifted toward Arwen. "And he'll take her if he can't find you."

"No, he will not." Azerdash used his magic to camouflage himself, then pointed to Arwen's multitool.

Nodding, she activated her own camouflage.

Willard lowered her phone. "You two half-dragons need to get out of here—off Earth—and take that assassin with you. There are more of you than of him. Go gang up on him. Set a trap. Drop a boulder on his head. Whatever it takes. Don't come back here until he's dead or no longer a threat for another reason. Stop embroiling Forester in your nonsense."

"Our mission is far from *nonsense*," Azerdash said.

"Whatever it is, leave her out of it. Forester has enough on her plate." Willard pointed at his nose. "And she's not available to be kidnapped."

Azerdash's second sigh was closer to a growl. As much as Arwen wanted him to stay around and help her—or just share his company with her—it might be better for everyone if he didn't come back to Earth until he dealt with the assassin somehow. Or maybe until the entire insurrection he was planning was over.

*You wish me to go,* Azerdash whispered into her mind. It was a statement of certainty. Maybe he'd caught the gist of her thoughts.

*It's not what I want,* Arwen replied silently, aware of Willard glowering at him, *but it's probably for the best. If I can find my missing friends and get the dark elves to leave me alone, I'll be happy to join you for negotiations, even though I'd be horrible at them.* She smiled at him. *Unless you think cookies would move the dwarven king.*

*I think your desserts might very well move a dwarf.*

*Matti does like everything I make, and she's half-dwarven.*

*Yes. And gnomes also enjoy sweets. I must return to negotiate more with them. Further, your mushroom medley is excellent. Perhaps feasting on it would prompt King Eireth to soften his stance about elven involvement.*

*Maybe you* do *need me to help sway the world leaders.*

*As I have been informing you.* Azerdash returned her smile, then clasped her hands and kissed her.

Normally, Arwen might have felt too shy to kiss someone in front of the stern and disapproving Colonel Willard, who stood close enough to see through their camouflage, but this was a goodbye kiss, and she didn't know when she would see Azerdash again. What if Saruknorath caught up with him, and she *never* saw him again?

Arwen returned the kiss, wishing they had more than a moment, wishing... for so many things that the world wasn't willing to give right now. Maybe she had to do more to earn it—to earn him.

Willard sighed dramatically.

Gondo squeaked.

Yendral formed a portal, said something in Elven, and poked Azerdash in the shoulder. Hard.

Azerdash tenderly brushed Arwen's cheek as he drew back, managing to give her a gentle look of longing while he also shot Yendral a dark glare and muttered, "We are going to test your fire retardancy later."

"Saruknorath will test *both* of our retardancies if we don't leave."

"Yes, yes." Azerdash released Arwen as Yendral leaped through the portal. He looked like he might say something. Maybe that he loved her? But, after a pause, what he whispered telepathically was, *Be careful, and please don't cause me to regret not kidnapping you.*

*I'll do my best. And you'd better solve all your problems and come back to me. My father will be disappointed if the farm has to carry on with a completely mundane mulcher.*

After giving her a solemn nod, Azerdash sprang through the portal after Yendral and disappeared.

"Grab your bow, Forester," Willard said. "We're going to visit a Mill-Creek-adjacent sinkhole."

# 18

Arwen had never been in Willard's SUV, a practical and impeccably clean Honda. Sarrlevi wouldn't have been able to find even a speck to wipe with his magical kerchief. Climbing and camping gear were stacked tidily in the back, strapped down so they wouldn't shift during turns. Arwen wagered a military colonel wouldn't have a lightsaber tucked in with her tent and dehydrated rations.

On the freeway on the drive up, Willard tried dialing Val twice. Each time, the call went to voicemail without hesitation. Willard scowled, knuckles tight where she gripped the steering wheel.

"Maybe she's fine but something happened to her phone," Arwen offered.

"*Her* phone doesn't hate her the way yours does you."

"Ah." Arwen thought about clarifying that she meant Val's phone might have been broken, but Willard radiated irritation—or maybe frustration—and Arwen was sure she'd thought of that.

"Look, Forester. I apologize for being short with you this morning. I'm just..." Willard released the wheel with one hand to grasp at the air. Yes, that was frustration. "Thorvald is... a good agent. Despite being a big mouth and a pain in the ass."

Arwen translated that to Val was Willard's *friend*. From what Arwen had heard, Val had worked for Willard for years and they'd been through harrowing adventures that went beyond what employees and employers usually experienced together.

"I understand, ma'am."

"The office can't lose her," Willard said.

Translation: *I* can't lose her.

"The entire situation is vexing," Willard added. "It would be a blow to lose Thorvald. Even Zoltan is useful, if outrageously over-priced. And I'm frustrated that our biggest dragon ally, Zavryd, is never around anymore because he's busy at home dealing with the fallout from your boyfriend's insurrection." Willard shot her the tenth or twelfth dark look of the morning.

So much for her apology.

"Even Sarrlevi is missing at the moment. I tried calling Matti this morning to get some magical backup strong enough to stare down dark elves, and she said he didn't come home last night."

"He should be back soon, if he's not already there." Arwen was glad she could offer some good news. "He helped me last night. I don't think Amber was willing to give him a ride home, but he can make portals, so I assume he stopped somewhere on the way." Possibly to shop in Arwen's pantry. She *had* extended that offer to Sarrlevi.

"Oh." Did Willard's hunched shoulders lower an iota? "Was he too tall to fit in that hatchback of hers?"

"No, that wasn't the problem. In related news, he's going to bring you a head."

Arwen expected Willard to request clarification—maybe Arwen should have been blunt and said *severed dark-elf head*—but Willard only grunted and asked, "Another one?"

"Sarrlevi thought the dark elf that he defeated might be a

known criminal and that you'd want to record the death and possibly reward him."

Willard grunted again. "How can that guy be such a ruthless cutthroat at work and then dote on his family at home like a normal loving male?"

"I don't know, ma'am." Arwen bit her lip, groping for a way to lessen Willard's ire with her. "Have you seen the baby carrier he made from vines?"

"Yeah." Willard signaled for the exit near McCollum Park. "It's cute, isn't it?"

Arwen nodded.

"Have you seen their nursery?" Willard added. "The crib hangs from vines in the ceiling. Apparently, babies with elven blood need to sway in the breeze, like they're being cradled in the branches of treetops."

"Are there a lot of breezes sweeping through Matti's house?"

"I understand she leaves the window open if the weather is nice."

The park was close to the freeway, and Willard turned into it, then tapped Matti's number on her phone.

"Hello, Colonel," Matti answered. "Do you need me for a job? I'm expecting my babysitter home soon."

"Is that Sarrlevi?"

"Yes. He won't yet allow anyone else to watch our children, but I wouldn't mind a break. I haven't thumped anything in days."

"While I do like to encourage my operatives to thump regularly," Willard said, "I'm actually looking for him. Thorvald is missing, and we expect dark-elf foul play. A deadly former assassin would be useful."

"Val is missing? And you don't think *I'd* be useful?"

"You would be, but if the mission goes long, I'd hate to have to send you away in the middle to nurse your babies. You've only *just* had them, you know. I gave you two months of maternity leave."

"Yeah, but I didn't ask for leave."

"I know. Because you're a hard worker."

"Varlesh asked for paternity leave. I'm not sure how long."

"Two years' worth." Willard surveyed a number of grassy athletic fields full of kids playing sports, with no sign of a sinkhole in view. She parked by a Snohomish County Parks and Recreation SUV in front of a trailhead leading into a wooded area. "I denied it."

"Where are you?" Matti asked. "I can send him your way when he gets back. He mentioned something about bringing back a few groceries."

Arwen snorted. Her pantry *was* being raided. She envisioned Amber and Sarrlevi standing shoulder to shoulder with grocery totes, making their selections.

"McCollum Park," Willard said. "According to Gondo, there's a suspicious new sinkhole up here. Forester and I are taking a look."

"I'll tell him, but if I'm stuck at home, I insist you send me someone to thump."

"Be careful what you wish for. That dragon assassin is still lurking around." Willard grabbed an Army tactical vest, checked her gun, and fished out some extra ammo to stick in her pouches.

"Dragons aren't as easily thumpable as you'd like," Matti said.

"Tell me about it."

Bow in hand, Arwen stifled a yawn, slid out of the SUV, and headed toward the trailhead. The sun was out, beaming through the branches and creating dappled shade, so they wouldn't see any dark elves, but... She knelt and rested her hand on the worn dirt path.

Brakes squealed as a commuter bus pulled into a park-and-ride on the other side of the fields. Laughter came from the kids playing sports.

As busy as this park was, Arwen was sure hundreds of people used the trails each day. She doubted she could find any physical signs to indicate dark elves specifically had passed through, but she used her tracking magic on the trees, hoping one would have noticed if suspicious activity had gone on during the night.

Unlike orcs, who often carried huge axes, and goblins, who tended to break branches to use in their shelters, dark elves rarely disturbed trees. Their interests were all underground, not on the surface. Even if they'd been here, it was possible nothing growing in the woods would have taken note. Still, Arwen made the attempt. Apology or not, Willard was frustrated with her, or at least that she was at the center of all the trouble, and Arwen wanted to prove that she was useful. And, of course, she wanted to find all the missing people.

A maple growing near a creek wakened at her touch. Aware of Willard standing behind her, Arwen hurried to ask if it had seen hooded people at night.

The tree showed her an old man shambling through the park and setting up a tent to sleep in. Then it shared a bunch of teenagers with baseball bats, likely up to no good. A pair of men in heavy coats met on a bridge, possibly engaging in a drug deal. Unfortunately, dark elves didn't appear in the tree's memories.

"Learn anything?" Willard asked when Arwen rose, brushing off her hands. She had her phone out, a call in progress.

"Only that this park may see a lot of petty crime at night."

"*I* could have told you that." Willard shook her head and passed, leading the way down the trail. Someone spoke on the phone, and Willard described Val's black Jeep, giving whoever it was the license-plate number. "Let me know what you hear," she finished and hung up. "The sinkhole is back this way."

Disappointed that she hadn't learned anything, Arwen walked silently after her.

"Was that soul tracking?" Willard asked after they'd walked a ways, the traffic noise lessening.

"No. If you think Val was here, I could try using that. All I heard was that she was checking for dark elves in Mill Creek." Arwen didn't mention that Val was striking enough with her magical sword, gun, and tiger that the trees would have noted her if she'd passed through.

"That's the last I heard too. It's all I was able to give her as a clue yesterday, and she didn't mention where she was going to start looking, other than questioning the locals. I've got the police searching for her Jeep. That'll at least let us know where she started."

In the back of the park, a little ways off a loop trail, they found a couple of dog walkers and a uniformed man who must have come in the parks-and-recreation truck. He was talking on the phone while one-handedly stringing caution tape from tree to tree around what did indeed appear to be a sinkhole. The faintest whisper of magic about it promised it hadn't occurred naturally. It was dark-elven magic.

Arwen clenched her fist at this first proof that the map had been accurate. Her mother's people were in the area.

"Yeah," the park guy was saying. "Maybe send some police out here. And a team to fill this in. It's *big*. It looks like a UFO landed."

Arwen raised her eyebrows, disagreeing with the assessment. With uprooted ferns and trees dangling over the jagged edge, it looked exactly like a sinkhole. Something had happened down below to cause it. That was where the magic came from.

Since the trees hadn't noticed dark elves in the park, Arwen suspected their tunnels traveled under it. Maybe Val had gotten in a big fight with someone down there, and the unleashing of magic had caused the sinkhole.

"Yeah," the guy said, still on the phone. "Oh, we're going to need a tow truck too. I don't know how we'll get it back here, but there's a Jeep at the bottom of the hole."

Willard's eyebrows flew up.

"Shit," she swore and ducked under the caution tape to get close.

"I have no idea how *it* got back here. Maybe the UFO dropped it." The park guy had been paying more attention to his phone than the spectators, but he spotted Willard creeping toward the edge. "Ma'am, get back. That's unstable." He lowered his voice to mutter, "Idiot civilians," to whoever was on the line.

Willard, her eyes locked on the bottom of the hole, didn't respond to the comment.

"Lady, don't be stupid." After demoting her from *ma'am* to *lady*, the park guy picked his way around the hole and through ferns toward her.

Arwen activated her camouflaging charm, then crept under the caution tape toward Willard. When the park guy tripped over a root and glanced down, Arwen gripped Willard's arm to extend the influence of the spell to her.

The guy looked up, then stumbled again.

"Where'd they go?" He glanced wildly around. "Did they fall in?"

"They disappeared," a dog walker standing farther back said.

"Oh, sure. *Disappeared*. Damn it." The guy inched closer to the hole and peered in. Dirt crumbled, and he skittered back, swearing again.

Willard didn't respond to Arwen's touch, other than to quietly say, "I don't see a body."

Arwen peered past a fern dangling over the edge. The sinkhole was deeper than she'd expected. Twenty feet down? Twenty-five?

Given how many layers of dirt and rock lay between the surface and the top of a tunnel that disappeared into the darkness below, Arwen decided magic must have made the hole. Or maybe a magical explosion. Nothing about it looked natural.

At the bottom, Val's black Jeep lay on its side, not as smashed as Arwen would have expected from a vehicle that had fallen that far, but the front fender was crumpled, the winch broken off, and one of the windows shattered.

"Can you tell from up here if there are footprints?" Willard asked.

"My eyes are good but not that good. I'd need to climb down." Arwen waved her bow, silently asking if she should.

"Give me a minute. This looks..." Willard squinted around at their surroundings, especially back at the trail.

"Like a trap?" Arwen suggested.

"Yeah. Val didn't *drive* back here. There weren't any tire tracks on the trail, and it wouldn't have been wide enough regardless, not without the Jeep tearing up the brush and leaving paint on the logs."

Arwen nodded. "No, I saw nothing like that. The only thing I can imagine is that someone levitated it back here."

"Unless the UFO hypothesis has merit."

"Levitation still would have been involved, just not the magical kind, right?"

Willard grunted. "I don't know what kind of technology *aliens* use to levitate things."

Arwen tilted her head back to examine the canopy above them and spotted numerous broken branches. "There. Someone dropped it—or lowered it—from above."

"To send a message to us?" Willard asked. "To lure us down there to investigate?"

"I can look for her. I have camouflage." Arwen patted the multitool, then pointed at the hole.

"Yes, thank you." Willard nodded to indicate she understood Arwen was sharing it, then glanced at the park guy.

He'd gone back to his phone conversation, though he did keep glancing around in puzzlement.

"I don't think you should go," Willard added. "If this is meant to be a trap, something to pique our curiosity and lure us in... that's what they want."

Azerdash quoting one of his dead military leaders came to mind. *More successful traps have been baited with mystery than meat.*

"At this point," Arwen said, "maybe I should give myself to them. It would be worth trading my life to free everyone else."

"That plan's dumber than a mud fence, Forester."

"I know, but I'm tired of people being hurt because the dark elves want me." Yet... if Arwen let them have her, and they figured out a way to compel her to do their bidding, even more people would be hurt. She rubbed the back of her neck, frustration and weariness leaving knots there.

"That's a reason to blow them to smithereens, not give in to their desires. You need some military training, Forester. Trotting around in the forest like a fae hippy hasn't hardened you enough."

"They must teach you to speak your mind in the military."

"That's a perk of rank."

After taking a couple of photos, Willard gripped her arm and started to back away from the hole, but Arwen held up a hand when she sensed a dragon. She groaned. Not the assassin again.

# 19

As Saruknorath flew closer, making Arwen believe he was not only looking for her but had a good idea where she was, a second guy in a parks uniform came up the trail, carrying four cones.

"How are *those* going to help?" the man with the caution tape asked.

"I'll block off the trail."

"Azerdash's stalker is here," Arwen warned Willard quietly, keeping a grip on her arm to share the camouflaging magic.

She didn't know if the assassin had visited the Army office, but Saruknorath might know who Willard was, even if she didn't have a magical aura to sense.

"Seems he's *your* stalker," Willard said without asking for clarification.

"I'm an easier target. Unfortunately. I lack talons, fangs, and a giant magical sword as a deterrent."

"You should have kept that sword for yourself, especially since you did most of the work to get it."

"I don't know how to fight with swords."

"As I've advised Thorvald before, the pointy end goes in the dragon." Maybe reminded of her missing comrade, Willard frowned down into the hole. "Even if it's a trap, I'm thinking of getting my rope from the car and going down there. There might be clues in the Jeep."

Arwen nodded but didn't let go of Willard. Saruknorath had flown close enough that he could come into view at any moment.

*Mate of the insurrectionist mongrel, Starblade,* the dragon said into Arwen's mind. *I have come to speak with you.*

She grimaced, debating whether to answer. He might be able to use her telepathic voice to pinpoint her location. The fact that he could speak with her didn't mean he knew exactly where she was; he might have sensed her before she'd camouflaged herself. Unfortunately, his aura promised he was heading almost directly toward them. It probably wouldn't matter if she replied.

*You will wish to have this discussion with me,* Saruknorath added.

*I doubt it,* Arwen said.

Willard poked her in the shoulder. "Did you hear me? Let's go back to the car to grab the gear."

"Sorry," Arwen whispered. "Saruknorath wants to discuss something with me."

"If it's about how he'll pin you to the ground with his talons and painfully extract information from your mind, you may want to bow out of that conversation."

*I am surprised,* Saruknorath said, *that Starblade did not take you with him when he left this world. One should keep one's mate close in times of turmoil.*

Arwen nodded to Willard and kept a hand on her as they retreated from the sinkhole.

*He wanted to take me,* she told Saruknorath, *but I'm on a mission. If you'd like to help me infiltrate a dark-elf lair and rescue my friends, I could then fully attend to your discussion needs.*

The dragon would never agree to help—nor could she trust

him if he did—but the thought made Arwen wistful. If she could talk Saruknorath into striding into the dark-elf tunnels ahead of her, she could sneak in camouflaged and search around while his great aura distracted the inhabitants.

Saruknorath soared overhead, visible through the branches to those with the power to see him. Fortunately for them, the park guys lacked that power and had nothing more pressing to worry about than how to strategically place four cones to deter visitors from getting close to the sinkhole. One of the dog walkers, however, had a smidgen of magical blood. Her eyes bulged as she looked up through the trees. She pulled on her pup's leash, tugging him toward the park exit at top speed.

*A lesser being should always attend a superior being, no matter what.*

*I'm sure that's true.*

*Were I to assist with these nefarious dark elves, would you agree to come with me to the dragon funeral caves of Irathidor so we could continue our discussion uninterrupted?*

Arwen had no idea where Irathidor was but assumed it was on a different world and that going with Saruknorath would involve betraying Azerdash. As useful as a dragon's help would be in the tunnels, especially if he would actually give it, she had to say, *No.*

*I see.* Saruknorath flapped his wings and flew out of view. *Since I am an honorable and magnanimous dragon, I will allow you to complete your mission.*

Willard stopped on the trail. They were only halfway back to the parking lot, but a soft clanking came from around a bend ahead, and she dropped a hand to the holstered pistol under her jacket.

Arwen sensed someone and *something* magical approaching, but she lifted a hand. It felt like gnomish rather than dark-elven magic.

"Have they got a tow truck or a crane coming back here to pull out the Jeep?" Willard wondered.

"No. I sense magic and..." A beeping noise grew audible over the clanks. It was familiar. Where had Arwen heard that before?

"An alarm clock?" Willard asked.

"No. It's gnomish magic." Arwen stopped as a four-foot-tall figure covered from head to toe in gray magical armor, including a helmet with a clear faceplate, clanked into view.

The armor was like nothing Arwen had seen before, except perhaps in a science-fiction movie. It was fully contained like a space suit but appeared sturdier, with magical gizmos attached to the arm coverings. Distracted by the outfit, she didn't realize right away that she recognized the aura of the person wearing it.

"That's Imoshaun's husband. Gruflen."

He stopped on the trail ten feet away, frowning through his faceplate at an amulet gripped in his armored hand—it was the source of the beeping. Arwen almost laughed. It was one of the dark-elf detectors he and his wife had made.

"Aren't you a little short for a stormtrooper?" Willard asked.

Gruflen, who hadn't seen them through Arwen's camouflaging magic, jumped at her voice. The suit must have been heavy because his jump turned into a wobble, and he flailed his arms for balance. Something in the armor whirred, and it helped him stay upright.

Willard elbowed Arwen. "Val would have been proud of me for knowing that line."

"What line?"

"Never mind."

"Arwen Forester?" Gruflen peered at her. "Are you the reason my dark-elf detector has been going off?"

"I may be *a* reason." Arwen remembered how delighted Imoshaun had been that the amulet they'd made using some of *her* blood had gone off not only when dark elves were close but even when Arwen was nearby and camouflaged, as she was now. "We believe there are dark elves in the area though."

"Excellent." Gruflen stepped closer until he could see them. "I've been using Imoshaun's ring to determine her location, and I should be getting close."

"Oh, good." When Arwen had dropped it off, she'd hoped Gruflen would somehow be able to use it to locate his wife. Maybe Arwen should have stayed with him from the beginning. Though he might have wanted to finish his armor before hunting for Imoshaun.

"There's a sinkhole back there." Willard pointed her thumb over her shoulder.

"Ah? Perfect." Gruflen lifted an armored hand in the air and clenched a fist. "I am not a warrior and admit to being wary of all the dangerous beings about—" he glanced skyward, though Saruknorath had disappeared from Arwen's senses, "—but I cannot abide the idea of dark elves experimenting on or torturing my wife. It was bad enough when they had *me*. I must find her, even if —" He paused and swallowed. "Even if it results in my death. I cannot invent and research alone. I must find Imoshaun."

"I'm looking for her now. I'll show you the sinkhole. We think it's a way into the dark-elven tunnels." Arwen released Willard and pointed back along the trail.

With Saruknorath gone, Arwen wasn't as worried about Willard being camouflaged, and it occurred to her that the armored gnome could be the distraction she'd been thinking about. She didn't want to use him in a manner that would result in him being hurt, but if he intended to go into the tunnels anyway... Maybe the dark elves would focus on him and not realize Arwen was camouflaged and walking behind him.

Willard lifted a finger, as if she might object to backtracking, but her phone buzzed with an incoming text.

"We'll wait for you to return with your rope," Arwen told her.

Willard waved an okay, but instead of continuing to the parking lot slowly followed them back down the trail. She was frowning at the message.

Arwen put a hand on Gruflen's arm and walked side-by-side with him to share her camouflage. He clanked noticeably, so maybe there wasn't any point in trying to hide him.

Back at the sinkhole, the park employees were shooing more walkers away. They lifted their heads in confusion when they heard clanks and beeps but didn't see anyone.

Ignoring them, Gruflen shuffled under the tape, barely having to duck, and peered into the hole. The beeping continued, coming from the amulet, until he pressed a circle in the center to silence it.

"Thank you," Arwen murmured.

"Imoshaun is down there?" Gruflen asked.

"I don't know for certain, but we have evidence to suggest dark elves are in this area."

"Yes, I sense traces of their vile kind. They made that tunnel." Gruflen pointed to the dark entrance Arwen had noted earlier. "I am prepared to infiltrate their base and find my wife. With luck, my magical suit will protect me and allow me to defeat them." He glanced at her. "I don't suppose you'd like to lead the way?"

"I do want to help you find Imoshaun. Zoltan and Val too, if they're down there."

"By leading the way?" Gruflen asked again hopefully.

Arwen remembered that he'd hidden behind his wife when Azerdash had come to their workshop. He did not have the soul of a warrior. That he was here, willing to sacrifice himself to try to find Imoshaun, spoke to how much he cared for her.

"I could walk at your side and shoot anyone who attacks us." Arwen didn't mention her plan to remain camouflaged, instead lifting her bow, hoping he would take heart.

"I wish the dark elves to be filled with many arrows."

"A lot of people do," Arwen said.

"Thorvald?" Willard asked into her phone. "This isn't your number. What happened to your phone? And *you*?"

Arwen looked at her.

"I'm at Hot Iron," came Val's voice with noise in the background making it hard to hear.

"I don't know what that is."

"A Mongolian grill. They're getting ready to open for lunch. I was lucky someone let me use their phone. The dark elves destroyed mine, and, uhm, I have some bad news about the Jeep you've been letting me use."

"Oh, we know all about the Jeep. How is it that *it's* in an underground tunnel, and you're—" Willard had typed in the restaurant while they spoke and frowned at the result, "—in the Mill Creek Town Center?"

"It's in a tunnel? Shit. The last I saw, they were levitating it into the woods to keep me from escaping in it. As to the Town Center, I sprinted across the McCollum parking lot with a giant fuzzy spider chasing me—unlike the dark elves themselves, some of their beasts are perfectly happy leaving their lightless tunnels—and happened to catch a bus as it was departing. I think the driver saw the spider because he wasn't willing to let me out until we reached the first stop."

"The Mill Creek Town Center?"

"You got it. Once I stopped bleeding, I figured contacting you was my priority. Did you know dark elves are perfectly happy being awake during daylight hours if they're in their dark tunnels? I blew up a couple of chambers—I'm so thankful Nin makes me magical grenades even though she's retired from weapons smithing now—and Sindari and I killed a few dark elves. That pissed off the others. I was lucky to get out."

"Did you find sign of Imoshaun or Zoltan?" Arwen asked, listening keenly.

Gruflen tapped her arm. "I must make my incursion soon.

They will be more likely to be asleep during the day, so it will be easier to find my wife—and I will hopefully have fewer enemies to battle."

"I'm sorry." Val probably hadn't heard Gruflen. "I think they may be down there, but I couldn't get to them. I should have waited until Zav was back on Earth and could help me. He *loves* annihilating dark elves."

"I'll come pick you up," Willard said, "and you can give me the rest of the details in a formal report."

"I do adore giving formal reports, especially when I'm bleeding."

"I haven't noticed that the lack or presence of wounds affects the length and usefulness of your reports."

"Was that an insult? Or a compliment about how delightfully succinct my briefings are?"

"I'll leave you guessing. I'm on my way."

Willard pocketed her phone and waved for Arwen to come with her.

"I cannot delay," Gruflen said, his armored boots not moving from the edge of the sinkhole, "especially not when a dragon is circling the area. That *never* bodes well."

"Like a single crow indicating a bad omen," Willard muttered.

Arwen was about to explain that the dragon probably didn't care about Gruflen and wouldn't pester him, but, after taking a deep breath, as if he were jumping into the deep end of a pool, he leaped into the sinkhole.

Startled, Arwen didn't reach for him until it was too late. She caught only empty air.

She leaned forward, afraid the gnome scientist would land as hard as the Jeep had and that far more than his fender would crumple.

But Gruflen landed on his feet in a deep crouch by the Jeep. If it hurt, he didn't give any indication, only spreading his arms for balance, then standing straight.

Willard, who'd also peered over the edge when he jumped, remarked, "That's more like science-fiction combat armor than what I usually see magical beings from other worlds wearing."

Arwen nodded, having had a similar thought.

"Maybe there *are* UFOs around," Willard added.

"I should go with Gruflen," Arwen said.

"*You* don't have combat armor. You've got—" Willard fingered the shimmery sleeve of Arwen's jumpsuit, "—bling."

"It can stop bullets. The same people made it." Arwen waved at Gruflen, who was already walking around the Jeep and toward the tunnel he'd pointed out. "Go meet with Val. Maybe she knows another way in, and you guys could storm the tunnels from another direction while Gruflen storms them from this end, and I... Well, I want to skulk around and find our friends."

"I do love it when operatives give me orders." Willard sighed but didn't look like she would object. Some of the tension had gone out of her face when she'd connected with Val.

Below, Gruflen clanked out of view.

"I'm going in." Arwen crouched.

Willard sighed again. "Don't get yourself killed, Forester."

"Because you'd care if I died?" Arwen smiled, certain Willard didn't feel as strongly about her as she did Val.

"Because that dragon wants to talk to you. If you die, he might start harassing the rest of us for the whereabouts of Starblade." Scowling, Willard walked toward the trail.

"She definitely cares," Arwen decided.

After taking a bracing breath, much as Gruflen had, Arwen tossed her bow and quiver into the hole and jumped after them.

## 20

Since Arwen's jumpsuit wasn't as impervious as Gruflen's combat armor, and didn't cover her moccasins at all, she landed with a roll meant to save her heels and joints. Her momentum swept her across the ground, dirt and rocks littering it from the ceiling collapse, but the jumpsuit protected against them. She barely felt the bumps through the material.

Once she grabbed her bow and quiver, Arwen reactivated her camouflage, made sure her phone was silenced, and jogged after Gruflen.

Surprisingly, he hadn't gone far. He'd only clanked a few yards up the tunnel before reaching a dead end. There weren't any other exits, as far as Arwen could see.

"I'm here with you," she whispered in warning before stepping close enough that Gruflen would see her through her camou-flaging magic.

"Excellent, but I must now command you to stand back." Gruflen spread a gauntleted hand on what appeared to be the solid dirt and rock of the dead end. "This is a magical barrier. I will knock it aside."

Now that he drew attention to it, Arwen could sense a hint of dark-elven magic in the dirt.

"Okay," she said.

Gruflen took several steps back, then lifted an arm and tapped what looked like a miniature cannon built into the suit. "If you have the capability to raise a barrier, you may wish to do so. It's possible the explosion will bring down the ceiling as well as the wall. Or... it may bring down *only* the ceiling."

Arwen eyed the dirt and rock above them, and the memory of the cedar that had almost smashed her and Amber came to mind.

"Heinous enemies could also wait on the far side," Gruflen said.

"I'm ready." Arwen formed a barrier and nocked an arrow, pointing her bow at the dead end.

Gruflen rocked from foot to foot while emitting a, "Beep, beep, *thwump!*"

Was that him making those noises? Or the armor? Either way, they were the only warning she got.

What she'd considered a *miniature* cannon unleashed a huge blue ball of energy. It slammed into the dirt wall with a great flash of light that would have made Arwen stumble back even if there hadn't been a shockwave. But there was. The energy knocked her back as the ground quaked, and dirt rained down from above.

She managed to keep her barrier up so the clumps bounced off—but barely. More dirt and rock blew outward from the wall Gruflen had targeted. Dust and spores and who knew what else clouded the air, flowing all the way back to the Jeep—maybe all the way up into the park.

A soft cackle came from Gruflen. Ensconced in his armor, he hadn't so much as stepped back.

When the dust settled, they could see twin red lights burning in the darkness of a tunnel behind where the magical wall had been. No, those weren't lights. They were *eyes*.

Between one blink and the next, Arwen sensed a *drykar*, one of the towering spider-like creatures that she and Azerdash had battled in the bowels of the dark-elf lair in Bellevue. Its jaws clacked, and it lumbered forward on eight legs, the furry tips barbed. Since Gruflen stood in front, it went toward him.

Arwen raised her bow and loosed an arrow well over his head. It landed between the spider's red eyes, sinking in deep. Unfortunately, that didn't stop the creature, only angered it. It reared up on its back legs, the two forelimbs raking the air like a horse's hooves. A barbed tip shot toward Gruflen.

"Look out!" Arwen barked, nocking another arrow.

He skittered back amid fast clanks. That didn't keep the tip from hitting him. The chest of his armor flashed blue and deflected the projectile.

The *drykar* opened its maw as it dropped back to all eight legs, hissing and showing fangs dripping with saliva. Arwen fired again, aiming for the back of its throat, hoping that would be a vulnerable target. She didn't have any arrows that were enchanted to defeat spiders.

This time, when her arrow struck, it hurt the creature. A pained shriek erupted from its throat, but instead of backing away in fear, the *drykar* charged in anger. Straight at Gruflen. The arrow protruded from its maw but didn't slow it down.

Arwen readied her bow again, afraid the spider would trample Gruflen and sink those jaws through his armor. But he must have reloaded his arm cannon, because he cried, "*Thwump!*" and the blue light flared again.

His magical ball of energy slammed into the *drykar's* open maw, striking the same spot as Arwen had. Light flashed, keeping her from seeing the fate of the spider.

Something spattered against her barrier—numerous somethings—and she focused on keeping her defenses up. When the light faded, she blinked a few times before her eyes adjusted to the return of darkness. It had grown quiet in the tunnel.

Gruflen cackled again. "Victorious!"

The spider lay on its belly, its legs crumpled underneath it, and its head...

"Uh, where did the head go?" More importantly, "Where did my *arrows* go?"

Her eyes focused on fleshy bits sticking to her barrier. Were those... pieces of the *drykar*? And... an *eyeball*?

"I believe one is up there." Gruflen pointed at the dirt ceiling of the tunnel where an arrow was embedded, fletching first.

"I'm glad that's magical," Arwen murmured.

After extracting it, she found her second arrow back at the Jeep, the head piercing one of Val's tires. Maybe Arwen could blame the dark elves for that.

"Thank you for distracting that beastly thing," Gruflen said. "I am, as I told you, not a natural warrior. For a moment when I saw it, I experienced... What is the human term for debilitating fear in which your every body part freezes up, except your bladder, which leaks its contents?"

Arwen stopped well away from Gruflen and any possible leaks. "A panic attack, maybe. Or shock. Terror."

"Yes, all of those things."

"You did well. That armor is amazing."

"Thank you, but I was considering improvements for the arm cannon while the spider was attacking me."

"*While*?"

"Yes. Gnomes are easily distracted by ideas, even while under duress. It's likely why our people are not known for going to war with other nations. Though I heard that Azerdash Starblade reached out to our leaders about acquiring siege equipment."

Arwen smiled. "I have no doubt. When he sees your armor, he'll want to see the schematics."

"They are a trade secret."

"He adores the roll of notes you gave him and has perused them often and lovingly. He used some of your knowledge to alter fae fertilizer machines in their realm."

"Oh, I'm familiar with the *dresdalatha*. Huh. Perhaps I *could* show him the schematics for my armor."

Arwen sensed Saruknorath had returned and activated her camouflaging magic again, certain the battle had knocked it out.

"What does that dragon want?" Gruflen whispered, clanking around the dead *drykar* and into the tunnel that stretched away into darkness.

"To chat with me, he said. He's being polite and waiting until I've rescued my friends."

Gruflen's faceplate turned toward her—bits of spider also adorned it. "Dragons aren't polite with lesser beings. I'm not certain they are even polite with each other."

"I know. He's tricky and sneaky. I'm afraid he's up to something." Arwen hoped he didn't plan to attack her—or mind-scour her from a distance—while she was in the middle of a battle for her life.

Gruflen tapped another gizmo on his armor, and a flashlight beam shot out, probing the darkness ahead.

Before they'd gone more than a hundred yards, Arwen sensed an energy field across the tunnel. Gruflen stopped, picked up a rock, and tossed it. Orange sparks flew as magic flared and disintegrated it.

"One moment." Gruflen waved for her to back away before reaching for his arm cannon again.

Once more, Arwen raised a barrier. He beeped to himself a couple of times and fired. She tensed, anticipating the backlash.

This time, the two magics simply met, flashing orange and blue and emitting sizzling noises before his ball of energy disappeared. The energy field also disappeared. Gruflen tested that by tossing a rock through. It thudded down on the far side.

"That's a versatile weapon," Arwen said.

"Yes. Imoshaun and I invented it together." Gruflen turned sad eyes toward Arwen. "I *must* rescue her."

"You will." She patted him on the back.

While they walked, it occurred to Arwen to wonder whose soul was in the third spider-shaped artifact, the one Willard had found. If it wasn't Val—and for that Arwen was glad—then who?

*You needn't skulk about in our tunnels,* a female voice spoke into Arwen's mind as they continued onward. *I've been waiting for you.*

A jolt of recognition went through Arwen. For the first time in twenty-three years, her mother was speaking to her.

# 21

———

ARWEN LICKED HER LIPS, HER MOUTH SUDDENLY DRY. THE URGE TO stay silent and not risk giving her position away came over her. No, her urge to stay silent was so she wouldn't have to deal with the cold dark-elf female who'd given birth to her.

But Arwen had come for Zoltan and Imoshaun, and her mother knew where they were. As much as she would have preferred to rescue them without dealing with her kin, she doubted that was an option. Besides, if Arwen was ever to be free, she had to find a way to permanently get the dark elves off her back. She either had to convince them that she couldn't be used in their plans, or, if they wouldn't accept that, she might have to destroy them. The thought sent panic surging through her in a way that facing a killer spider never would.

*I've come for the gnome and the vampire,* Arwen replied, doubting her mother knew their names.

*Yes, I'm aware. Given your aspirations regarding your tattoo, you need the vampire. I'm more puzzled as to why the gnome matters to you, but it seems Harlik-van was correct about that.*

Her brother. Unless her mother referred to a past conversation, her words were proof that he'd survived.

*I'm open to negotiating for both of their lives,* her mother continued, *providing you are ready to take your place at my side.*

*Their lives* and *their souls?* Arwen had no intention of standing at her mother's side, but she might have to pretend to consider it to get anywhere.

*Yes, of course. The crystals can be dissolved and the soul shards returned to the owners. If you promise to come back to us and work to help our people grow our population and recover the fertility we've lost.* Thus far, her telepathic tone had been calm and reasonable, but it turned cold when she added, *You will certainly stop opposing us or standing with those who oppose us, causing* deaths *of our kind that we can ill afford.*

*I never wanted to fight the dark elves.* That much was true. Arwen's hand had been forced at every turn.

*Then you shouldn't have sided with half-dragons and other ridiculously fertile beings that have no need of your assistance.*

*Where can I find Imo— the gnome and the vampire?* Arwen asked.

*Continue as you are going, and you will find them. And you will find me.*

Arwen swallowed, again fighting the panic that wanted to swallow her. Wasn't it the middle of the day? Why was her mother awake? She was old. She needed beauty rest, didn't she?

Gruflen's dark-elf detector started beeping again. This time, he didn't silence it.

They reached an intersection with fog creeping in from side tunnels, dulling the effectiveness of his flashlight.

He turned to the right. Guessing? Or guided by Imoshaun's ring? He didn't say.

Did Arwen's mother know Gruflen had a way to find her prisoners? She'd said to continue the way they were going.

"We're expected," Arwen whispered, realizing she should warn Gruflen of the contact. She was surprised when she could. Before, the various dark elves she'd encountered had used compulsion magic to keep her from warning her allies. This time, if her mother was doing something to affect her, Arwen couldn't sense it. That made her more uneasy than if her mother had been openly asserting her influence.

The tattoo on her arm warmed slightly and pulsed, but it seemed more content than irritated. That worried Arwen too.

After a couple more turns, the beeping of the detector growing louder, Gruflen touched it to silence it again. He pointed ahead. Though the fog had thickened, they could see that the tunnel widened into a chamber.

Arwen wiped one palm at a time on her trousers, careful to keep a good grip on her bow. They were only walking, but her heart pounded as if she'd been racing through the tunnels at a dead sprint.

Once they entered the chamber, Gruflen shining his flashlight around, he halted it with a gasp.

Three alcoves, with mist-shrouded spider statues on the ground between them, were carved into the far wall. All three alcoves had occupants. One held Zoltan, the vampire flat on his back. Was he resting or in a more ominous state? The second held a half-troll, also lying on the ground and unconscious, with a guitar next to him.

Arwen blinked. The dark elves had kidnapped that guy before. It was Willard's bard informant. Was *that* whose soul was in the other artifact?

More concerned about the occupant in the third alcove, Arwen squinted through the fog to pick out Imoshaun. She sat on the ground amid artifacts and tools, with her back to them. A tiny orange lantern glowed enough to brighten her work area.

"Imoshaun?" Gruflen whispered.

She spun, dropping a wrench, her eyes shining with delight behind her spectacles. "Gruflen! And the battle armor prototype!"

"Yes, we are both here." He chuckled, rapping a gauntleted knuckle on his chest piece, though he glanced around too, peering into the fog. Looking for other tunnels? He had to suspect a trap.

Arwen did too. She checked to make sure her camouflage was still activated.

"Which are you most excited to see?" Gruflen added, walking toward her alcove.

"Well, I'm less worried about the health and longevity of the armor. How did you get past the guards? Are you all right? Did you take your medicine before coming down here?"

"Yes, yes, of course. And we— I defeated the giant spider." He glanced into the fog again.

Expecting dark-elf spies and not wanting to give Arwen away? Gruflen might have silenced the detector, but the magical amulet continued to flash. Arwen doubted it was because of her presence.

"You defeated a giant spider?" Imoshaun asked. "Without growing distracted by an idea for a new project?"

"Certainly. It wasn't until after the creature was dead—mostly —that I considered a new idea, and the idea was quite logically about how to improve the armor, not some random doodad back on my workbench." Gruflen tapped his arm cannon as he approached.

Energy fields similar to the one they'd encountered in the tunnel secured the prisoners in their alcoves. Would Gruflen be able to use the cannon to free them? Without harming them?

Not sure if she should reveal herself or wait for her mother, or whichever minion her mother sent, Arwen headed for the other two alcoves. She would check on the bard and make sure Zoltan was okay.

She eyed the spider statues. Their eyes glowed a faint purple, the same hue as the artifacts. Were they related, with each tied to the soul of the prisoner in the adjacent alcove?

*You will not depart with the work you have done for us on the* thyamiliscar, her mother's stern telepathic voice spoke from nearby.

Arwen halted. The thya-what?

"I said I wouldn't," Imoshaun said, then repeated the words telepathically, and Arwen realized her mother had spoken to everyone.

Gruflen whirled toward a misty corner of the chamber. Arwen couldn't see or sense anyone there. The voice *had*, however, seemed to come from that direction. His dark-elf detector flashed faster now.

*Though I'm not sure why you're worried about wiping people's memories,* Imoshaun added, *when you said dark-elf fertility is your primary concern. I don't see how my work, which you're forcing me to twist to your own ends, will help with that.*

*You speak your mind too freely for such a weak being,* Arwen's mother said.

The fog thinned, and she came into view, her hood up, her albino skin barely visible. Her eyes didn't glow, like those of the *drykar*, but Arwen well remembered that they were red.

*You are fortunate another has made a deal for your life,* her mother added.

Imoshaun looked around. Arwen was still camouflaged, so the gnome wouldn't be able to see her.

*Reveal yourself, Vleesha,* her mother continued, using the name she had long ago given Arwen. *It is time for us to speak.*

*After you let my comrades go,* Arwen said.

After a long pause, during which Arwen expected a defiant answer or at least further negotiations, the energy fields imprisoning Imoshaun, Zoltan, and the bard disappeared. A small magical device that Arwen hadn't noticed but that was attached to

Zoltan's temple fell free, clinking on the ground. His eyes opened, and he sat up. The same thing happened to the bard. When he sat up, he clutched his guitar to his chest like a shield.

*They may leave,* Arwen's mother said.

*With their souls intact and pieces not stuck in those artifacts,* Arwen said.

Magic whispered across the chamber to the three spider statues. As one, they hummed for several seconds, and then their purple eyes darkened. *It is done.*

Was it? Arwen had no way to double-check. Afraid to break the artifacts that held pieces of Zoltan's and Imoshaun's souls, she had left them in her home. Willard had presumably tucked the third somewhere safe.

*Thank you,* Arwen made herself say, though her mother had been responsible for the kidnapping in the first place.

*I am not unreasonable, even though you befriend the most loathsome individuals.* She thrust an image of Val into Arwen's mind as she and Sindari slew a dark elf. *Had I captured that one, no promise of obedience would have convinced me to free her. I would sacrifice her soul. And that of the tiger too.*

Arwen didn't think she had promised *obedience,* but she didn't argue, simply willing the others to hurry and leave while they could.

Zoltan and the bard had already stepped out of their alcoves. Imoshaun, after giving a long look to the magical device on the ground that she'd been working on, sighed and stepped into the chamber.

"Has the sun set above this dreadful place yet?" Zoltan eyed Arwen's mother warily.

*Should it melt your bones, you would deserve it for attempting to make a potion to nullify a sacred dark-elf tattoo.*

"I am an alchemist. It is my duty to make formulas."

*You are an undead scourge on this world and should have turned to dust long ago.*

"I will not count you as a possible future customer," Zoltan said, "and I forbid you from watching my instructional videos."

*Take Imoshaun and the bard and follow Gruflen out of here, please,* Arwen whispered telepathically to her friends. She was still skeptical that they would be permitted to escape but, on the off chance that her mother was telling the truth, Arwen didn't want their words to change her mind. *Val and Colonel Willard are waiting at a Mongolian grill for you,* she added, though she had no idea if they were still there. She also doubted it was dark yet. Zoltan would have to wait underground until it was.

*Food?* That prompted Imoshaun to look away from her work. *The dark elves didn't feed us. I'm famished.*

*Come, my wife.* Gruflen raised his arms and waved for her to step behind his armor.

Arwen's mother kept her gaze on Arwen as the others departed, having no trouble seeing through the magical camouflage.

Arwen wished she could escape with her comrades but had no doubt that her mother could ensnare her. She wasn't doing anything to mask her powerful aura, and it was the equal of Azerdash's or Yendral's. Unless Arwen shot and killed her, she wouldn't be able to go anywhere against her mother's wishes.

Even as the notion of attacking crossed her mind, she shied away from it. As much as she detested her mother and the dark-elven ways, the thought of murder repulsed her. Of course, if her mother tried to kill her first, and she was forced to defend herself...

"Now it is time for our discussion, *Vleesha*," she said aloud in Dark Elven. With a flick of her fingers, the device Imoshaun had been working on floated across the chamber and into her grip. "Do you know what this is?"

"No." Arwen responded in English.

Her mother's red eyes narrowed with displeasure, but she didn't comment on the choice. "A *thyamiliscar*."

"That tells me less than you might think."

"One would expect you to be more aware of the work your strange comrades are doing. It combines gnomish and dragon magic and can restore the memories of one whose brain has been damaged from injury or age."

"Imoshaun did mention that. I believe she's been written up in a journal for the work."

"It can also *destroy* memories." Her mother smiled at Arwen, a cold smile.

Arwen shifted her weight. What did *that* mean? That her mother would use the device on someone Arwen cared about? Or to enact some nefarious plan?

As that cold gaze remained on Arwen, weighted with significance, an inkling of what her mother might intend came to her.

"I will give you two options." Her mother walked toward her, the mist curling about her long cloak. "You know by now why I brought human males into my lair and used them until I became pregnant with you."

"To create a daughter who looks human but is loyal to you," Arwen said.

"Essentially. You've learned to fit into their world. Now, you will use that knowledge to benefit us. You will bring human females with fertile wombs to us, and we will place our embryos, enhanced by the various scientific experiments we've been pursuing, within them. They will give birth to dark elves, and we will repopulate our species before taking over this world for ourselves."

"You can't do that without me?" Arwen didn't want them to do it at all, but she didn't know why she would be so integral.

"With your ability to walk in the sunlight and your knowledge of their ways, you can find the ideal specimens to bring to us. Now, you can either accept your fate and remain as you are—" the words prompted a lip curl, "—or we can use this device to selectively wipe your memories. We would leave enough intact for you to perform our missions but remove your recollection of your past and insert new memories, memories that would ensure your loyalty to me."

New fear swept through Arwen as she looked at the device. She wouldn't try to murder her mother, but she would have no qualms about destroying that. Imoshaun might have intended it to do good, but it wouldn't do anything but evil in the hands of the dark elves.

Before Arwen could reach for an arrow, the power she'd feared her mother would unleash swept over her. Not only did it grip her, holding her immobile, but it burned as it ran through her veins. On her forearm, her tattoo heated painfully, sending a jolt of energy straight to her mind that made her gasp and grab her temples.

Arwen struggled to focus, to create a barrier, but this wasn't an arrow or bullet that her magic might deflect. She willed her power to be enough to push back the attack, but she failed. The pain in her head intensified.

Even as she gasped again, Arwen decided it had been worth it. As long as the others had gotten away...

*Such strange thoughts your human half gives you,* her mother spoke into her mind. *It does not matter. You will serve our people, as you were made to do. I will give you one chance to do so voluntarily, to prove you are deserving of your memories. If you fail, I will use the* thyamiliscar *on you. One way or another, you will serve us.*

With a final pulse, tremendous power ran up Arwen's arm from her tattoo and overwhelmed the circuits of her brain. Her legs gave out, and she lost consciousness before she hit the ground.

## 22

For the second time that day, Arwen woke with her head throbbing and the coldness of stone seeping through her clothing and into her body. This time, Azerdash and her father weren't there, looking over her.

When she opened her eyes, utter blackness greeted her, making her wonder if it *was* still the same day. She didn't sense any magical beings around, and, other than a few traces embedded in the tunnels themselves, the only magic came from her arrows, her bow, and Azerdash's multitool.

Surprised her weapons hadn't been taken from her, Arwen sat up and patted around for them. Her bow was off to the side. Where she'd dropped it when she fell? Had her mother left her in the same spot? Arwen was surprised she hadn't woken in a cage—or one of the magically sealed alcoves—with a dark-elf guard. Maybe her brother.

Arwen reached for her quiver, since a couple of her arrows could glow in the dark, before remembering the multitool had that capability. With a soft murmur of, "*Eravekt,*" it emitted a flashlight beam that shone into the alcove Imoshaun had occupied.

The tools remained, the tools that had crafted the memory device, and Arwen shivered at the threat her mother had made.

After standing, Arwen probed the darkness of the chamber with the light, letting the beam linger on the tunnel her mother had probably entered through. Arwen had no desire to go that way or see her again, but was she free to return the way she had come? To leave?

"What's the trick?" she murmured.

Her mother's last words repeated in her mind: *One way or another, you will serve us.*

Why did she have a feeling her mother had set something in place? Arwen touched her head, the throbbing ache suggesting she'd hit it—or something worse had happened. She wondered if she would later regret not being able to shoot her mother.

Before leaving, she shone the light over the three spider statues. They remained dormant, their eyes no longer glowing. Hopefully, that meant her mother had truly released the pieces of her friends' souls from the smaller artifacts. Arwen would check them as soon as she returned home.

As she headed back the way she and Gruflen had come, she sensed a magical being, not in the tunnels with her but high above. Saruknorath.

Arwen frowned, remembering his promise of a chat, and activated the camouflaging magic that had likely worn off while she'd been knocked out. It probably didn't matter, since he knew where she was, but maybe she would get lucky, and he would go away. She had enough to worry about without dealing with assassin dragons.

Hoping Imoshaun and Zoltan had indeed made it out, Arwen pulled out her phone to call Val or Willard and check. But she was too far underground to get a signal. Either that, or the dark-elven magic of the tunnels was blocking it.

*You have completed your mission to free your comrades?* Sarukno-rath spoke into her mind.

Arwen frowned again. Could she get away with ignoring him?

*I have returned to inform you that I no longer need to discuss matters with you. For some time, you fell unconscious.*

*Yeah, I noticed,* Arwen caught herself responding before she'd decided whether it was wise to engage with him or not.

*During these hours, your mind was undefended, and the dark-elven magic that protects you abandoned you.*

Fresh unease crept into her. What was he getting at?

*I was able to read your thoughts.*

No wonder Arwen had a headache. Not only her mother but also a dragon had been rooting around in there. Maybe her brother had also shown up for the party.

*So?* Arwen tried to sound indifferent but failed. Still, what could he have learned? She didn't know where Azerdash was.

*I have learned what I needed to learn.* Saruknorath inserted a vision into her mind of Azerdash and Yendral standing in an underground assembly of gnomes, machinery and magical devices of all sorts around them. Most of the gnomes were older, with lined faces and wispy white hair, and a couple wore fine clothing, some of it glittering in a way that reminded Arwen of the jumpsuit Imoshaun had altered.

In the vision, Azerdash stepped forward and held out a tray of cookies. Arwen rocked back. Those were some of *her* cookies. Had Azerdash also raided her pantry? They *had* discussed using baked goods to help sway world leaders, but she hadn't yet given him anything. That didn't, however, mean he hadn't stopped by the farm. He might even have visited Sarrlevi and asked for some of the baked goods he'd taken.

Arwen shook her head. That didn't matter. What did was that Saruknorath knew Azerdash had wanted to negotiate with the gnomes, something he had mentioned to her. She feared she'd inadvertently betrayed him. Again.

*He didn't tell me he was going to the gnomish home world.* Arwen hoped Saruknorath had conjured the image from his fancy, but the cookies made her uncertain about that. They didn't seem like a detail he would have come up with on his own.

*No? Are you certain?*

A brush at her mind suggested he might be attempting to get more from her.

"Not fair that I can't get phone reception in these tunnels but a pestering dragon's signals can get through," Arwen grumbled.

*I now know where he is, and I've acquired what I need to capture him.*

*Watch out for his sword,* she warned, remembering that Saruknorath had been wary of it before.

*During our last meeting, I learned what I needed to learn of its capabilities. Defeating the half-dragons will not be difficult.*

*Uh-huh. I'll mourn your death after he drives it through your heart.*

Saruknorath chuckled into her mind. Arwen hated when enemies did that.

*If you know the full list of its capabilities,* he added, *I will accept that information from you. I understand you were instrumental in finding it.*

*I don't know anything about what it can do. I was told the pointy end goes in a dragon.*

*Such wit.*

More mental scratches at Arwen's mind made her flinch. She felt him rooting around, trying to stir up her memories of the sword.

*Yes, very good,* he said after a moment, though she was positive she hadn't given him anything about its capabilities. She'd seen it glow and shoot a beam, but Saruknorath had seen those things too. That wouldn't be new information. *That is all I need.*

He withdrew from her mind. *Once I kill him, before handing the corpse over to those who paid for it, I will bring you to him and allow you to offer whatever farewells are customary for your mixed-blood kind.*

*Thoughtful of you.*

*Indeed. Most dragons are not as gracious as I, but you have been instrumental in finding him.*

A squish under her moccasin made Arwen pause and shine her light around. She'd reached the spot where she and Gruflen had killed the *drykar*.

"Almost out." She broke into a run.

As the first whisper of fresh air reached her, she sensed magical beings ahead. Ahead and above. Looking down into the sinkhole from the park?

First, she picked up Imoshaun and Gruflen, the full-blooded gnomes having strong auras, and then Zoltan and Val.

It should have been a relief to confirm Val was alive and well, but a surge of irritation coursed through Arwen, and her tattoo itched, flaring with inner magic.

Frowning at her forearm, she slowed down. Had her mother done something to her while she'd been out? Something to ensure the tattoo could assert its power over her and make her do what it wished, whether dark elves were around or not?

The emotion disappeared as abruptly as it had appeared, and the itch faded.

Arwen bit her lip, not convinced that everything was okay, but Val spoke into her mind, distracting her.

*Arwen? Are you alone? And free?* Val must have sensed her. Had the flare from her tattoo broken her camouflage?

*Yes.*

With all her heart, Arwen hoped Zoltan could recreate that tattoo-removal formula, that she could finally get rid of the thing and its influence. In this case, it didn't matter that Val had sensed her, but she would prefer the tattoo not be able to knock out her camouflage when enemies were about.

*I'm alone,* Arwen added.

*We were about to hop down and rescue you. There's a gnome up here who, while not volunteering to lead the way, is in the process of drawing me a map.*

*That's Gruflen. He led the way when we went to get his wife.*

*Yes, apparently, he's not willing to go back in for your sake.*

*I don't mean as much to him as Imoshaun does.* Given that Arwen had seen Gruflen hide behind his wife before, she was impressed his love for her had driven him into the tunnels at all.

*Yeah. Also, venomous spider ichor has burned holes through his armor, so he's had to strip down.*

Arwen paused to glance at the sole of her moccasin and hope there hadn't been ichor on the piece she'd stepped on.

*Saruknorath was here flying around threateningly for a while,* Val added.

*I know. He told me he's after Azerdash.*

*He wouldn't answer my questions. He doesn't chat with me the way he does you.*

*A tremendous loss in your life.*

*Oh, yeah,* Val said. *A couple of minutes ago, he formed a portal and flew through it.*

*To the gnomish home world?* Arwen shook her head, telling herself that she hadn't known Azerdash's location, even if Saruknorath had taken every memory from her mind. Besides, Azerdash had already *been* to the gnomish home world, right? Even if he'd planned to return, she hadn't known when. She couldn't have betrayed him.

"Please let that be true," she whispered.

It grew a little lighter as Arwen reached the sinkhole but not much. The sun had set, and only someone's flashlight beam shining down from above provided illumination. Val's Jeep was still on the ground at the bottom of the hole.

"It's all right," her voice floated down. "Once Zav comes back to Earth, whenever that is, I'll bring him here, and he can levitate it out of the hole. He's *good* at throwing two-ton vehicles around."

"Are you certain?" came Imoshaun's voice.

Even though Arwen had sensed her, it was a relief to hear the verification that she'd escaped and was okay.

"With a few tools, one of these stout trees, and some basic materials, Gruflen and I could build a hoist capable of lifting it out."

"It would get pretty beat up bumping against the sides of the hole," Val said.

"How much more beat up is it going to get?" Willard asked. Since she was a mundane human, Arwen hadn't sensed her up there. "It fell twenty feet into a hole."

When Arwen reached the Jeep and looked up, she could see Val and Willard at the edge, gesticulating as they spoke. Val spotted her and tossed down a rope.

Arwen climbed up and blinked when she spotted Gruflen, naked except for a brown loincloth. His armor lay in the ferns beside him, its flashlight glowing to provide light. Tongue stuck between his lips, he hummed to himself as he drew in a notepad.

Imoshaun lifted a hand to Arwen and patted Gruflen on the bare shoulder. "I don't think we'll need your map after all, dear."

"Not now, not now. I need to be precise while it's in my memory. Oh, and that energy field might be back up."

Imoshaun's pats turned into pokes. "Arwen has rescued herself. Unless you found a treasure vault of power crystals while you were exploring down there, we don't need to go back down."

Gruflen's ears perked, and he sat up. "Crystals?"

"I didn't see any," Arwen offered.

"Oh, you were already rescued?" Gruflen scratched his jaw with the pen he'd been using, leaving an ink stain. "But that dark-elf female was so powerful. I didn't think you'd be able to get away from her."

"How *did* you get away, Forester?" Willard shone the flashlight toward Arwen and looked her up and down. "After the harrowing escape Thorvald underwent, we thought we'd need a dragon to get you out."

Willard waved the flashlight at Val, who must not have had an opportunity to go home and change—or apply bandages—yet. Her clothing was ripped and bloody, and soot caked her cheek and the side of her neck. The people in that Mongolian grill must have gaped when she'd walked in.

"Dark elves are *always* harrowing," Val said.

"As I well remember." Willard raised her eyebrows toward Arwen. "I'm a little surprised you're not dead."

Her expression was more curious than suspicious, but something about the situation made Arwen feel guilty. As if she'd agreed to do her mother's bidding and was in collusion with the dark elves.

"They want to use me," Arwen said.

"I assume you object to that."

"Vehemently." Arwen glanced at her forearm, but her tattoo had been quiet since that initial surge when she'd sensed Val.

Val followed her gaze and pointed. "I've got some good news on that front. Zoltan said he sensed the dark elf coming for him and had time to hide your ingredients and the completed formula. He doesn't think his kidnapper found them."

Arwen brightened. That was the first good news she'd heard in ages. "You mean I won't have to go back to the fae realm and get Azerdash to forage all over the Cosmic Realms to find the ingredients again?"

"As long as Zoltan is right and the dark elves didn't find his stash hole. He—" Val looked into the woods. "Where did you go, Zoltan?"

"I am here." Zoltan stepped out from behind the dark trees, holding a prize aloft. Mushrooms? In the dim lighting, it was hard to tell. "Were you aware that stump puffballs have already started to come into season? These have medicinal qualities and are called for in several of my formulas. What a delight to find them in these benighted woods filled with dog excrement and human trash, with the roar of the freeway assaulting my sensitive ears."

"Zoltan was going to play a small but crucial role in your rescue," Val told Arwen.

"I can understand being distracted by a good foraging find," Arwen said. "Stump puffballs aren't the most delicious of mushrooms, but people eat them because they're supposed to help with nosebleeds and skin disorders."

Zoltan squinted at her in surprise, then looked at Val. "Dear robber, I wasn't aware that you had any acquaintances who actually read books and have useful knowledge."

"*I* read books," Willard said dryly.

"About military history and other pugilistic topics, no doubt." Zoltan sneered at her. "And the half-dwarf, when she isn't doing menial handiwork, is hurling hammers and threatening to break things in my laboratory."

"Matti is a talented artist and craftswoman," Val said, "and she's never threatened anything in your lab, much less *actually* broken anything."

"The way she loses her temper and stomps around and glowers at my breakables is quite threatening. I am pleased that you have made the acquaintance of someone with an education—a *useful* education." Zoltan shot a glower at Willard, who glowered right back at him.

"Did you *have* to rescue him?" Val asked Arwen.

"He was in the cell next to Imoshaun."

"Hm. I—" Val paused and looked toward the night sky.

Arwen winced, afraid she had sensed Saruknorath again. But Val's face brightened with pleasure. The assassin's appearance wouldn't evoke that expression.

Soon, Arwen sensed Zavryd approaching.

"The savior of my Jeep is coming." Val smiled.

"You *can't* be talking about Zavryd," Willard said, "the *destroyer* of your first Jeep."

"He's changed his ways."

*It is good that you are with the half-dark-elf mongrel, my mate,* Zavryd reached out telepathically, including them all.

*Yes, and her name is Arwen, remember?*

*I do remember this. I have news from the Dragon Council that she will desire to hear.*

Arwen slumped against a tree trunk. She doubted she wanted to hear anything that the Dragon Council had to say. For all she knew, one of their members had hired Saruknorath to hunt down Azerdash.

# 23

---

ZAVRYD TUCKED IN HIS WINGS SO HE COULD DROP BETWEEN THE trees and land near the sinkhole opposite Arwen, Val, Willard, Zoltan, and the gnomes. Before going into detail about what the Dragon Council had said, he peered into the hole.

*That is not the typical type of place where you park your conveyance, my mate,* he told Val.

"That's because the dark elves parked it," Val said. "They didn't know about my preference for spots far from store entrances where the doors won't get dinged."

Zavryd's long neck lowered, and his head disappeared through the hole as he examined the Jeep. *The conveyance has gained dings.*

"Tell me about it," Val said.

Arwen shifted impatiently from foot to foot. "The Dragon Council, Lord Zavryd? News about Azerdash?"

His head rose, and he considered Val, looking her up and down. *You have been injured, my mate.*

"Yup, I've got dings too."

Zavryd shifted into his human form and walked around the

hole to rest a hand on her shoulder. Healing magic flowed from his fingers, and Val slumped in relief.

Arwen corralled her impatience—she well knew how helpful it was to be healed by a dragon—but Willard didn't.

"What's your council have to say that affects us here on Earth?" she asked.

Zavryd gave her a baleful look, probably affronted that a lowly human dared question him while he was busy, but Val said, "We'd like to know, Zav," and he relented.

"The full council, many Stormforges and representatives from other clans, was in session," Zavryd said, "when Saruknorath opened a portal and flew into the area. He stated that he'd captured Azerdash Starblade and would soon also have the half-dragon Yendral. He has Starblade imprisoned in a cave. He said he would give the location to the highest bidder—apparently, a Silverclaw dragon *and* a Stormforge dragon offered Saruknorath a reward for Starblade independently of each other. My kin wished him brought in alive." Zavryd nodded to Arwen, having told her that already. "The Silverclaws want him dead. Understandable, given what he desires to do."

Arwen shook her head. Wanting Azerdash dead *wasn't* understandable. He didn't want to kill any dragons, just keep them from ruling over worlds that weren't theirs.

"Is he still alive?" Val asked.

"He has to be. Saruknorath was *just* here—" Arwen pointed at the sky, "—digging into my mind and trying to figure out where Azerdash is. When did he show up at the Dragon Council? That had to have been before he came here. He must have been lying to them."

Unless he'd been lying to *her* and had already captured Azerdash when last he'd shown up. But if so, why bother reading her mind?

"There are very few who would dare lie to the queen," Zavryd said, "and his reputation suggests that he acts with honor in his dealings with other dragons and even those lesser species that he stalks."

"Are you sure he was still looking for Starblade when he spoke to you?" Val asked Arwen.

She hesitated. Was she? Saruknorath had asked about the galaxy blade's capabilities. What if, when he'd come to speak with her, he'd had Azerdash trapped but not yet defeated? Maybe he'd wanted to know about the sword's weaknesses before their final confrontation. And maybe she'd inadvertently given Saruknorath a key that he'd gone back and used to defeat Azerdash.

"No," she whispered in response to Val.

"His time left to live may be limited," Zavryd said. "Saruknorath flew off with the Silverclaw who hired him. If their clan outbids the Stormforge, then Saruknorath will return to the cave and slay him."

Arwen shook her head, distress bunching her shoulders and making her want to shoot someone.

"Do you know where that cave is?" Val asked. "Will you take us there?"

"No, my mate." Zavryd lowered his hand from her shoulder. "I will not take you. My mother, the queen, has forbidden me to interfere. She would have attempted to rehabilitate Starblade, since he is kin, in a manner of speaking, but she will not risk starting a war with the Silverclaws over him. Or sowing discontent among the others in our clan who do not feel that my uncle's illegitimate mongrel offspring should be protected. Already, they have questioned the queen over her decision not to have Starblade slain."

"Just give us a ride there, and then you can leave. We'll handle this." Val nodded toward Arwen.

"As my mate, you are also forbidden to go," Zavryd told her.

Val propped a fist on her hip. "Is that so?"

"It is."

"By you?"

"By the queen. You do not wish to cross my mother."

Arwen grimaced, wanting to find and help Azerdash, but also not wanting to get Val in hot water.

"You will *not* go," Zavryd stated slowly and firmly, holding Val's gaze.

"Fine, fine." Val lifted her hands in defeat. "Why'd you even come here to tell us if you're going to forbid us to help him?"

"I have only forbidden you, my mate."

Arwen looked at him, though he was gazing intently at Val and ignoring her. Did Zavryd *want* Arwen to go get Azerdash?

"My uncle has stated that it would be rude not to allow the mate of his offspring to go find him and retrieve his remains for a respectful funeral pyre."

It sounded like Ston'tareknor might want Arwen to get Azerdash. He *had* to want her to do more than grab his body for a funeral pyre.

"Where *is* the cave Saruknorath mentioned?" Arwen asked. "Do you know?"

"I do not," Zavryd said.

"Wait." Arwen lifted a finger. "I may know. Saruknorath wanted me to come with him to the dragon funeral caves of... Irathidor, I think it was."

"Yes, I know of the place," Zavryd said. "Those caves are on the world of Zokthoran."

"Isn't that where the Assassins' Guild is headquartered?" Val asked.

"Yes. It is an unclaimed wild world. The caves are not on the same continent as the guild headquarters."

"Well, Arwen doesn't know how to make portals to wild worlds or anywhere else, so if you're not taking her to those caves, how's she supposed to retrieve Starblade's remains?"

"Mongrels can be resourceful."

"Can't you help at all?" Val asked.

Zavryd lifted an arm, and his magic swelled. A grinding noise came from below, followed by the crunch of glass falling out, as his levitation magic swept down and lifted the Jeep.

Val pointed in the direction of the parking lot.

Once the Jeep disappeared over the trees, Zavryd said, "Come, my mate," and shifted into his dragon form again.

Val held up a hand. "I need to see if the Jeep will run and, if not, have it towed to a repair shop."

Now towering over her as a dragon, Zavryd gazed into her eyes. *You will not assist the mongrel in aiding the half-dragon.*

"Of course not," Val said. "I'd be foolish to piss off your mom."

*It is foolish to irritate any dragon.*

"Oh, I know."

*Hm.* Zavryd gave Arwen an indecipherable look before springing into the air and flying away.

"Are you going to assist Forester?" Willard asked Val when he was out of earshot.

"Of course. That's what friends do." Val gave Arwen a thumbs-up.

"Even when their mates have forbidden them to help?" Willard asked.

"Nobody forbids me to do anything."

"I have on occasion."

"Yeah, and how did that work for you?"

Willard considered some memory. "Not well. You're a recalcitrant subordinate and stubborn as a mule."

"I'm an independent contractor, not a subordinate." Val winked and pulled out her phone.

"Who are you calling?" Arwen asked.

"Someone who's familiar with that world *and* who can make portals."

"Matti?" Arwen guessed, though she didn't know if Matti had ever visited the Assassins' Guild. "Or Sarrlevi?"

"Matti has a portal generator that her mom gave her, but I think it can only go to places that have been preprogrammed into it, so we'll need Sarrlevi, yes."

Arwen couldn't keep from feeling wistful about a mother who gave her daughter gifts instead of wanting to use her to find fertile wombs and take over the world.

"Sarrlevi wasn't that delighted to go with me on my last quest," Arwen said. "Tell him I'll bake him his choice of cookies, and I've got a fresh batch of pickled carrots. Oh, and I can offer him goat cheese for Matti. I know she loves cheese."

"Is that all?" Val asked, eyes twinkling.

"They might like some more of my goat truffle butter."

"I'll let him know."

"Better tell him Amber won't be coming along," Arwen said. "She wasn't as properly respectful toward him as he prefers."

"I'm sure she wasn't, but he shouldn't complain this time. It'll just be you and me, and Sarrlevi *loves* me." Val slapped Arwen on the shoulder.

An indignant pulse of magic came from the spider tattoo. The uneasy feeling returned again, and, as much as Arwen appreciated Val's willingness to help, she worried about what her mother might have done to her. Her escape had been far, far too easy.

## 24

"HOW LONG DOES THE TATTOO-REMOVAL FORMULA TAKE TO WORK?"
Arwen asked Zoltan as Willard drove them to Val's house in Green
Lake.

The Jeep hadn't been operable, so Val had called for a tow
truck before they'd left. Imoshaun and Gruflen had arranged their
own transportation back to Bellevue with gnomes who lived near
the park. The couple had thanked Arwen for her help but had
been unwilling to go on a quest to battle dragons and save Azerdash. Understandable, but Gruflen in his battle armor *had* been
handy. Arwen would have been glad to have his assistance.

"I am uncertain," Zoltan said, from beside her in the back seat,
his undead shoulder cold when she brushed it, "and I believe you
will need a tattoo artist with magical blood to apply it—your
muscular green-skinned friend, perhaps. Let us first ascertain if it
is indeed where I secured it."

Arwen hoped so. She fidgeted with impatience, wishing she
were already on Zokthoran and looking for Azerdash.

Would Sarrlevi help her again? He didn't owe Arwen anything,
nor, as far as she knew, did he owe Azerdash any favors.

As Willard drove off the freeway and into the Green Lake neighborhood, Arwen shifted in her seat, nervous.

"Zoltan?" Arwen looked at the vampire again, though his eyes were hidden—he'd found a cap and pulled it low, complaining about the obnoxiousness of the intrusive streetlamps that slashed their lights into the car. "Do you have any formulas that could nullify my tattoo, even if only temporarily, in case it, uhm, acts up while I'm trying to reach Azerdash?"

Arwen hadn't told Val about the flashes of irritation she'd felt toward her earlier, but she needed to if they were going off on an adventure together.

"A tattoo nullifier?" Zoltan asked.

"Or something that nullifies power in general." Arwen described the gunk the dark elves had been using to subdue Azerdash when they'd captured him in their Bellevue lair. "When I smeared it over my tattoo, it made it harder for them to control me for a bit."

"Perhaps, my foraging mongrel, you should have brought me a sample."

"I didn't think of it at the time. Also, I didn't know you then."

"You were not aware of the famous vampire alchemist who lived in Val Thorvald's basement? You knew of *her*, did you not?"

"Of course," Arwen said. "Everyone in the magical community knows the Ruin Bringer."

"Everyone in the *alchemical* community knows of Zoltan and the many, *many* excellent formulas he's created, not to mention the award-winning papers he has published." Zoltan placed a hand on his chest, the cap still covering half his face, leaving only his lips and indignant nostrils visible.

"When he says *alchemical community*," Val said over her shoulder from the passenger seat, "he means his teenage followers on YouTube. I'm sure he tells them all about his publications."

"I speak not only of my devoted followers, dear robber, but people of standing in the field."

Arwen lifted a hand. "I apologize that my ignorance in alchemistry meant I didn't know about you, but *do* you have anything that might perform a similar function? I'd pay, of course. I need to make sure the dark elves aren't able to control me at an inopportune time. Or at *any* time, ideally."

"Then you should have shot the dreadful female in charge of imprisoning us."

"That was my mother."

"I stand by my statement." Zoltan shuddered.

Arwen wondered what her mother had done to him.

"Let me consider what I have prepared in my laboratory for a moment," Zoltan said. "Also, I will need to see what damage the kidnapper did as she dragged me away. I remember glass breaking. Such terribly brutish behavior. As if I'd been kidnapped by ogres instead of agile people with elven blood. But she was deliberately abusive to my laboratory. The dark elves are a *dreadful* people."

"Yes," Arwen murmured. "Val? Did you get in touch with Sarrlevi?" The last she'd heard, Val had been speaking with Matti. "Will he help, or do we have to figure out a different way to get there?"

"Matti was going to check with him and get back to me," Val said. "Sarrlevi was out taking the babies for a stroll before bed. Apparently, they like it when he shows them the oaks and maples in the neighborhood and speaks about how inferior they are to elven trees."

"Do they know the difference between trees and mailboxes at this point?"

"Well, they're half *elven*, so probably. I think it's coded in their DNA to hug trees and sneer haughtily at mailboxes and everything else made by humans." As they drove closer to her home,

Val leaned forward to peer through the windshield. "Good. I don't sense Zav. If he were here, he would again be forbidding me to go."

"Would he?" Willard asked. "He didn't have to come and let you—and Forester—know about Starblade's ensnarement, but he seemed to be making a point to share the information."

"With Arwen, maybe. I'm sure he doesn't want me to go against his mom's wishes. In dragondom, it's bad form when your mate defies the queen."

"I think that's true in human monarchies too. But maybe his uncle wanted to give Starblade a chance and leaned on Zavryd."

Arwen couldn't imagine the laid-back dragon who'd lounged in her rejuvenation pool *leaning* on anyone. Except maybe a pillow.

"It could be they just don't want a Silverclaw to get to him," Val said.

"Those Silverclaws *are* irritating and obnoxious," Willard said.

"You think all dragons are irritating and obnoxious."

"That's right. Can you provide evidence that would prove me wrong?"

Val scratched her cheek. "No."

When Willard parked in front of Val's home, Sarrlevi was standing on the sidewalk across the street, wearing a cloak, a magical travel pack, and his longswords. The twins were in their house with their mother, hopefully sleeping peacefully after learning about the inferiority of Earth trees.

Arwen slid out of the car while Zoltan hurried to his basement laboratory and Willard spoke to Val.

"You'll help us?" Arwen asked, joining Sarrlevi on the sidewalk, a breeze ruffling his short blond hair.

"Mataalii has forbidden me from being eaten by a dragon."

There was a lot of forbidding going on.

"If it helps," Arwen said, "I think dragons mostly chew people up and spit them out. I haven't heard them suggest humans—or elves—are delicious."

"That is correct."

"Even if you can just open a portal to the place we need to go —is there a chance you know where the dragon caves are on that world?—that would be amazing." Arwen looked at the sword hilts poking over his shoulder. He was dressed to go on an adventure, not wave his hand to open a portal. He could have done that in bare feet and pajamas.

"I will assist you with opening a portal *and* finding Starblade," Sarrlevi said.

"Thank you. Is there anything I can give you—*bake* or *make* you—to show my appreciation for your assistance?"

"That is unnecessary. What he is trying to do..." Sarrlevi gazed around the neighborhood, but she thought he might be looking for possible spies instead of considering the local flora, especially when his gaze lingered on the goblin-filled urban sanctuary. Goblins were, after all, known gossips. "Few will admit, except in the most private of gatherings with trusted individuals," he said quietly, "that they long for an end to dragon rule, but most do, whether they be elf or dwarf or gnome or troll. There are some who've gained power because they were deemed suitable to be placed in important positions by the dragons, and they would tattle on those who plotted against the current order, but..." Sarrlevi spread his hand, palm toward the night sky.

"You care about what happens on Veleshna Var and in the Cosmic Realms? Even though you live on Earth now?"

"My mother lives on Veleshna Var, and, even though I was in exile for centuries, it never stopped being the home where I grew up." Sarrlevi's eyes grew a little wistful. "I care."

Arwen was surprised to see him opening up, especially when he was usually haughty and aloof around her, but maybe her relationship with Azerdash made him more inclined to look past her dark-elfness. Or maybe he'd accepted her because she was becoming friends with Matti and Val? They seemed to accept her on her own merits, which she appreciated. Plying them with pickled and baked goods perhaps helped.

"I hope Azerdash is okay," she said.

"Yes. The movement needs him. For a long time—for *centuries* —it has awaited a catalyst."

"And a half-dragon is it?"

"A half-dragon with a legendary sword."

Zoltan returned from his laboratory, cursing under his breath about the execrable state the kidnapper had left it in, not to mention the experiments he'd left in progress that hadn't been tended.

"Is that what prompted the odd smell from the basement?" Val asked, waving a farewell to Willard and joining Zoltan as he headed toward Arwen.

"If the smell wasn't one of a great scaled dragon, then perhaps so," Zoltan said.

"Dragons don't smell, and Zav doesn't come in the house in dragon form anyway. This was more of a rotten-egg odor that was wafting up through the furnace vents, even though we didn't have the heat on."

"If it was bothering you, perhaps you might have cleaned the mess down there."

"The rent that you don't pay doesn't include housekeeping." Val started to thump him on the shoulder but noticed that he carried a vial and pointed at it instead. "What's that?"

Zoltan handed the vial, a green liquid sloshing inside, to Arwen. "A formula that may help weaken the bonds of a magical compulsion. You must consume it and give it approximately ten minutes to seep into your bloodstream from your digestive system —twice that if you have food in your stomach—so time your dosage appropriately."

"Better not eat any cookies before going into battle," Val told Arwen.

"I don't know if it will be as effective as the nullifier that you described," Zoltan said, "since, as we discussed, you so rudely did not provide me with a sample of that to study, but it may assist you."

"Thank you," Arwen said.

"We're ready, Sarrlevi," Val told him, standing beside Arwen.

Irritation swept through Arwen, originating at her tattoo. She didn't know if its magic was irked because it somehow understood what was in the vial or if it was displaying the same irritation with Val as it had earlier in the night.

"Maybe you shouldn't go," Arwen blurted with foreboding.

Val blinked and touched her chest. "Me?"

"Yeah. I have a bad feeling about this."

"But I come with a magical tiger and a badass gun and a sword."

"I know, but I think..." Arwen pushed up her sleeve, expecting to find the spider tattoo glowing, if not hissing and spitting power at Val, but it lay dormant, not even itching as it often did in the presence of dark-elven magic. "I think my mother may have done something to me when I was down there. I've had an urge to... I don't know, but I'm finding you irritating. I've never felt that way before."

"No?" Zoltan asked. "She irritates me a great deal. When we first met, she slew my loyal guard spider, and she and her beastly mate make so much noise upstairs that it is difficult to concentrate on my very important work."

"And you wonder why housekeeping isn't included for you," Val said.

"If you swept my laboratory now and then, I might feel more kindly toward you."

"I'll get you a Roomba for Christmas." Val glanced at Sarrlevi before focusing on Arwen again. "I think you're going to need all the help you can get. Also, Willard wants me to keep an eye on you."

This time, Arwen touched her chest. Why would her desire to help Azerdash have anything to do with Willard or the work of her office? *She* shouldn't care about insurrections in the Cosmic Realms, unless there ended up being ramifications to Earth.

"We think it's weird that the dark elves let you go. *And* let Zoltan and Imoshaun go. Though it is possible that Zoltan was obnoxious enough that they were glad to get rid of him."

"Really." Zoltan sniffed.

"I think it's weird too," Arwen said. "That's why you shouldn't come."

"But Sarrlevi can?" Val raised her eyebrows.

"I don't feel irritation toward him."

"None at all? Even though he's haughty and full of himself?"

Sarrlevi's eyes narrowed. Val might end up with *two* people ready to punch her.

"The dark elves don't hate him for ruining their plans multiple times," was all Arwen said.

"Are you sure about that? He decapitated one of them last night."

Arwen bit her lip. She *wasn't* sure the dark elves didn't now have Sarrlevi on their shit list. What if she ended up turning on both of them?

"Look," Val said, "we're going to another world. The dark elves won't be there and won't be able to control you. Nobody can enact magical compulsion from another *planet*. I don't care how powerful they are. I'll grant that once we're back on Earth, you might be a threat to me, but this should be fine." She waved at Sarrlevi.

He nodded, and magic swelled as he formed a portal, the silvery disc floating in the air above the street.

"Be careful out there," Willard said from her SUV. "I'd like all of my operatives to come back intact."

Val gave her a thumbs-up. Sarrlevi nodded gravely, then jumped through the portal.

Hoping she wouldn't regret not going alone, Arwen leaped through after them.

## 25

HOT, DRY AIR AND INTENSE ORANGE SUN GREETED ARWEN WHEN SHE arrived on Zokthoran. They'd landed in a canyon, the ground dusty with red rock formations rising up all around. The hazy sky was as orange as the sun, with the air thick with the scent of wood burning somewhere. It reminded Arwen of wildfire season back home, though she didn't see much foliage. A few stunted trees similar to pinion pines grew along the bottom of the canyon, and a dry gully that probably held water part of the year meandered through the center.

"Good thing we didn't bring Zoltan," Val said. "He would have disintegrated instantly under that sun."

Her voice brought a fresh flash of irritation to Arwen, and she took several steps to the side and wrapped her fingers around Zoltan's vial in her pocket. Since he'd only given her one dose, she couldn't take it until she was *sure* her tattoo would affect her. She hoped Val was right, though, and that the dark elves wouldn't be able to compel her from across the galaxy.

"Elves also do not enjoy the intense climate of Zokthoran, but I have been to this world often. The Assassins' Guild headquarters is about eight hundred miles away atop a pillar that can only be reached by flying or levitation magic." Sarrlevi pointed to what might have been something similar, a red-rock column that rose hundreds of feet from the bottom of the canyon with a plate-like formation at the top. A bird's nest perched on it was so large that Arwen imagined something like a pterodactyl using it.

"Mundane assassins not allowed, huh?" Val smirked.

"An exception might be made for the *Ruin Bringer*." The emphasis on the term and a mocking eyebrow twitch suggested Sarrlevi didn't think Val worthy of the moniker. Either that, or he wanted to irk her. She'd called him haughty, after all.

"Would the other assassins mock me if I had to get a ride from my mate?"

"Vociferously and often."

Arwen let them walk ahead of her, but the itch to find Azerdash made her want to rush into the lead. Since she'd never been here and had no idea where to go, that wouldn't work. She couldn't yet sense Azerdash or anyone else. The barren landscape didn't seem to hold much life of any kind.

Between one step and the next, that changed. Arwen halted because she *did* sense Azerdash.

His aura was faint and came from... It felt like somewhere high up and inside the rock wall of the canyon. A cave.

Val and Sarrlevi also stopped and looked in that direction.

"There are many dragon funeral caves scattered over dozens of miles along this canyon," Sarrlevi said. "I did not expect to find him that quickly."

"Could it be a trap?" Arwen asked. "Were we *meant* to sense him right away? Because the dragon assassin wants..."

What? If Saruknorath wanted Arwen, he could have snatched her up numerous times. And he shouldn't care a whit about Sarrlevi or Val.

"I won't say that's impossible," Sarrlevi said, "but I don't know how Saruknorath could have anticipated where my portal would drop us. It might be luck."

"I'm not a lucky person," Arwen said.

Sarrlevi looked at Val, as if *she* might be a luck magnet.

She only shrugged. "Let's check it out. I don't sense Sarukno-rath or any other dragons, do you?"

"Not at this time," Sarrlevi said.

Arwen shook her head.

"How do you think Saruknorath imprisoned Starblade without a guard?" Val asked.

"Not in a stasis chamber, hopefully," Arwen said. "He hates those."

Telepathically, she reached out to him, but if he were conscious, wouldn't he have already sensed her and reached out himself? *Azerdash? Can you hear me?*

He didn't answer. That worried her, but his aura felt strong, not diminished as it would be if he were severely injured or ill.

"I believe his aura would be more muted if he were ensconced in a stasis chamber," Sarrlevi said, "but I am not that familiar with the magic or technology. If it wouldn't have interfered with her nursing schedule, Matti might have been the better person to bring."

"Gotta get her a breast pump so she can store her milk for later," Val said. "Then you can feed the kids while she goes out and thumps things. Or you could get a nanny. Maybe one of the goblins down the street would help out."

Sarrlevi gave her an appalled look, though Arwen didn't know if it was prompted by the breast pump or the goblin nanny idea. Maybe both.

"What?" Val asked. "Busy moms with bad guys to hunt down have to make use of modern technology. She can fill containers and pop them in the freezer."

"Never would I have expected someone with the moniker *Ruin*

*Bringer* to bring up such topics on a mission," Sarrlevi murmured, then waved a finger. Levitation magic swirled about them, lifting them into the air.

"Hey, I'm a mom too."

"Also, no goblin will be left to watch over my children," Sarrlevi said as they rose above the dry gully and floated along the wall of the canyon in the direction of Azerdash's aura.

"No? What about me? I haven't babysat in a long time. It might be fun. Zav could help."

Judging by the second appalled look, Sarrlevi didn't intend to invite Val and Zavryd over to babysit. "I would bring my mother from the elven home world if we needed someone to watch them."

"Oh, sure. That's a practical commute."

They reached the top of the canyon and levitated over the rocky ground on one side. Arwen hadn't yet seen any caves.

"I recommend camouflaging magic." Sarrlevi dropped them down on the lumpy earth, the red rocks as predominant there as in the canyon. The only life existed in dust-filled crevices where a few stalwart shrubs grew.

"Okay," Arwen said, realizing he'd already activated his own. Just because she didn't sense magical beings around didn't mean they weren't in the vicinity and hidden themselves. Since Azerdash was a valuable prisoner, Saruknorath probably hadn't left him unguarded.

"One moment." Val reached not for her camouflaging charm but the cat-shaped trinket that dangled on her thong with many others. "I have a hunch we're going to find trouble lurking beside our half-dragon."

In the harsh sun, the silver mist that always formed when Sindari arrived was barely perceptible, but once he appeared, his striped silver form was impossible to miss.

"We're going to free a half-dragon so he can go back to an

insurrection meant to oust full-blooded dragons from ruling worlds that aren't theirs," Val told him.

*Since my kind—* Sindari pointed a paw at Val's charm, *—were long ago crafted by dragons to serve them, I should not fight in battles that could lead to a war against them.*

"But you will, right?" Val activated her own camouflage.

*My duty is to protect the one who wears my charm and summons me.*

"Perfect. My ass is always in trouble."

*I am aware.*

Sarrlevi walked off and drew his swords, one glowing as he lowered it into crevices in the rock.

"I guess we're searching now." Val tapped her thong. "I'll see if my charm for revealing hidden doors and passageways comes up with anything."

Arwen nodded and padded in the direction of Azerdash's aura. It ought to be as likely to lead them to a cave entrance as anything.

*Azerdash?* she tried calling telepathically again.

Nothing.

Arwen stopped walking when she sensed his aura below her. Thirty feet down? Forty?

She drew an arrow and tapped the head on the ground, hoping it would pierce an illusion. The way it *tinked* suggested nothing but solid rock. She moved around, trying different spots.

Sarrlevi and Val were doing the same with their swords, perhaps thinking their magic might nullify, or at least more easily find, a hidden entrance.

It occurred to Arwen that if Saruknorath had trod across these rocks on the way to the cave, she might be able to track him. Thus far, she hadn't spotted any footprints in the dusty crevices, but the breeze that swept through periodically and tugged at her hair was probably enough to whisk the dust around and eliminate prints. It was also possible he'd flown the whole way with his prisoner.

Arwen crouched, touching the ground. She glanced toward Val and especially Sarrlevi, experiencing that familiar fear that others would sense her using dark-elven powers and not approve, but they'd moved far enough away that she could no longer see them through their camouflaging magic. Using her power would dissolve her own camouflage, but oh well. She had to do this. Azerdash was in danger.

"I'll check the cliff face more closely," Sarrlevi called, his voice indicating he was walking or levitating down into the canyon. "The entrance may be in a vertical section."

"Okay," Val replied.

Arwen didn't reply. She focused on drawing on her own internal power as well as what she could take from the ground. A surprising amount of magic surged out of the rock and into her, and she teetered backward, off balance for a moment. She'd forgotten how much more magic was inherent on other worlds. This wasn't as profound as in the fae realm, but it gave her extra energy, and when she called upon her soul-tracking ability, the dimness that came to her vision was startling, especially in contrast to the brightness of the sun.

At first, when she gazed around, looking for the photolumines-cent tracks that revealed themselves once her eyesight changed, she didn't see anything. The wind wouldn't have swept the residue from one's soul away, but it was possible Saruknorath hadn't been up here. Maybe, as Sarrlevi had suggested, the entrance was in the cliff.

She was about to head in that direction when she spotted a glowing green scratch on the rocky ground. When she padded over, she picked out a few more scratches. They weren't footprints, but a hint of Saruknorath's essence clung to them, and she real-ized they were talon marks.

"I think I've got something," she called, trusting Val was still nearby.

Encouraged, Arwen jogged toward another scratch. She hadn't yet spotted talon marks that indicated Azerdash had set foot here, but Saruknorath might have had him trussed up with magic and been levitating him. The thought filled her with indignation.

When she reached the last visible talon mark, her foot came down on what looked like solid ground but was empty air.

Reflexes kicking in, Arwen flung herself backward, twisting to grip the rock behind her. But even as she caught the edge, stone snapped and crumbled, then gave way. She flailed, trying to grasp something stable, but her fingers caught nothing but rock falling along with her.

"Arwen?" came Val's call from the distance.

Arwen was too busy plunging into darkness to answer.

## 26

ARWEN TWISTED IN THE AIR AS SHE FELL, TRYING TO GET HER FEET under her, but the darkness made it hard to tell how far down the bottom was. Light slashed into the cave from above, but after being out in the bright sun, her eyes couldn't adjust quickly enough. The ground startled her when it came.

She landed feet-first and hard, pain lancing up her legs. A head-sized stone clubbed her shoulder as it also tumbled down. The armored jumpsuit protected her, but the blow threw her off balance and pitched her sideways.

Though she tried to turn the fall into a roll while protecting her head from more plummeting rocks, her quiver and bow made it awkward. She landed in a heap on her side, more of the ground above—the roof of the cave—falling around and on her.

Belatedly, she remembered she could make magical barriers. Fighting the pain to concentrate, she managed to draw upon her power and focus enough to wrap one around her. A single rock, the last remaining, landed on top and bounced off.

As pain reported in from all over her body, Arwen groaned and wondered when making barriers would come instinctually when needed. Right now, she still needed concentration, something that was hard to find while plummeting.

"Arwen?" came Val's voice from above.

With her camouflaging magic engaged, she wasn't visible at the edge of the hole, but it sounded like she was peering down.

"I'm still alive," Arwen croaked. "There's a hole there." Okay, that was obvious. She took a pained breath to clarify that more rock might fall, so Val should be careful, but Val spoke first.

"Yes, thank you for finding that for us. But you could have marked it better. Thanks to this illusion magic, it's hard to tell where the edge is."

"No kidding."

"Maybe you could bring some orange traffic cones along next time."

"Do your other allies appreciate your wit?" Arwen fought the pain to find her bow and push herself to her feet.

"Terribly so, yes. Sindari is a tremendous fan of my humor and is bereft every time he has to leave me to return to his realm."

*Yes, I miss you like a burr in my fur.*

"*Incredibly* bereft," Val said.

A pebble fell, the only warning Arwen got that the camouflaged tiger was coming down. He landed a few feet to the side of her, close enough to appear to her eyes. Her soul-tracking magic had faded, her vision returning to normal, and she peered around the dark cave, looking for Azerdash.

Even if the fall had hurt, and she felt foolish for having stumbled into the trap, she was at least closer to his aura. So much so that she was surprised she didn't see him slumbering in a stasis chamber or some other device that could magically ensnare him.

Other than his aura, she didn't sense a lot of magic nearby, though there was an artifact off in his direction. Also, now that she was in the cave, she could detect magic in the roof above—probably whatever had triggered the rocks to fall.

"Sarrlevi is investigating something in the canyon," Val called down, "but heard the rock fall and wants to know if you need to be levitated out."

"Not yet." Arwen headed toward Azerdash's aura, feeling bolstered that Sindari strode beside her. She dug out her phone and activated the flashlight app.

*I sense the aura of the half-dragon but do not see him,* the tiger noted.

"Maybe he's being hidden by camouflaging magic."

There were also numerous rock formations inside the cave, columns, pillars, and mounds that made it hard to see everything or tell how far back it went.

*Hm.*

They paused when they reached the artifact that Arwen had sensed. A small cube resting on the ground, it didn't glow or look like anything special. She had no intention of touching it, but she did bend over and peer at it, wondering if it was responsible for hiding Azerdash or even keeping him trapped and unconscious. Its magic was weak, however, and she couldn't imagine it having the power to ensnare him.

"Do you want me to come down?" Val called from the hole.

"No." Arwen continued to worry about that irritation she'd been feeling toward Val and didn't want them to be trapped together. Just in case. "I'm bonding with your tiger," she added so Val wouldn't think the refusal odd.

"Oh? Has he threatened to gnaw your foot off yet?"

"He hasn't."

*She does not presume to pet me without permission,* Sindari said. *Nor does she intentionally irritate me by dangling foul-smelling trees in her conveyance.*

"I think he likes you," Val said.

"I'm honored."

The cube lacked writing or any identifying marks. Arwen was

about to leave it and continue on when brilliant white light flashed from it, filling the cave and half-blinding her. She stumbled back, lifting an arm as she squinted her eyes shut, but the light faded as quickly as it had come.

*What was that dreadful flash?* Sindari asked.

"Everything okay?" Val called down.

With the cube seared in her retinas, Arwen had to blink several times before her vision returned and the dark cave came back into focus. The dark cave and an image floating above the artifact. An image of her face.

"Are there such things as magical cameras?" she called to Val.

"I can't remember running into any, but Matti can do a lot with her enchanting magic, so I wouldn't be surprised."

A click-hum came from the cube, and the image disappeared.

"Odd," Arwen murmured.

Had the device stored her picture in its memory? So Saruknorath would know who came to free Azerdash while he was away?

Arwen was still surprised she hadn't run into any guards—or guard devices. Maybe the collapsible cave ceiling had been meant to kill intruders. If she hadn't been wearing her armored jumpsuit, the fall might have done her in.

*I would flatten the odious thing with my paw, but there may be repercussions.* Sindari flexed his claws at the cube.

"Yeah." Arwen gave it a wide berth, regretting that she'd gotten close enough for it to take a picture, and headed toward Azerdash's aura.

*I have located a cave entrance hidden by illusion magic,* Sarrlevi spoke telepathically to them.

*We don't need another entrance,* Arwen replied. *I already made one.*

*So I heard.* After a pause, Sarrlevi added, *I sense a dragon approaching. Saruknorath.*

Arwen glanced back at the cube sitting dormant on the cave

floor. Damn it, maybe it had magically transmitted her image, letting the dragon know she was in the area.

Picking up speed, she hurried around a rock formation. She had to reach Azerdash and get their group out of there—or at least find a way to wake him up in time to help defend against the assassin.

*Is he alone?* Arwen asked telepathically. *Or is there a Silverclaw dragon with him?*

What if the dragon from the clan that had outbid the Stormforges was coming to kill Azerdash?

Sarrlevi responded, but Arwen didn't register the answer, because more snapping and cracking of rocks thundered from above.

"Shit." Fearing another ceiling collapse, she sprinted forward.

There was nothing to hide under, but she sprang behind a thick column, hoping it would offer some protection. This time, she had the wherewithal to raise a barrier around herself before the first rocks slammed down. The first of *many.*

Sindari blurred past, also rushing to get past the rock-fall area. But if the ceiling of the entire cave collapsed, he wouldn't be safe.

*Here,* she told him as more rocks pounded down, some as large as Val's Jeep. *You can get in my barrier.*

But his instincts made him beeline for the back of the cave, and he disappeared from her view.

Beams of sunlight slipped through as more rocks fell from above, but dust soon clouded the air, dimming the cave. As more and more rubble piled around Arwen, some rocks thudding against the column and making it shudder, it grew darker and darker. The dust cloud became so thick that she couldn't see more than three feet. Rocks settled atop her barrier and piled all around it before they finally stopped falling.

"Val?" Arwen croaked, her mouth dry even though her barrier had kept out the dust. "Sindari?"

Val didn't respond. Arwen couldn't see the place where she'd fallen in anymore. She couldn't see anything in that direction but a wall of rubble. The ceiling directly above her column hadn't collapsed, nor had rock fallen in the back of the cave where Sindari had run, but they couldn't get out, not unless there was an exit in the back. Did the opening Sarrlevi had found lead into this cave? Or another?

*I believe you are trapped,* Sindari spoke into her mind.

*Just me?* Arwen looked in the direction of the cube. It had been buried, but she had a feeling that second rockfall had been as calculated as the first, intentionally sealing her in.

*Val can dismiss me from this world, and the magic of the charm will return me to my realm.*

*So, no need for you to die buried alive with me, huh?*

*I would not even volunteer to die buried alive with Val, whom I've known for many years.*

*That doesn't seem very loyal. Maybe she should get a dog.*

*Do not remind me of the odious canine of her mother's that so often rides in her conveyance and leaves fur and odor everywhere. Ah.* His tone changed. Had he found something? *You may want to come back here.*

Reminded of Azerdash, and worried he lay helpless with Saruknorath on the way, Arwen almost released her barrier before she remembered the rocks over her head. She plastered her back to the column and attempted to tilt the top of her protection so that the rubble slid off. It somewhat worked, but manipulating her barrier was difficult.

Meanwhile, Saruknorath flew close enough that she could also sense him. It wouldn't be long before he arrived.

Impatient, Arwen let the barrier collapse, using her arms to protect her head. A few small rocks remained and struck her, but it wasn't bad. A lot less painful than her original fall had been.

*Arwen?* Val asked telepathically. *There's a dragon coming, and I can sense you.*

*I'm fine. Thanks for asking,* she replied dryly but did hurry to activate her camouflage as she climbed over rocks.

*Sindari told me you're okay and being snarky with him.*

*I was almost buried alive. Snark seemed right.*

*It usually is. Have you found Starblade?*

*I'm almost to him.*

Arwen rounded a bend in the cave, and Sindari came into view, sitting on his haunches next to... What was that? Clothing?

Sindari hooked the item with a claw and lifted it into the air. *This is the source of what we believed was the aura of the half-dragon. It carries his scent and the remnants of his aura that has, through some magic with which I'm not familiar, been amplified so we believed we sensed him.*

Arwen stared, the memory of Saruknorath leaping on the bench and flying away with Azerdash's pants coming to mind. She hadn't thought much of it at the time and never would have guessed clothing could be used in a trick.

"To bait a trap," she whispered, glancing at the caved-in rocks.

# 27

"So, where is Azerdash?" Arwen looked around the cave, half-expecting to find him tucked away in a stasis chamber. Then, with a realization that struck like the banging of a gong, she swore. "*I'm* the bait, aren't I?"

Sindari lowered the pants and gazed at her.

"The aura trick—and maybe even the announcement to the Dragon Council—was to lure me here, but am I meant to lure *Azerdash* here?" Maybe that cube had transmitted the magical photo of her to more than Saruknorath. Could it have also shared the image with Azerdash, wherever he was? "Probably not on this world."

Sindari walked around the back of the cave. Searching for the exit Sarrlevi had mentioned? *I do not know this assassin dragon, but it seems that if he spoke to the Dragon Council and said Starblade was trapped here, he believed Starblade would truly be trapped here. If not at that moment, then soon.*

"Yeah, once he learns I'm here and comes to save me." Groaning, Arwen bent and gripped her knee. "What if there are more traps around to attack *him* if he shows up? Or is Saruknorath going to lie in wait?" She sensed him flying closer and didn't know what to do.

Could Val and Sarrlevi win a battle against a full-blooded dragon? A crafty one that liked to use trickery and set traps?

*I briefly sensed another dragon,* Sarrlevi said, presumably talking to Val as well as Arwen, *but he must have camouflaged himself. He was flying behind Saruknorath.*

*A Silverclaw?* Val asked.

*I believe so.*

*We need to get you out of there, Arwen,* Val said. *Sindari says Starblade isn't down there—was* never *down there.*

*Not yet,* Arwen replied grimly. *I'm bait for his trap.*

*Not if we get you out of there before he gets here. Sarrlevi, can you levitate over to the far side of the canyon and distract Saruknorath?* The origin of Val's telepathic voice had changed. She had to have jumped down into the hole.

Arwen groaned again at the idea of Val being trapped down here with her once the dragons showed up.

*How do you propose I distract a dragon from his mission?* Sarrlevi had also moved, and his voice came from farther away now.

*You're a big fan of dueling with their kind. Why not challenge him?*

*Shall I also challenge the Silverclaw?*

*I wouldn't recommend taking on two at once.*

Or even one, Arwen thought. She joined Sindari in looking for an exit. She had to get out of here. The idea of being helplessly stuck while leading Azerdash to his demise was too much to bear.

*Stand back, Arwen,* Val said from the other side of the rockfall. *I can blow some of these boulders away with my sword's magic.*

*I'm back.* Arwen patted along the wall of the cave, hoping to find another illusion. Where was that other exit Sarrlevi had mentioned?

*It's going to get a little hot in there,* Val warned.

A muffled snap came from the other side of the rockfall.

Arwen imagined a beam shooting out of Val's sword and breaking boulders in half. She had no idea if the blade had that capability but knew it was powerful. Even if it could break boulders, though, would Val be able to get through fast enough for it to matter?

*What are you doing here, elf?* Saruknorath boomed telepathically. *This is not your battle.*

*The fate of Azerdash Starblade is now of concern to many.*

*Only those who are foolish. Never will lesser species cast aside dragons as the rightful rulers of the Cosmic Realms. Our kind are too powerful.*

*But there are relatively few of you,* Sarrlevi replied. Chatting up Saruknorath to buy them time? *You may find that even the mighty can be overcome by the weak, when their numbers are far greater.*

*Greater but insignificant. Lower your blades, Sarrlevi. You do not wish to die protecting an enemy to dragons. Have you not squalling infants that require your presence?*

Sarrlevi didn't respond right away. Maybe he *was* thinking about that.

Arwen had to find a way out of here before they started fighting. *Especially* if a Silverclaw dragon lurked nearby, prepared to jump in. Arwen didn't want to have to explain to Matti that her husband had died, and it was her fault.

But she'd checked every crevice in the back of the cave. Whatever entrance Sarrlevi had found, it had to lead elsewhere.

*Nothing is here.* Sindari sounded equally frustrated.

Boulders shifted on the other side of the rockfall, and one clunked. Val was making progress, but Arwen feared it would take far, far too long.

She had to help. Unfortunately, none of her arrows could split boulders.

She set aside her bow and drew the multitool, remembering how she'd poured her own power into it and tunneled through rubble the day before. It might take a while, but she could do it again.

*I'm going to try to tunnel out,* Arwen warned Val, rushing to the rubble and stuffing one of the multitool blades into a gap.

*I highly recommend that,* Val said. *I think Sarrlevi is fighting Saruknorath up there. I hear battle sounds. And insults.*

Abruptly, the Silverclaw revealed himself, and Arwen sensed him in the air above their cave. Was he coming for them? Or had his camouflage dropped because he'd joined in the battle? As talented as Sarrlevi was, there was no way he could survive against two dragons.

*Shit.* Val must have thought the same.

"Now or never," Arwen whispered.

Closing her eyes, she drew upon the power within her and also pulled from the ground, forming as much energy as she could into a ball, then channeling it into the multitool.

*Yes,* a dark-elven voice whispered into her mind, speaking in that tongue, *accept your power and use it. You don't need that toy. Simply accept the demons as your guide, and their power will infuse yours.*

Gritting her teeth, Arwen ignored the words. Her power flowed into the blade, and a great beam burned into the rocks. Dust and powder flooded the air, shards striking her face. She tried to create a barrier while continuing to focus on tunneling. As always, performing two separate magical activities at once was almost impossible, but extra energy flowed from her tattoo—not, she prayed, from some demon—and into her. Concentrating so hard it made her head throb, she continued to burrow into the rockfall while forming a barrier around herself.

Sweat snaked down her spine, but the effort was worth it. Her magical defenses deflected shards that flew as her power bored deeper into the rubble. Rocks fell down, gravity trying to block the hole she was making, but raw white energy flowing from the blade blasted the obstacles away.

*Arwen?* Val asked. *Is that you?*

Fresh irritation swamped her along with the desire to blast Val as she was blasting the rocks.

Horrified, she shook her head. *Yeah. You need to move out of the way. Go up, and help Sarrlevi. Please.*

*We need to work together to dig you out of there so we can all take a portal and get the hell off this world.*

*I've got it under control. But you're in danger.* Arwen dashed sweat out of her eyes. The arm holding the multitool trembled under the strain of all the power flowing through it, but she was making progress, burning a hole wide enough to escape through. Just a little farther... *I'm using my dark-elven magic,* she added in case Val didn't understand. She was stubborn and would want to keep helping. *Go. Please. For both our sakes.*

Val didn't answer. Arwen hoped it was because her friend was busy climbing up to help Sarrlevi, but she couldn't know for certain.

Remembering the vial Zoltan had given her, Arwen paused to dig it out. She worried this wasn't the best time, that it would wear off before she needed it most, but she couldn't risk her magic getting the upper hand and making her do something she would regret.

It tasted awful, like a corpse that had been rotting in a swamp, but she made herself choke it down. Her tattoo burned in indignation.

*Continue using your power,* the voice speaking in Dark Elven urged. *Free yourself. Don't allow yourself to be a weak damsel who must be rescued.*

Arwen agreed with that sentiment a lot more than with the idea of attacking Val, and she renewed her efforts, again chan-neling her power into the multitool.

Black mist flowed up around her, seeming to come from the ground, but she'd seen it before. It was a side effect of calling on her dark-elven power. She sensed Sindari pacing behind her, watching her. Warily?

More irritation arose in her. He was Val's ally, and he'd helped destroy dark elves. She knew it.

"And I don't care," Arwen snarled, wiping her face again and pouring more magic into the idiotic obstacle that she'd triggered, the trap *she'd* walked into.

Her frustration made her power stronger, and she blasted through the last of the resistance, meeting the tunnel that Val had been excavating from the other side.

Relieved to see daylight, Arwen grabbed her bow and squished her barrier enough to surge into the tunnel. Steam wafted from the sides, but her magic protected her. Black mist flowed through with her.

When she didn't see Val on the other side, Arwen was relieved that she'd obeyed, but as soon as Arwen emerged from the hole, she spotted Val still down in the cave. She'd backed up, and her sword glowed in her hand, sweat beading her own brow.

Fury came not only from the tattoo but from the back of Arwen's mind. Imagery of Val and Sindari and Zavryd stomping through tunnels and slaying dark elves washed over her. Along with such intense anger and hatred that it overwhelmed her.

Before Arwen could stop herself, she rushed forward, raising the multitool and sending deadly power at Val.

# 28

V̲a̲l̲'̲s̲ ̲e̲y̲e̲s̲ ̲w̲i̲d̲e̲n̲e̲d̲ ̲a̲s̲ ̲b̲l̲a̲c̲k̲ ̲m̲i̲s̲t̲ ̲r̲o̲l̲l̲e̲d̲ ̲o̲u̲t̲ ̲o̲f̲ ̲t̲h̲e̲ ̲t̲u̲n̲n̲e̲l̲ and a white beam shot from the multitool toward her, but she wasn't caught off-guard. Her sword glowed an intense blue, and a magical barrier protected her. The beam hit with enough power to make her step back, her barrier wavering, but she gritted her teeth and reinforced it.

"This isn't a good time, Arwen." Val pointed her sword at the hole in the ceiling, now three times as large as it had been.

Silhouetted against the hazy orange sky, a black-scaled dragon with topaz eyes flew over it and roared. Out of sight, Sarrlevi cursed in Elven. He was still alive but needed help. Why hadn't Val gone up to assist him, damn it?

Arwen tried to shift the multitool aside, but power flowed from her tattoo, and something in the back of her mind also held sway. As if a powerful dark elf were standing behind her, magically compelling her to attack her friend.

"Arwen..." Val's cheek twitched, her face strained from the effort of keeping her barrier up. She shifted her sword, as if to aim it at Arwen, but hesitated.

"Stop me," Arwen managed to rasp as black mist flooded the chamber, wrapping around them both.

Why hadn't she taken Zoltan's concoction earlier? He'd warned her it would take some time to work. If it even did.

Panting, Arwen stepped closer, and her tattoo throbbed, amplifying the power blasting into Val's barrier.

"Shit, Arwen." Val lifted her sword but again paused.

She didn't want to attack. Arwen understood, but she needed Val to defend herself. If Val attacked, she had the power to defeat Arwen. That would be for the best.

*No*, the voice that had been plaguing Arwen whispered. *With the aid of the demons, we have the power to defeat the Ruin Bringer.*

A roar came from above them. *Is that the mate of Zavryd'nokque-tal? And also the wench that holds Starblade's tail?* A silver-scaled head lowered through the hole, glowing yellow eyes fixing on them. *A great victory it will be to destroy them. Worth every gold nugget scrounged for this prize.*

Even as Saruknorath and Sarrlevi battled above, the Silverclaw descended through the hole, talons extended.

Arwen should have felt nothing but terror, but relief was her predominant emotion. The dragon had the power to stop her attack, to knock her into the rubble pile and keep her from hurting her friend.

But the Silverclaw dove not for Arwen but for Val.

Sindari streaked out of the tunnel behind Arwen, a silver blur as he passed her and sprang for the dragon.

He struck the Silverclaw as Val dove away. Her defensive barrier remained intact, but maybe she'd worried it wouldn't hold up to attacks from two directions.

Arwen, treacherous magic forcing her hand, shifted her multi-tool to continue targeting it—targeting *her*.

Protected by a barrier of his own, the Silverclaw reached the bottom, landing without trouble. Sindari was deflected away, no different from an arrow or bullet. He landed on his feet, snarling, but the dragon, after glancing at Arwen, focused on Val.

*Your ally has turned on you,* he spoke with amusement, flicking a wing at the black mist.

Arwen panted from the mental effort of trying to turn the multitool away. She needed to attack her enemy, not her ally. Worse, she sensed Val's barrier weakening. All it would take was a slash from the dragon's talons to collapse it.

The Silverclaw hurled a magical attack instead of a physical blow. It knocked Val into the rubble pile. Fortunately, it clipped Arwen too, diverting her attack for a second.

Sindari crouched to spring at the Silverclaw but glanced at Arwen when her compulsion forced her to turn her beam back on Val, to again blast her.

Val had landed on her feet, but her barrier wavered as she struggled to keep it up. Cursing, she threw a glower at Arwen, then leaped at the Silverclaw with her sword.

Magic flared above. A spell cast in the battle? No, that was a portal forming.

A second later, as she battled with herself, striving to turn aside her attack so Val could focus on only the dragon, Arwen sensed Azerdash.

At first, she felt relief, but that quickly turned to fear for him. He'd flown right into the trap that Saruknorath had set.

Sindari sprang for Arwen, claws raised to swipe at her.

Instinctively, she funneled magic into her barrier. Thanks to the tattoo, she had more power than usual, and the tiger bounced off it.

Growling, Sindari ran in front of the multitool, trying to block Arwen's attack on Val. But he didn't have a magical barrier, and the beam singed into his fur.

Arwen cursed, frustration and guilt making her wish she could turn the weapon on herself. But the tattoo wouldn't allow that.

Roaring with pain and fury, Sindari sprang again, claws swiping at Arwen's defenses. Magical and powerful, those claws left gouges in her barrier, but it didn't fall completely.

*Arwen?* Azerdash spoke into her mind. *Are you uninjured?*

*Yeah, but I'm attacking my friends and can't stop,* she cried in frustration.

*I suggest you desist.*

*No kidding!*

When Sindari sliced his claws at her barrier again, it disintegrated.

After drawing upon so much power, Arwen struggled to recreate it. Her legs felt heavier than granite, her knees weaker than straw.

Once more, Sindari slashed, trying to knock the multitool away, or maybe tear her entire hand off. Arwen barely found the wherewithal to leap back and evade his claws. Her heel clipped a rock, and she almost fell.

*No,* the dark-elven voice spoke, and fresh power surged into her. *You will slay the Ruin Bringer and her companion. She is distracted. Strike now.*

Val was more than distracted. She'd sliced into the dragon's barrier, and almost managed to draw blood, but he blasted her again. The powerful magic knocked her across the cave and into a rock column. She almost lost her sword as her own barrier disappeared.

The Silverclaw roared, spotted Arwen, and hurled power at her like a hurricane gale. With her barrier down, she was vulnerable. She flew through the air, then slammed into the cave wall. Her armored jumpsuit wasn't enough to completely dull the force. The air whooshed from her lungs as pain hammered her back, running up her spine to stab her head and make white dots swirl before her eyes. She crumpled to the ground, her multitool and bow falling from her grip.

Roaring again, the Silverclaw stomped toward her. Recreating his barrier, he sprang and landed over her, forelimbs planted to either side, trapping her. His huge maw lowered, fangs stretching toward her. The anger in his eyes promised he would rip her head off. His power rippled over her—he was so close that she was inside his protective barrier.

Arwen struggled to push aside her pain, to focus on raising her defenses. As his maw descended, she managed to get a barrier up, but he popped it with his power.

*No!* a telepathic cry came from above as a shadow fell over the hole. Azerdash.

The Silverclaw paused to glance up. Arwen rolled out from between his forelimbs and snatched up her multitool. She stabbed the dragon in the foot, the blade finding flesh between scales.

He jerked it up and stepped back as gunfire came from the side —Val firing at him.

Arwen staggered to her feet, intending to help, to launch another attack through the multitool, but her tattoo throbbed, working against her again.

*Kill the Ruin Bringer,* the voice plaguing her ordered.

Arwen started to shift the multitool toward Val but glanced up at the hole. Azerdash had landed, and one of his violet eyes peered down at her.

Utter shame filled Arwen, the shame that she couldn't defeat the dark-elven magic, that she was giving in to their demands, that she wasn't strong enough to defy them.

"*No!*" she cried in pure frustration.

From deep within, she found the strength to turn her shaking arm toward the dragon again. She aimed her power not at Val but at the Silverclaw's barrier. If she could weaken it, maybe Val could land a sword strike. Maybe Azerdash could fly down and help.

She'd no sooner had the thought than the black-scaled Saruknorath flew into Azerdash from the side. He'd been focused on her and hadn't seen him coming—or had but hadn't been willing to leave Arwen when she was in trouble.

The thought that her situation might result in him being killed gave her more fuel to fight the tattoo and the dark-elven urges that wanted her to keep attacking Val. Arwen stepped toward the Silverclaw, again channeling her power into the blade and this time succeeding in keeping it aimed at him.

Sindari was poised to spring at Arwen again, but he saw that she'd stopped attacking Val and instead turned toward the dragon. He leaped, claws raised and jaws parted to reveal his fangs.

Though her power was ebbing, maybe because the tattoo had stopped helping her, Arwen's assault burned a hole through the dragon's barrier. It collapsed an instant before Sindari struck. He reached the Silverclaw's scales and slashed and bit, fangs sinking into flesh.

Val charged and swung, her magical blade also landing, slicing into the dragon's shoulder.

The Silverclaw roared. *Saruknorath, you lied. They are not defenseless, and Starblade isn't trapped down here.*

Saruknorath didn't respond. Roars, thumps, and screeches came from above.

Swirling magic surged from the Silverclaw, knocking Val and Sindari back. It hadn't been aimed at Arwen, but it also clipped her, making her stumble. She didn't have energy to continue to channel into the multitool, and the beam flagged, growing more feeble.

She sheathed the weapon and reached for an arrow.

Before Val could recover and charge back in, a portal formed next to the Silverclaw. He cast his magic at them all one more time, his power making more rocks fall from the cave ceiling, then sprang through it to escape.

As more rocks tumbled down, one almost smashed Arwen.

She tried but failed to raise her barrier again. She didn't have the energy left to even raise her arm.

Power wrapped around Arwen, and she tensed, afraid a new attacker had entered the fray, but she recognized it as Sarrlevi's magic. From somewhere above, he used it to levitate Val and Arwen upward as more rocks fell. Was the whole cave going to collapse now?

"Sindari," Val called, reaching back toward the tiger. He remained on the ground. "Dismiss yourself."

A moment later, as Val and Arwen were whisked into the daylight, the rest of the cave collapsed.

Roars and screeches sounded as two dragons battled in the light above, Azerdash and Saruknorath.

Sarrlevi, one of his sleeves ripped off and with blood staining his blond hair and running down his arm, still had his swords, but he couldn't reach the aerial battle to help.

A portal floated in the air near Sarrlevi. Did he want them all to flee? To leave Azerdash to face Saruknorath alone?

No. Arwen had finally found Azerdash. She wasn't about to leave. Besides, he needed help. Saruknorath was twice his size and killed people for a living.

Though she'd taken numerous blows, and her shoulder twinged agonizingly as she reached for an arrow, Arwen nocked her bow and targeted Saruknorath. Val took several steps from her, giving Arwen a wary look, before she raised her gun toward the dragon.

But with Azerdash and Saruknorath entwined in the sky, rolling about as they snapped their jaws and slashed with their talons, they couldn't get off safe shots. At least Azerdash's protective barrier was intact, deflecting fang and talon. It seemed stronger than Arwen had noticed before, and Saruknorath snarled in frustration when he couldn't get through.

Was the galaxy blade lending Azerdash power? In his dragon

form, he couldn't wield it, and Arwen had no idea where it was, but he must have had it, tucked in some magical storage cubby.

Saruknorath's barrier was the one to fall. He snapped to keep Azerdash's jaws from reaching his vulnerable neck, then hurled power, knocking Azerdash back.

As soon as the dragons separated, Arwen and Val fired, arrow and bullets hammering into Saruknorath's side. His flapping wings faltered, and one clipped the ground. He somersaulted clumsily over the lumpy rocks.

Azerdash could have zipped in, maybe even finishing off Saruknorath, but he paused and gave his enemy a chance to get to his feet.

"This isn't the time for honor, Azerdash." Arwen drew another arrow from her quiver.

A silver-scaled dragon flew out of the portal, startling her. She shifted her aim, thinking another enemy had arrived. Then she recognized Yendral.

Surprisingly, another dragon—no, a half-dragon—flew out after him, this one with golden scales. Arwen had never seen the male before but remembered Azerdash mentioning that another half-dragon had battled with them on Veleshna Var, one in addition to Gemlytha.

Azerdash, now flanked by his two allies, landed and surrounded the wounded Saruknorath.

The assassin managed to get to his feet and stood taller than the three half-dragons, but blood ran from deep gouges between his scales, and his barrier remained down.

*I am defeated,* Saruknorath admitted, lowering his head.

*Despite the tricks and treachery you used to bring me here. Despite trapping Arwen Forester and using her as bait, like cheese to lure in some rodent.* Eyes glowing violet with indignation, Azerdash looked over at her.

*Stubborn and irritating cheese, yes,* Saruknorath said.

Val snorted. "Better than being pliable and easily captured cheese."

*Will you leave me be, Saruknorath?* Azerdash turned his gaze back to the bigger dragon, studying him intently. *If not, we must slay you.* As Commander Aylida Alonsha said, 'Leave no enemies at your back, or they will plant a dagger in your spine at an inconvenient moment.'

*You quote inferior elves? What a strange creation you are.*

*I embrace both halves of my heritage. I can also quote the ancient dragon king, Aridestylar. 'If you cannot remove the talons of your enemy, you must slay him.'*

Saruknorath huffed out a breath, almost a wheeze. Maybe there was a bullet lodged in his lungs. Arwen hoped so.

*I wish to leave, so I will give you my word that I will hunt you no more as an assassin.* Saruknorath's eyes closed to slits. *But if you lead an attack on all of dragondom, I will join my kin to battle you.*

They held each other's gazes in silence.

Val fingered the trigger of her gun. "I'd get rid of the bastard to have one less dragon to face later," she muttered.

Arwen might have too, but she wasn't surprised when Azerdash stepped back and flicked a wingtip, indicating that his allies should let Saruknorath go.

Yendral hesitated. *Are you sure?*

*Yes,* Azerdash said. *And so are you.*

Arwen had never seen a dragon roll its eyes, but Yendral came close as he looked toward the blazing orange sun. The other half-dragon only opened his maw in what looked like a laugh.

Saruknorath flexed one taloned foot in a gesture that might have meant something to the half-dragons. Whatever it was, they didn't attack, merely taking another step back as he formed a portal.

Before stepping through, Saruknorath looked toward Arwen. *My apologies for ensnaring you. I knew the galaxy blade made my target powerful, and I had to employ sneaky methods in an attempt to outmaneuver him. I have no adoration for Silverclaw dragons and did not mind seeing you stab that one.* One of his lids drooped over his topaz slitted eye in an approximation of a wink before he leaped through the portal and disappeared.

Val lowered her gun and looked at Arwen. "Are you done trying to kill me?"

Arwen winced. "I hope so."

"I'm glad you thought to ask Zoltan for a potion."

Was that what had finally given Arwen the strength to defy the dark-elven programming? Or had it been the shame she'd felt at knowing Azerdash was watching her doing their bidding? She didn't know, but she was glad she hadn't succeeded in hurting Val.

"Yes. I did warn you to get out of there. I could feel..." Arwen lifted her tattooed forearm. "I had a hunch."

"All along, I know. You did try to warn me." Val pointed to something singed tied around a boulder that had barely missed tumbling into the cave during all the rockfalls. "Someone up here burned my rope, so I couldn't get out."

"You need to learn how to levitate."

"Oh, I know, but it's harder than it looks."

"It is a skill that generally takes the power of a full-blooded magical being," Sarrlevi said, joining them.

"Because haughtiness is required?" Val asked him.

"A certain confidence in one's abilities can assist in casting difficult magic."

Val nodded. "Haughtiness."

"Will you apologize to Sindari for me, Val?" Arwen could no longer sense the tiger and assumed he'd returned to his realm. "I singed him."

"I will, but it probably won't matter. He'll make snarky comments about your failings for the rest of your days."

"Do you think there's a way I could make it up to him?"

"It's doubtful," Val said.

"What if I use my magic to destroy your air fresheners every time I get in your Jeep?"

"That actually might do it."

"*I* would forgive her all grievances if she did that." Sarrlevi wrinkled his nostrils toward Val. "You park close enough to our home that I can smell that odious thing."

Azerdash shifted into his elven form, revealing the galaxy blade in his hand, and walked toward Arwen. Relieved to see him and glad he didn't appear too wounded, other than a few gashes and a bruise swelling on his jaw, she didn't hear Val's response to Sarrlevi.

When Azerdash sheathed the sword and lifted his arms, Arwen ran toward him for a hug. He pulled her in tight—tighter than she would have expected. Maybe he'd been afraid for her life when the Silverclaw had loomed over her. Understandable, since *she'd* been afraid for her life.

"I'm so glad you survived," Azerdash whispered.

"I'm sorry I walked into his trap like a big dummy. I was— Well, Saruknorath led me to believe *you* were the one trapped."

"I know." Azerdash leaned back enough to gaze into her eyes and lift a hand to the side of her face, his thumb brushing her cheek tenderly. "And you were not a dummy. You cared." He smiled. "As *I* care."

A lump in her throat made it hard to swallow. She could only grip him, longing to kiss him, but he wasn't done speaking.

"I did not fully realize how much you've come to mean to me until I saw that Silverclaw standing over you, about to—" His throat must have formed a lump too, because his voice was tight. It took him a moment to finish, emotion bringing moisture to his eyes. "When I thought I was too late, that he might kill you before I could do anything... I realized I love you."

Arwen blinked, tears welling in her own eyes.

"I do not have any more confusion about... the past. About how I feel about *you*."

"I love you too," she whispered, wrapping her arms around his shoulders.

"Good." Azerdash kissed her with great longing in his touch, as if they'd been parted for ages, as if he'd needed nothing more than to be with her again, to say these words.

Though she was vaguely aware of Val and Sarrlevi standing nearby, and the two half-dragons shifting into elven form, Arwen didn't care that they witnessed the kiss. If anything, she wanted everyone to know about this, to know Azerdash loved her. And that she loved him.

For a time, the others left them alone until Yendral walked up and punched Azerdash in the shoulder.

"You said there'd be taycos."

A rumble—or maybe a growl—emanated from Azerdash's chest, and his grip did not loosen.

Only because Arwen wanted to get back and have her tattoo removed did she break the kiss, though she hoped her eyes promised she wanted to return to it and more later.

"Tacos," she said, correcting Yendral's pronunciation without looking away from Azerdash. "Crispy corn tortillas holding a seasoned meat or fish filling with lettuce, cheese, and salsa on top."

"The meat component is large?" That was the other half-dragon, now a blond elf standing at Yendral's side. "And seasoned deliciously? Like the meat shavings that the half-dwarf brought us before the great mountain battle?"

"Is food the only reason you came back to join us, Sleveryn?" Yendral asked him.

"I came because Azerdash found his sword and needed me." Sleveryn paused. "Humans do have tasty food."

"The meat component can be large," Arwen said, "though the shells tend to break if you stuff them too full."

That elicited a frown from Yendral. Arwen would have to make sure to cook up a *lot* of meat for the meal she'd promised Azerdash, one that would apparently, once again, involve other dinner guests.

"You can also make a filling from vegetables such as sautéed mushrooms," she told him.

Azerdash nodded his approval.

Yendral frowned again while Sleveryn curled a lip.

"Why would you use your special cooking powers to such an evil end, Chef Arwen?" Yendral asked.

"To make Azerdash happy."

The two half-dragons shook their heads and walked away.

Sarrlevi, who was gripping one of his wounds and probably wanting nothing more than to go home to his family, lifted a weary arm and formed a portal.

"Come on, lovebirds." Val pointed specifically for Arwen to go through it. "Zoltan is waiting."

"I'm ready," Arwen said.

More than ready.

# 29

Sarrlevi's portal delivered them to the street between Matti's and Val's houses, a soft rain falling and the clouds almost hiding that daylight had returned. Exhaustion made Arwen wonder when the last time she'd slept had been. With her senses dulled from fatigue, she almost missed noticing Zavryd's aura in the turret bedroom he shared with Val.

Val sighed as soon as they arrived. Was he already speaking telepathically with her? Berating her for not obeying him?

Arwen looked warily at Azerdash, hoping Zavryd wouldn't feel compelled to take him to his mother. Even though Saruknorath was, if he kept his word, no longer hunting Azerdash, that didn't mean anything had changed for the rest of dragonkind.

Perhaps having similar thoughts, Azerdash camouflaged himself, pointing for his comrades to do the same. They waved an acknowledgment but barely looked at him. Their heads were bent as they discussed something in Elven, pointing to the portal and also off to the north.

"Can your tacos accommodate any type of meat?" Azerdash

murmured to Arwen as Val headed into the house, hopefully to keep Zavryd from coming out and challenging the half-dragons.

"I suppose," Arwen said. "I might have to play with the seasoning blend to make sure it goes well with an atypical filling, but people make chicken and pork tacos. And I told you about the fish and mushrooms."

"Yes." Azerdash pointed as Yendral and Sleveryn shifted into their dragon forms, then took off, soon disappearing since they had obeyed the suggestion to camouflage themselves. "Those two, especially Sleveryn, are excited about the prospect of a feast."

Feast? Arwen hadn't been planning to prepare a *feast*. Would a few side dishes and a dessert be sufficient? She had better make multiple desserts since the half-dragons had proven that they, unlike full-blooded dragons, enjoyed sweets.

"They plan to hunt down fresh game for your dish," Azerdash added.

"Not another yeti."

"I believe they will bring whatever looks interesting and is a suitably challenging prey to hunt down. They were discussing whether to seek game here or on another world. I did remind them that we are being hunted ourselves and will have to return to our mission to unite the intelligent species of the Cosmic Realms against our dragon overlords, but we will enjoy the feast first. Also, it would be greatly helpful if the alchemist's formula works not only on your mark but on ours." Azerdash lay a hand across his pectoral, the dragon tattoo that allowed others to track him hidden under his shirt.

"Let's find out." Arwen gestured toward the gate in the fence.

Azerdash gripped her hand, giving her a lopsided smile as if he were shy about doing so, and nodded for her to lead.

Arwen grinned, feeling that something had changed since he'd proclaimed his love. The thought of making delicious tacos with a mushroom filling just for him excited her. She crossed her fingers that the tattoo removal would be successful and that, without it, the dark elves would struggle to control her again. She looked forward to spending many relaxed meals with Azerdash. Someday.

Sensing Zoltan in the basement, Arwen led the way to the backyard. Someone else with a magical aura was down there. Mark, the half-troll–half-elven tattoo artist. That brought hope to her heart. Zoltan must have found his formula and called him over.

Before they reached the basement door, Azerdash squeezed Arwen's hand, making her pause. When she turned, he kissed her, smiling as their lips met.

Basking in his new—or at least newly clarified—passion for her? How long had he been conflicted about his past and not certain if he could trust what he felt for her?

Arwen rose on tiptoes to return the kiss. She knew they shouldn't make Zoltan and Mark wait, but a little smooch wouldn't take long.

Val came out through the back door, close enough to the stairs to see through their camouflage to their lips molded together. Blushing, Arwen drew back.

Azerdash's eyes, his lids drooping as he watched Arwen through his lashes, suggested he was thinking of ignoring Val and returning to the kiss.

"I've assured Zav that he was sleepy and mistaken that he briefly sensed Starblade here," was all Val said, though her eyebrows rose, and she glanced at their handhold.

"I'm not well versed on dragon romantic relationships," Arwen said. "Is it allowed to lie to your mate?"

"For the female, yes. She's in charge and has to do what she must to keep her male in line."

Arwen blinked and looked to Azerdash. "Is that true?"

"Well, Zav might not put it *exactly* like that, but he has admitted that female dragons usually rule and outrank their male counterparts."

Azerdash nodded.

"Zav jumps to obey his mother, though he assures me that his younger sister isn't old enough yet to have the wisdom needed to order him around. I haven't noticed that keeps Zondia from trying." Val pointed at their linked hands. "Be careful walking down stairs like that. You might trip."

"Our elven agility gives us sure feet," Azerdash stated.

Since Arwen was battered and bruised after falling through holes and being hurled about by a dragon, she didn't nod. She hadn't felt that agile lately.

"Uh-huh," Val said. "Does it make your lips sure too?"

Azerdash smiled. "Very much so."

Blushing even more, Arwen hurried down the rest of the steps and knocked.

*Yes, yes, do come in,* Zoltan said telepathically. *We have been wondering what was causing a delay.*

Not explaining, Arwen opened the door, and she, Azerdash, and Val squeezed inside. Having three people in the lightlock made for a tight fit, but Arwen didn't want to risk irritating their alchemist with further delays, not when she was so close to finishing her quest.

After Val closed the outer door, Arwen opened the inner and almost sprang into the basement laboratory. The red glow of Zoltan's special lights showed a few cardboard boxes that had appeared and been packed since Arwen's last visit. Mark stood beside his portable tattoo table with his tools.

He grinned when he saw Arwen, though his grin faltered when Azerdash followed her in, their hands still linked.

"Uhm, hi, Mark." Seeing him reminded Arwen of the letter

he'd sent and the gift of a tattoo he'd promised, and she realized she hadn't seen him to thank him since then. She extracted her hand from Azerdash's grip, though it was probably already obvious that she wouldn't go on a romantic interlude with Mark.

He sighed wistfully. Maybe he'd already known there was someone else—after all, Arwen hadn't accepted any of his invitations for coffee—because he forced the grin back onto his face. "Hello, Arwen. I'm delighted to see you. I hope you and your, ah, powerful friend there can keep this vampire from waylaying my veins. I understand he enjoys the blood of magical beings, due to health benefits involving increased vigor and mental acuity." Mark shuddered. "Apparently, he's never enjoyed the blood of a half-elf–half-troll before and is curious."

"*Achingly* curious." Zoltan gazed at Mark's neck, the half-troll's lean build making the arteries stand out. "Since I'm allowing you to set up your entire workshop in my laboratory, you should give me a gift of blood. Your body would soon replenish the mild loss you would take."

"How do you live with a vampire in your basement?" Mark asked Val.

"He's afraid of Zav and doesn't come upstairs," she said.

"We must discuss the living arrangements soon, dear robber. I have some news to share with you."

Val eyed the boxes. "Are you moving out?"

She sounded more hopeful than disappointed.

"As soon as I can secure new lodgings, yes. As much as I enjoy some of the city conveniences—easy access to blood, for example —" Zoltan waved to indicate neighboring houses, and Arwen shuddered, thinking of the poor, mundane people who lived in the area, "—I find that I am a target for kidnappers here."

"You're catnip to their kind," Val said.

"Indeed. I understand from my vampire comrade, Jimmy, who moved into the carriage house I used to enjoy in Woodinville, that the whole area has grown far too busy for our kind. I must seek a more rural setting to enjoy peace." Zoltan looked at Arwen. "Your Carnation is full of farms, is it not? Perhaps that is a locale to consider."

"Lately, it's been full of yetis, dark elves, and dragons." Arwen didn't want a vampire as a neighbor, but if his formula worked to remove her tattoo, she might feel compelled to help him find a place.

Zoltan's top lip curled back.

"Maybe try Mt. Vernon or Sedro-Woolley," Val said. "It's pretty quiet up there. Willard hardly ever sends me to deal with magical beings committing crimes."

"These are quiet rural areas? With good internet? I must have excellent internet for the live-streaming of my instructional videos to my followers."

"I'm not sure *rural* and *good internet* go together, but they're sedate towns, aside from some tourist stuff. How do you feel about tulip festivals?"

The lip curled again, though it might have been more for the idea of substandard internet than flower celebrations.

"If you'll help me load your formula into my tattoo machine, we can get started," Mark said to Zoltan, then patted his table and nodded at Arwen.

"Is there any possible danger?" Azerdash, who hadn't voiced an opinion on rural living, eyed Mark's tools.

"The formula is untested." Zoltan shrugged.

"I will go first then." Azerdash stepped past Arwen.

"The entire Cosmic Realms is waiting for you to lead a joint army against the dragons," Arwen said. "Don't you think it makes more sense for me to be the guinea pig?"

"No." Azerdash removed his shirt and lay on the table, tilting the glowing dragon tattoo toward Mark.

Zoltan came over with a beaker, the blue liquid inside as

appealing as Drano and with a similar smell. Arwen hoped it only went under the skin, like tattoo ink, and not into a vein. It was bad enough Zoltan wanted to sink his fangs into their veins.

Mark held the beaker up to one of the red lights, which did nothing to improve the appeal of the contents. "This would be perfect if I wanted to do a Smurf tattoo." He smiled at Arwen, as if she might want to take him up on that.

"A what?" she asked.

"Arwen isn't old enough to know the Smurfs. They were a part of *my* youth." Val pressed a hand to her chest. "Though admittedly not until Mom moved us from that converted school bus into a real house. Once we had a TV, I had to play catch-up for all the cartoons I'd missed. Willard is a Smurf fan though. Maybe she'd like a tattoo. I know she has a mug."

"Oh." Arwen's memory conjured an appropriate image of a blue cartoon character. "We didn't have a TV when I was growing up either."

"Do you have a TV *now*?" Val smirked at her as Mark swirled the dubious magical ink—the ink *remover.*

"Yes, but it's my father's. He uses it to watch *Jeopardy.* We do have a computer. I think you can watch cartoons on it."

"Have you ever done so?"

"I... have not. There's an excellent YouTube channel called Eat the Weeds that my father and I watch. We already know about most of the foods one can forage, but the instructor covers other interesting topics too. Have you ever made your own vinegar?"

"You're kind of a nerd, Arwen," Val said.

"Yes."

Azerdash, who had probably never seen a cartoon, rested a hand on Arwen's arm and glared at Val. "Arwen Forester, schooled properly by her father, watches and reads about educational matters that are important for surviving and thriving in the world —and the Cosmic Realms. She is a superior individual."

"Oh, I'm sure." Val smirked again.

"You forgot that I admitted to reading *Twilight*," Arwen told him, patting his abdomen and letting her hand linger. For emotional support, of course, not because he was appealing shirtless and she hadn't yet gotten many opportunities to touch him.

"I do not know what that is," Azerdash said. "A romance, you said?"

"With *vampires*." Mark smirked as well.

"How do you know about these things?" Val asked him. "You're not from Earth, right? And are you old enough for *Smurfs*?"

"I run a tattoo shop. My clients gossip about a great many things. And Smurf tattoos are a frequent request, usually from forty-something women who want to relive their youth." Mark nodded at Val before lifting a hand. "I must concentrate now."

Val and Zoltan stepped away. Since Azerdash's hand was on Arwen's arm, she stayed. A wrinkle of concern creased his brow as he watched Mark load the tattoo machine with the magical concoction.

"You recall my wishes if I die?" Azerdash asked Arwen gravely.

"You're not going to die. You battled multiple dragons today. You can't be concerned about a little blue liquid."

"It smells like sulfuric acid and more ominous ingredients."

"Such as the ingredients we foraged? One was cave-corn husk and is edible, remember?"

"Some were poisonous. You recall my wishes?"

Mark, unconcerned about this talk of death from the ink remover, set to work on Azerdash's pectoral.

"As I recall," Arwen said, "we discussed moving the airplane project you've been working on from the goblin sanctuary to my farm."

"Yes."

"Yendral was going to do it. Have you let him know about that duty yet?"

"I have. He may also bring you some of the literature I've acquired. There are notes in the margins. You may find them interesting remembrances of me."

Arwen imagined Yendral showing up at her father's house with the airplane project floating behind him and the toilet-paper roll filled with gnomish notes in hand.

"My writing is in Elven though," Azerdash added. "You'll have to have the writings translated. Or learn to read the language."

"A hobby I may feel compelled to take on in the event of your death."

He nodded, apparently finding that reasonable. "I regret that there wasn't time for me to repair your mulching device."

"My father will be disappointed, but we'll get by." Arwen patted his abdomen while noting some eye rolls from Mark at all this talk of post-death plans. He had to be fairly certain Zoltan's concoction wouldn't kill his client.

"The tattoo is resisting me, but the formula is powerful," Mark said, "and I'm not without magic of my own."

"I could lend you the power of my sword," Azerdash told him.

"I'm not interested in your sword. I lament that others are." Mark glanced at Arwen.

Even though she wasn't the swiftest when it came to innuendos, she grasped that he wasn't referring to the galaxy blade.

"The sword is a boon and a bane," Azerdash said, *not* catching the innuendo. "I have been surprised by how many rulers and generals have agreed to meet with me now that I have it. Some of them had no interest in speaking with me before, not that I was attempting to foment a rebellion then. I was only seeking asylum for my fellow half-dragons and myself."

"Is the legend of the sword that great?" Arwen asked.

"There are many tales about the galaxy blades, but I believe it is as Admiral Hashyvar said. People pledge themselves to a commander not because he is ready to lead but because they are ready to be led."

"I have gotten the gist that many magical beings," Arwen said, "even if they haven't spoken against their dragon rulers before, would prefer they not be there."

"Yes."

"Sarrlevi didn't come along to help you because I promised him cookies," Arwen said.

"*Did* you promise him cookies?"

"And pickled carrots, yes. And goat cheese for Matti. And truffle butter."

Azerdash smiled. "Naturally. After the tacos, I desire you to bake many delicious desserts and accompany me to visit the more recalcitrant rulers, to woo them to our side. As we previously discussed."

"I look forward to it." Arwen thought about pointing out that she still had to worry about her mother and brother. They were going to be pissed when they learned she hadn't killed Val. And if she successfully removed the tattoo? They would be *extra* pissed. At least she should be beyond their reach if she was visiting other worlds with Azerdash. She would have to worry about her father if he stayed on Earth though. Unless he came too. "My father might enjoy seeing new places."

Azerdash raised his eyebrows.

"We could bring him along to hold the cookie trays."

"He would be welcome to join us if he wishes," Azerdash said. "I have found your father to be an apt model to observe and emulate in my efforts to fit in on this world."

"Yeah, he likes you too."

"I'm done." Mark leaned back.

The dragon tattoo had disappeared, no sign of it left behind, not even a scar.

"Wow." Arwen leaned close to examine the spot more closely.

"Usually it's a good sign when a female looks at your chest and says *wow*," Mark told Azerdash, "but she's admiring my work."

Azerdash lifted his chin. "Arwen has admired my work before."

"You work?" An eyebrow twitch suggested Mark believed all dragons—and half-dragons—existed only to use their great power to force others to serve them.

"I have built magical and mechanical items from scratch and made existing mundane creations sentient so as to be more reliable and functional."

"Yes," Val said, coming over to inspect the now-bare pectoral. "I understand Thad has been forbidden by the homeowners' association from unleashing his robotic mower anywhere but in his own backyard. That looks good. Arwen?" Val pointed to her forearm.

Azerdash slid off the table and grabbed his shirt. "Yendral and Sleveryn will also need their tattoos removed," he informed Mark, "but you will apply the formula to Arwen first."

"Please," Arwen said, since Mark was already bristling at the order. "I'll bring you cookies."

"That's not necessary." Mark waved her to the table. "The *half-dragons* better bring me cookies."

"They are hunting fresh meat for tacos," Azerdash said.

"You may get a yeti haunch," Arwen told Mark.

"My troll half would find that appealing. My elven half thinks I should hold out for the cookies."

Val nodded.

Nervous, Arwen sat on the table and pushed up her sleeve. When Mark leaned forward to examine her spider tattoo, it itched and throbbed.

The desire to spring from the table and attack him swept over her, the longing to knock the tattoo machine out of his hand and jab the needle in his throat.

"Hurry, please." Arwen clenched her jaw and squeezed her eyes shut.

Azerdash leaned close to her, resting a hand on her shoulder. His powerful aura wrapped around her, and a trickle of his magic curled around her forearm, soothing the itch and more. It felt like he'd laid one of his elven regeneration pads over it, tamping down the vile magic trying to escape. The violent urges continued, but they were less powerful and easier to ignore.

Arwen slumped against him. "I wish you'd been there when I was trying to stab Val."

"Me too." Val watched from a distance, maybe worried she might still be a target. "I won't tell Zav about that, or he would want to adjust the wards and topiaries to keep you from visiting."

"Wouldn't he forgive me if I brought him some skewers of seasoned meat?" Arwen kept her eyes closed as Mark started to work, the tattoo machine tracing the lines of the spider, inserting the removal formula. Memories of when the spider had originally been inked came to mind, the dark tunnels of the lair, the cold red watching eyes of her mother.

"Yeah, probably. For the record, *I'll* forgive you if you bring me some of those pickled cherries. Amber never lets me have any of hers. She's willing to drive an employer to dangerous remote mountains and risk her life, but don't ask the girl to share a snack."

Arwen sensed her tattoo protesting, its magic lashing out at Mark. He paused and clenched his own jaw a couple of times, but Azerdash helped quash the dark-elven magic each time it rose up.

Sweat broke out on Arwen's forehead. As if *she* were the one doing the work instead of sitting still. Hours seemed to pass though the clock on her phone promised it was minutes.

Finally, Mark leaned back, wiping moisture from his own brow. "I'm not going to put magical tattoo removal on my list of services. It's too difficult."

"I had not intended to supply you with more of the formula, regardless." Zoltan rubbed his hands together. "I have uses for it."

"They're going to love you in Mt. Vernon," Val said.

"Naturally."

"Thank you for doing this, Mark," Arwen said. "Let me know how much I should pay you."

"That's not necessary. I owe you and *him*—" Mark nodded at Azerdash, "—for keeping that dark elf from slaying me."

"But you'll accept that batch of cookies, right?"

"Of course. Two batches."

Hesitantly, Arwen ran a hand over her forearm, finding the bare skin warm but smooth and free of tattoo ink. The blue stuff had disappeared. So had the hair on her arm.

"Is that normal?" She looked toward Azerdash's pectoral, but he'd put his shirt back on. "For the hair to fall out?"

"A side effect, probably," Mark said. "That formula has some powerful magic in it."

"Yes. It can be used for hair and wart removal. The annihilation of all manner of growths." Zoltan beamed a smile at Arwen. "That is one of the many reasons I am eager to put it to use."

"You have growths you need removed?" Val asked him.

"Some of my clients do." Zoltan nodded.

Arwen looked at Azerdash's chest again, then up at him. "You're lucky you didn't lose your nipple."

"It was a risk I was willing to take to keep dragons, elves, and others who wish me ill from tracking me down," he said.

"Can you still lead an army with only one nipple?"

"Of course. Great leaders are able to overcome tremendous adversity."

After admiring her bare forearm for another moment, Arwen pushed her sleeve down and slid off the table. "Will you give me a ride home? After I get some rest, I need to start working on a taco feast."

"Yes. And this time, you will not invite *other* dragons, correct?" Azerdash looked upward in the direction of the turret.

"I won't, but you did tell Yendral and Sleveryn about the tacos, so I think we have to invite them."

"It's true that great leaders must also feed their troops, but once they have dined, I will send them away, and we will enjoy the rejuvenation pool, this time *without* interruption."

Arwen kissed him. "I look forward to it."

# EPILOGUE

Since Arwen had promised to make tortillas from scratch for her tacos, it was a couple of days before she could invite the half-dragons for their meal. Fortunately, some of the heirloom corn varieties that grew on the farm were ready to harvest. While she boiled the kernels and turned them into nixtamal, she shared everything that had happened with the dark elves with her father and showed him the bare spot on her forearm.

Since the tattoo removal, Arwen hadn't had any urges to attack Val, but she also hadn't seen her. Willard had sent Val, Zavryd, and Sarrlevi to flush out the dark elves under Mill Creek—or at least try. From what Arwen had heard, the team had returned to the sinkhole and also the exit that Val had used to escape and found no sign of the access points. Arwen didn't know if that meant her mother's people had left the area, knowing their cover was blown, or if they'd used their magic to make all evidence of the tunnels disappear. Unfortunately, she worried she hadn't seen the last of her dark-elven family.

A loud grinding came from the front of the property, followed by her father cackling. Arwen had sensed Azerdash arriving earlier, but he hadn't come to see her yet. He'd probably been distracted by repairing—or *improving*—something. The mulcher was her guess.

After taking a pan of cookies out of the oven—Arwen was working on desserts to bribe world rulers as well as tortillas to reward half-dragons—she went outside to check. She spotted Azerdash and her father, both shirtless as they carried a log over their shoulders toward the mulcher.

The device glowed and hummed with magical vigor. Previously, the opening for wood had only been about a foot wide since it was for breaking down *branches*, not entire fallen trees, but the funnel had been expanded. As Azerdash and her father approached with the ridiculously large log, the machine trembled, like a dog eager to be released to hunt, and glowed brighter.

Arwen watched with her chin clasped in her hand as they angled the end of the log into it, Azerdash's magic helping lift the heavy weight. Intense grinding drowned out every other noise on the farm.

Arwen thought about pointing out that they should be wearing ear protection, but the log went through so quickly—a dragon chomping with its great maw couldn't have destroyed it faster—that there wasn't time for warnings. As sawdust spat out the opposite end of the machine, forming a mountain of wood shavings, her father cackled again and clapped Azerdash on the shoulder.

"Come in the barn," he said. "I have *more* tools that would be improved by a—what did you call it?"

"A sentience."

"The cider press might need one of those."

Azerdash gazed at Arwen, lifting his eyebrows in a silent inquiry. Asking if the tacos were ready?

Father headed toward the barn, but Azerdash didn't follow. His gaze dropped to admire Arwen's curves, though she wasn't wearing anything sexy to cook in. An apron with dancing cartoon cookies read, *Bakers gonna bake.* Even so, Azerdash seemed to appreciate the view, and Arwen smiled warmly. Maybe he was more interested in visiting with her than with the rusty implements?

Her father looked back when he reached the barn and noticed Arwen—and Azerdash gazing at her. He grunted and went inside by himself.

"I've prepared four meat fillings," Arwen told Azerdash as he strolled toward her, "two with the elk and caribou that your friends hunted down and dropped in the driveway." She waved at the spot, though she and her father had broken down the carcasses and prepared the meat the day before, so little of the mess was left visible. Father was talking about making caribou jerky to try to sell at the farmers market along with their apples, pears, cabbage, and broccoli. "I've also made a vegetable filling heavy with mushrooms."

"I look forward to trying those foods." Azerdash climbed the steps to the deck, clasped her hands, and kissed her. "Then spending the night with you, if you'll have me."

Arwen swallowed, nervous anticipation and excitement filling her. "Of course I'll have you."

"In your home, not on your roof," he stated, as if she didn't know what he meant.

"You *can* spend time on the roof if you want, but I would be happy to invite you inside for the night."

"Excellent." Azerdash wrapped his arms around her, resting a cheek against hers. "Many duties remain for me, with Yendral and Sleveryn attempting to arrange a meeting with the dwarven king, so I dare not stay long, lest others who might be hunting me seek me out here, but... I have longed to be with you."

"I long for that too," she whispered.

"Yes. I know."

Arwen snorted, tempted to punch him for being full of himself, but with his penchant for reading minds, her desire for him had never been a secret.

He brought his lips to hers, warm and gentle and full of promise. *With your tattoo gone, I am more easily able to read your thoughts.*

*The noble thing would be for you to refrain in order to give me my privacy.*

*I will instruct you on how to raise effective mental barriers to keep out mind readers.*

*So, you're* not *going to be noble?*

*I am ever curious about what you are thinking, so it is difficult to refrain. Better for you to learn to protect your mind. Then you will also be less easily controlled by dragons and other powerful beings.*

*I would like that. Dragons are rude.*

*Extremely so.* Azerdash smiled against her mouth. *You have impressive power for a half-blood, even without the dark-elven tattoo. You will be able to learn to protect yourself.*

*I hope so.* Arwen pushed her fingers through his hair, more interested in him spending the night than in learning mental self-defense, at least at the moment.

Their kiss might have led to a before-dinner visit to her home, but they sensed Yendral flying toward the property.

Arwen sighed when Azerdash pulled his lips back, but she trusted his comrades would fly off once she fed them. Then, she could finally have a night with Azerdash.

Yendral soared over their heads to land on the roof. His head lowered on his long neck to regard them.

*Sleveryn will be here shortly and has news for you, Azerdash. I have arrived early to enjoy caribou taycos.*

"Tacos," Arwen murmured.

She released Azerdash and went inside to stir the meat and prepare the toppings while wondering how she would explain the concept of build-your-own-tacos to half-dragons. Maybe she would make the first ones herself so they could get the gist. But did half-dragons like salsa? Or spicy things in general? What about guacamole? She had to include some of that, since she'd gone through a lot of trouble to coerce a couple of avocado trees to grow in this temperate climate.

Not certain if they wanted to sit down and eat at the nook indoors, the dining room having long ago been sacrificed to expand the kitchen, or outside at the picnic table, Arwen prepared a couple of plates and put them on a tray. When she stepped back onto the deck, Yendral had taken his elven form and was in a heated debate with Azerdash. Both paused, nostrils twitching, and looked at the tray.

"You brought five for Azerdash?" Yendral pointed, immediately noticing that one plate held an extra taco. "Because he's the commander?"

"Because I didn't think you wanted to try the mushroom filling," Arwen said. "These four have only meat."

"Ah, yes, quite. But you could have brought a fifth filled with the elk or caribou."

"There's plenty more meat inside if you're still hungry after this." Arwen handed them the plates and waved toward the picnic table. "Normal humans usually only eat a couple."

"A couple? Two? Of these tiny snacks?" Yendral held up thumb and forefinger, holding them together an inch apart. The tacos were much larger than he indicated.

"I stuffed them as full as I could. That's the elk and the caribou. My favorite is the duck chorizo filling." Arwen pointed to the tacos on their plates as she spoke. "It's my father's favorite too. The last one is a traditional beef taco that's popular in this country."

"Hm," Yendral said.

With far less complaint, Azerdash selected the mushroom-stuffed taco, shifting it around as he debated how to eat it. Maybe

Arwen should have brought a serving for herself so she could have demonstrated.

Yendral opted for grabbing one and taking a giant bite, stuffing falling out of the end and juices dribbling down his chin.

"Oh, this caribou is delightful." He finished it with another bite.

"I do not know what chorizo is," Azerdash said, "but it's delicious, as are the mushrooms. Naturally."

"You're the oddest commander," Yendral told him. "Do you really think the dwarf king will speak with you?"

"Once he stops referring to me as a criminal who escaped his people's stasis-chamber prison, it's possible he will. His daughter, Princess Rodarska, is much more reasonable and is inclined to like me since I assisted in *her* release from a similar prison. A good deed that I did not at the time know would prove useful later. This is beef?" Azerdash asked, biting into his third taco. "From the ungulates that graze by the river?"

"Yes." Arwen was debating whether to prepare a plate for her father—and another for the half-dragons—when she sensed their comrade flying in their direction.

"It is also delicious." Azerdash gazed lovingly at her through lowered lashes.

"*Most* delicious," Yendral agreed, giving her a similar look.

She'd forgotten that feeding dragons—and apparently *half-dragons*—could make them randy.

"If she were not such an odd female," Yendral said, glancing at Azerdash, "I would resume my attempt to woo her."

"You will not," Azerdash stated firmly. "I will claim her soon. She is *mine*."

Maybe the caveman talk should have offended Arwen, but she'd wanted him to *claim* her for a long time and couldn't keep from gazing at him with love, looking forward to their night together.

"I suppose." Yendral sighed. "She likes you for your weird quirky interests, not your great power, and she is also quirky. You must have her."

"*Yes.*" Azerdash chomped into his taco, watching Arwen intently.

For some reason, she flushed with heat. How quickly could she feed the other two half-dragons and get rid of them so she and Azerdash could... claim each other?

Sleveryn came down in the driveway, shifting into his elven form as he dropped, and landing in a crouch.

"Azerdash," he said, then spoke in Elven.

Whatever he said shocked Azerdash, who rocked back, his jaw dangling open.

"You're sure?" Azerdash asked, first in English and then in Elven. He looked at Arwen, a strange impossible-to-read expression in his eyes.

Sleveryn also looked at Arwen, then hesitated. *I am not sure,* he spoke telepathically. So she could understand? *It is a rumor that we must confirm.*

*Yes.* Azerdash set his plate down on the railing, so distracted that he almost dumped it off.

Arwen reached out to steady it and the remaining taco.

*We must find out,* Sleveryn said.

Yendral scratched his jaw. *This is not the news I expected you to bring.*

*If it is true, we must retrieve her,* Sleveryn said.

*Yes, of course. As soon as possible.* Azerdash took a deep breath and looked at Arwen.

"Retrieve who?" A weird premonition fluttered in her gut, making her worry that she wouldn't get to claim Azerdash tonight after all.

"Sleveryn has heard a rumor," Azerdash said slowly, his gaze dropping to the deck boards, "that Gemlytha may have been found by the dragons before she died—or shortly after—and revived."

Arwen stared at him. Gemlytha? The half-dragon–half-dark elf subordinate that he'd had feelings for but never acted on? And that he'd *regretted* not acting on? The woman who'd been in his heart to such an extent that he hadn't been certain he was developing genuine feelings for Arwen?

Gemlytha might be *alive*?

"How can one be revived from *death*?" Arwen asked, feeling like someone had punched her.

Admittedly, even on Earth, without magic, it was sometimes possible to resuscitate someone whose heart had stopped, so the possibility didn't stun her. No, what stunned her was that she might have finally won Azerdash's heart only to lose him to someone else, someone he'd loved before he'd ever met her.

"With powerful enough magic, it is sometimes possible with one who hasn't been dead for long—and who died of an injury rather than an incurable disease." Azerdash spread a hand and looked at Yendral.

"Even if there's a chance, we have to check." Yendral also set aside his plate. "There are so few of us left, and if she's a prisoner..."

"We can't leave her in enemy hands," Azerdash said.

"No. Definitely not. She would come for us."

"She would."

Yendral hopped down from the deck, joining Sleveryn, and they both turned into dragons.

Azerdash faced Arwen.

She forced a smile for him, but anguish twisted her insides. She'd finally gotten rid of that tattoo, finally had Azerdash realize he loved her, and now... She doubted she was able to hide the emotion in her eyes and in her mind—the mind he now had no trouble reading.

"I will return," he told her, clasping her hands, "but I need to find out if there is any truth to this rumor."

Arwen nodded, though it took a moment before she could say, "I understand."

And she *did* understand. Even if she was devastated.

Azerdash opened his mouth, as if he might say nothing had changed. Arwen *hoped* nothing had changed.

But he didn't speak right away, and when he squeezed her hands, it wasn't as reassuring as she wanted.

"I will return," he repeated softly, kissing her on the cheek before joining the others in the driveway.

Arwen believed he *would* return, but would he still want to be with her when he did?

She could only watch bleakly as Azerdash turned into a dragon and flew off with his comrades.

THE END

Thank you for reading!

To find out what happens next, you can order the final installment in the Tracking Trouble series, Tested by Temptation.